The Cartoon Life and Loves of a Stupid Man

MARC JOAN

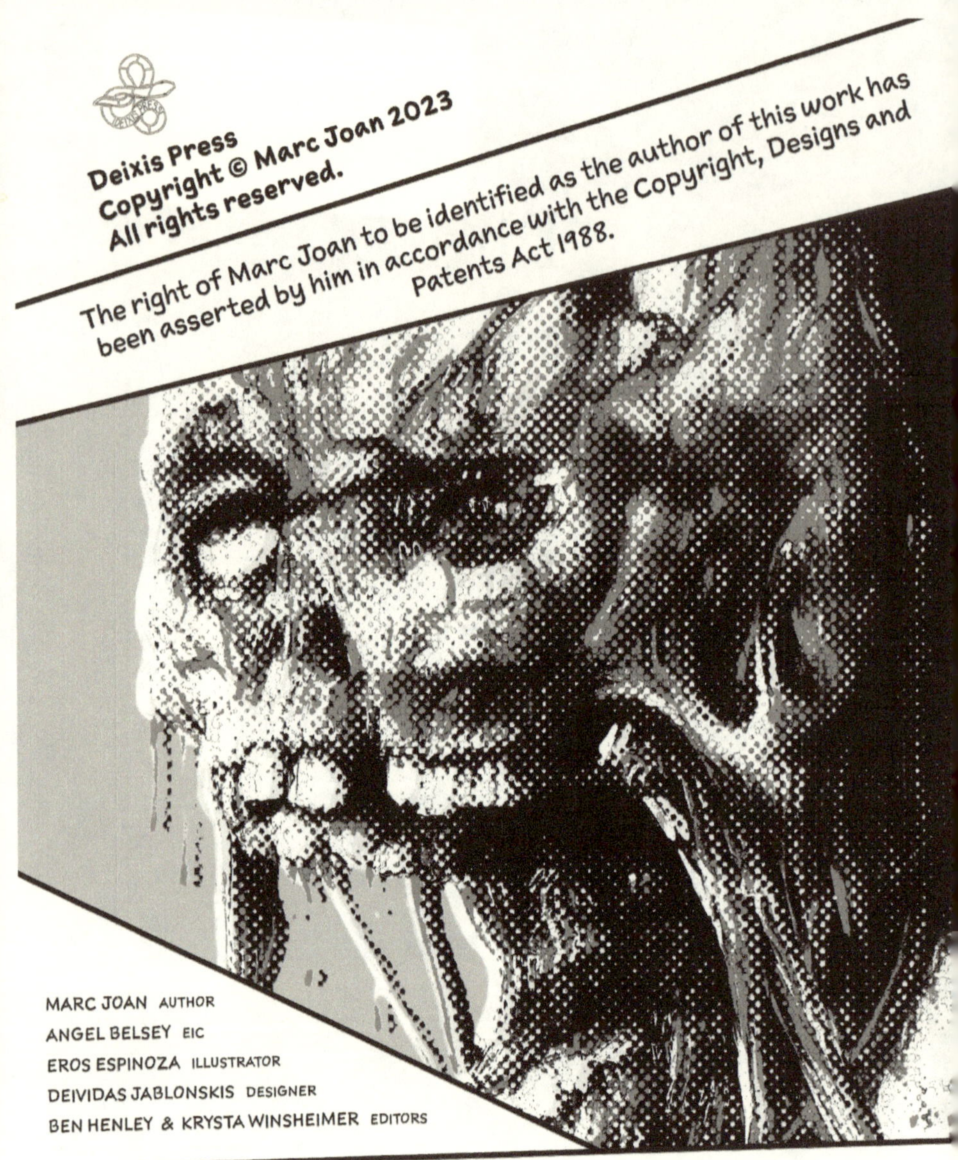

MARC JOAN AUTHOR

ANGEL BELSEY EIC

EROS ESPINOZA ILLUSTRATOR

DEIVIDAS JABLONSKIS DESIGNER

BEN HENLEY & KRYSTA WINSHEIMER EDITORS

First published in 2023 by Deixis Press
www.deixis.press

ISBN: 978-1-7397081-8-4 (HB)   978-1-7397081-9-1 (PB)

The Cartoon Life and Loves of a Stupid Man

MARC JOAN

*To my family – thank you for being
so unfailingly patient and supportive.*

Chapter 1

To recall the day I first saw another's head on my shoulders is both simple and precise. It is no harder, and no less exact, than reading a glossy, hard-backed *bande dessinée*. It is like perusing a flat-packed reel of sequential art and speech bubbles, a Book that traps all my sins and sorrows in exaggerated perspective. And the Book's font is Laffayette Comic Pro, as used by Marvel Comics and Roy Lichtenstein.

Well, of course it is.

Look. Here is that much-thumbed page. I know it, and each of its panels, perfectly; I believe I could draw an exact facsimile of the original. Its sequence of images starts with a drone's-eye view of Geneva's Old City, drawn in three-point perspective. On one of the tiled roofs, light spills from a dormer window. The drone moves closer: we are looking at a bathroom window. A shadow against the obscured glass shows it is occupied. Cut to an inside view. A man is standing in the bathroom. It is I, Philippe Favrier, and my anger is evident. Thick brows beetle, bald head shines, ears steam, teeth grind, and I curse Marilyne in a Comic Pro whisper. My bladder is close to bursting; the toilet's clean white ceramic invites, but I resist the urge. And with this small rebellion, I defy both body and wife. Why *should* I be beholden to drugs and doctors forever? Unfair! I clench my fists and shake them at the ceiling; I bring them to my chest and bend into a tense crouch, grimacing with fury. I punch at the air, again and again, left hand and right, as fast as I can. I rip a hand-towel from its rail and hurl it away.

And there! Do you see? A corner of the thrown towel catches at the little pedestal mirror on the windowsill. Had I knocked the mirror from the sill and broken it, all would have been well. But I only set it moving. That's all I did; set the mirror moving. And as the mirror rocks and jigs around the vertical, it sways towards that most precious jar that sits next to it and my speech bubble grows a muted shriek: "*Non!!*"

Comic Pro. Naturally. After all, my whole life has been – *is* – in so many ways, nothing but a comic strip. Just a long, long comic strip.

'Just', I say; but oh, the fatal vitality of the Ninth Art! Look: each panel, demarcated by linear borders and painted in bright primaries, is shot through with the pixellated hues of slow death – aconite blue and arsenic yellow, bryony red and belladonna black. To turn the Book's pages is to see my life extend, frame by printed frame, in all the colours of poison. Could any medium be more vivid? Could any twist the knife more exquisitely? Look again, at this page or that. There, Clooney kisses my lovely Marilyne while Yves smirks fatly. There, I vomit into the cold Arve while Laurence bellows at my back. There, I kneel before the oleander tree in Geneva's Jardin Botanique, as if in thrall to a green-skinned, yellow-eyed, apricot-scented demon.

And there, *there*, I glance in the mirrored mirror and see another's profile – so familiar, and yet so foreign. Damn him. Damn me.

But wait. I am getting ahead of myself. Return to the page, Philippe!

It wobbles, the mirror; it sways, and it turns on the edge of its circular base, round and round, like a flipped coin settling. It seeks the perpendicular but fails to find it. It pushes at the jar (*Non!!*) – it shimmies to the drop – and I grab it before it can lemming its way over the sill's edge to shatter on the tiled floor. My pulse kicks: suppose it had been *that* jar, the container that holds the most dear of Marilyne's collection, that had been dislodged! I carefully reposition both jar and mirror on the windowsill. But – and here is the happenstance to note – I replace the mirror both at a different angle and the wrong way around. Instead of being turned to the window, the mirror now faces the room!

In the Book, memory's artist makes my clumsiness painfully clear: the mirror's silvered surface, clearly visible, reflects my surroundings. Such glassy images! The beast inside Marilyne – the one that hated her and her beauty – would have erupted at the sight. What had she said to me, all those years ago? *We have mirrors, Philippe, because sometimes we need them, but they must never be casually displayed. D'accord? Always inside cupboards, or turned to the wall, or otherwise hidden. Only expose them when strictly necessary.* And when some strict necessity required her to use one, she would, as penance, bite at the inside of her lip – later, her kisses would taste of iron – or score her stomach with Yves' knife until the bright blood ran.

So: the Book's artist shows the pedestal mirror displaying its back-to-front world. And that world includes the closed doors – *closed,* mark you – of the wall-mounted bathroom cabinet. The other mirror – the one on the inside of the cabinet door – therefore remains hidden. As it should be. *Whatever you say, Marilyne.* So how then did it come about, that I saw – yet did not recognise – the face that grew upon my own? Read on, Philippe!

It seems that my sudden urgency, briefly forgotten, returns, stronger than before. I struggle spastically with fly and pants; I take aim; I release the unstoppable flow. I curse my father and Favrier Pharma and the damned pills that Marilyne had insisted on prescribing and their damned diuretic side-effects. And this, it seems, acts as a reminder, for I reach to the bathroom cabinet, and open its little double-doors.

Doors of which the left-hand one has a mirror on its inside surface. Look. There it is. There it is.

I scrabble at the cardboard packet with its personalised, stick-on pharmacist's label: *M. Philippe FAVRIER, 2 x daily*. I press a yellow tablet from its silver blister and place it on my tongue. The formulation's hinted flavour – chalky-bitter, almost emetic – pulls my mouth into an arc of distaste. I swallow it quickly with a mouthful of water, bending to drink from the tap. Then I raise my head, intending to close the bathroom cabinet, to conceal its mirror once again. *Yes, Marilyne, it shall be as you wish*. But as I take hold of the cabinet door – it happens. I look at the mirror. I catch sight of my profile. For by chance – by the *conspiracy of events* – the angle of the cabinet mirror, to my left, and the angle of the displaced pedestal mirror, on the windowsill to my right, are such that I can see my own side-view in each.

I had no Understanding that day, only the merest Inkling. An idea that something was awry. As though someone had breathed in my ear, with quiet wonder: *But who was that? Who was that, that you saw?* And that innocent question, I felt, threatened to uncover a dark, unformed answer, to disturb a *something* that might rise from Geneva's cellars and drag its aborted shape up the stairs to the very door of our apartment. An answer that, if I dared look at it, would plunge me, I somehow knew, into the deepest, blackest black pit of hell. I shuddered, and pushed thought away, and blocked my ears, and squatted in the corner like a trapped animal, hugging my knees and fighting the urge to shriek out for Marilyne and beg her to come for me, come for me, that minute, that very minute, oh please Marilyne, I am alone again, so alone, just like in Paris, but now it is worse because you are receding, I cannot see your face, and I have seen mine and it is not mine, and I cannot draw, oh Marilyne!

The Book's colours are transiently more vivid in that panel, and its palette more varied; outlines are clearer, and the font bolder. But then, as commanded by Favrier *père*, neuropharmacology bleeds the colours away; my shivering ceases, the whispers go, my fear sleeps again. I pull at my ears, but hear nothing beyond the sounds of dull Normality. And a knock on the door.

"Philippe?"

"Yes."

"You have been in there a very long time. Are you well?"

"Oh, very well, Marilyne. Very well indeed."

Perhaps I should study the Book's earlier panels: for example, those where I set up La Market Jaune, my little *bandes dessinées* shop behind Geneva's Cornavin station. Or those that depict our move from Paris to Geneva, when Marilyne joined the cardiosurgery team at Les Hôpitaux, closely followed by Yves and Pretty-boy Clooney (my fists clench with a cuckold's rage). Or those that illustrate the events in Paris that led to Marilyne and I leaving that city: events that almost broke the delicate, reciprocal supports by which we survived in this dully Normative world. Or even (to regress into still older pain) those that outline the Philippe Favrier childhood, where Favrier *père* amassed a fortune from the chemistry of despair, from patents that paper over mental fractures. Hail, Favrier Pharma! Your pills dull all saw-edged lives.

Your *shares*, however, will sharpen life's savour, and make all things possible. Oh come, come, vesting day!

Stop. I am jumping from page to unrelated page again, like a child with its first picture book. This will never do. I close the Book; I almost hear the pages slap each other – *snap!*

The questions remain. *How* did my head and the Other's come to elide, thereby making of *him* something near human and of *I* something almost monstrous? And how would that make of me a cuckold and of Marilyne a deceiver? What were the logical links that dragged me along an irrevocable course that I still do not fully comprehend?

Let me think. Let me *think*. I am not stupid.

I am not.

Very well. This is what I will do. Now that all has changed – to find out *how* everything changed, and *who* changed it so – I will return to the Book, but calmly and logically. I will turn a page, and another, and more pages still – forward and back, here and there – until I find among this colourful collection an image, a remembered starting point: a *how* from which one can extrapolate the *who*.

For example – here.

Ah, yes.

Chapter 2

A sunny spring day, seven months ago. Behind the Geneva skyline, late snows painted Mont Salève titanium white. Mid-morning light, like summer's shy proposition, beamed through the kitchen window of our top-floor flat in Geneva's Old City. It caught the empty spice rack and made the oak glow blondely gold. On the kitchen table, it found my *petit dejeuner*: croissants basking on pale china, black coffee steaming white. On the shelf above the work surface, it found a refracted path through Marilyne's jars of animal hearts, picking out tones of butter and coral, and casting pale, dappled shadows on the wall. One heart per jar, arranged by date of dissection, taken from an eclectic range of species: mouse and rat, rabbit and hamster, toad, hen, even a lizard. All had had their little red pumps carefully excised by Marilyne's delicate scalpel and now sat, foetus-like, in colourless preserving fluid. Time's chemistry had faded their bloody acrylics to pastel pink or yellow, but each little fist of tissue remained a work of art; even the tiniest had been mounted on card, its vessels pinned back to fully expose the heart's secret form.

Before and beneath these little anatomies, I slumped at the table, all disarrayed pyjamas and tufty bed-hair. One hand supported my head; the other fidgeted with Yves' knife. Fragrances of pastry and arabica piqued me, but my breakfast remained untouched. Why? The Book does not specify, but I can see that something unrecalled gnawed at my sensibilities; my irritation was profound, yet unfocused. I knew I was angry, but could not remember why.

I blew on the coffee, but I blew gently, so as not to break the skin of silence that had grown in the flat since Marilyne had left three hours before. I rubbed at my eyes. I stood Yves' knife on its tip in a patch of sunlight, to admire the blade's serrated shadow. I yawned at the framed print of *Mad Magazine*'s Alfred E. Neuman hanging on the kitchen wall. And, as usual, I listened, ears cocked for the whispers I hadn't heard since Paris. Nothing. The goblin murmurs remained hushed by the famous Favrier Pharma pill. Favrier *père* had made it, Marilyne had endorsed it, Philippe had swallowed it.

Yes: Philippe was good. Philippe behaved. Philippe *fitted in*.

I tore off a croissant tip and ate it; I ate its twin; I ripped the remaining pastry into bite-sized chunks. Idly, I pulled at the kitchen table drawer. It opened by a small centimetre, and shiny chrome peeped out at me. I recognised that sterile gleam: a sternal retractor, brought back from the hospital by Marilyne for God knew what purpose. I shut the drawer as carefully as if a baby slept above it, but the Book emphasises my irritation with a dark and corrugated brow. More tiresome medical impedimenta! Why can't she hide it in the cellar with her other acquisitions?

I sighed. I yawned. I flicked at the knife's pommel so that it spun on the table, making the illusion of a wheel, its quillons the hub. I swirled coffee dregs as if panning for hope. Something yellow – most divine of colours! most devilish hue! – nagged at my peripheral vision: a little square on the fridge to my left. Now that I noticed it, I could not forget it; nevertheless, I refused to acknowledge it. I am a Favrier, and I will *not* be dictated to by notelets.

I knew what it would say, anyway; it would say exactly what Marilyne had said to me as she was getting dressed that morning. As if I needed Post-it reminders of everything! Sometimes she acted as if I were stupid.

"Don't forget to take the recycling down," she'd said. "They're collecting it today."

"I know."

"And make sure you tie the paper and card into a bundle, or they won't remove it. You know what the Swiss are like."

"Believe me, I know."

"And we need to do some laundry. It's backed up again. You'll have nothing to wear."

"I know."

"So that means doing the laundry this morning."

"I know! I'm not stupid!"

"Mm-hm. Just don't forget, that's all. And don't forget to take your mobile phone with you. Don't forget *anything*. You know."

"Darling, I wish you would consider the possibility that, having reached thirty-two years of age, I am capable of carrying out some small matters independently and without instruction."

"Darling, *sans* prompting, you will wander around in your own dream-world all day, and nothing will get done." She pulled blonde locks back into a Betty Cooper ponytail, achieving – as always – effortless chic. "I've fed Infelix, by the way, so *that's* done, at least. Bye, *cheri*. Have a good day in your shop!"

Dream-world, indeed! The injustice of it! Sometimes Marilyne was extraordinarily insensitive. She *knew* what the pills had taken from me. My slumbrous wanderings, my visions more vivid than any live-long day. The distant planets I'd trod; the unimagined futures I'd found; the unforgettable characters I'd sketched and set free to walk streets graffitoed with undiscovered colours! Where now were these more-than-real worlds? Gone, gone, gone. Like food without flavour, love without delight: under the drug, life's spectrum was restricted. As if the finest of scalpels had excised both *ultra* and *infra*, and thereby sliced away my inspiration, my ability to create. Cruellest orchidectomy!

I drained the coffee, and then, defeated, leant over to the fridge and peeled the Post-it from the door. (That yellow! It was like a slap on the retina). Marilyne's neat cursive was succinct: *Recycling. Laundry. Have fed Infelix.* Ah: a breakfasted, bloated Infelix; so unless I wanted a full litter tray to deal with very soon, I should put the creature out. But how does evicting the cat work on the top floor of a five-storey apartment block, one might ask? Easy: one uses the roof. You see, in our part of the Old City, time had made demands of space, such that buildings had clustered together over the centuries, their roofs connecting to form a land-locked, high-cliffed island, like the tepuis of the South American rainforest. Through the dormer window of our bathroom, the eye met a continuity of gutters and gables, terracotta peaks and stone plateaux, wood-clad cupolas and lead-flashed walls, spread out like a cubist landscape. What better playground for a cat? Each day, I would encourage Infelix through the bathroom window, to take his place – the bane of fledgling sparrows and pigeon squabs – in the rooftop ecosystem that spread its links across the tiled slopes and tarred, aerial-scattered savannahs of the Old City. And truthfully, he always seemed okay with this arrangement; he'd eagerly disappear among the angles of the city's ancient carapace, like a sarcoptic mite scrabbling over the flaking hide of some vast, decrepit animal. It gave him, I was sure, an interest in life, and it relieved me of much of the litter tray burden. Everyone was happy; Marilyne didn't need to know, and I didn't tell her.

As usual, then, I put Infelix out on the roof, that sunny spring day. I closed the bathroom window; on the sill, I gently touched the jar containing that most dear of all hearts, and stroked its hand-written label. I took a pill. I dressed, shrugged on my coat and checked that its pockets still held my tram pass. Most importantly, I ensured that I had my phone. Marilyne liked to be able to contact me at any time, no matter how much I told her not to worry.

In theory, therefore, I was ready to head off for another day at La Market Jaune. In practice, however, I was not. That undefined care gnawed at me still. My feet took me to the kitchen, the bedroom, the living room; in each, I admired one piece or another of my collected graphic art. A Frank Quitely here, a Stan Lee there. Over there, Alfred E. Neuman again. With his tousled hair, mis-set eyes and goofy expression, *Mad Magazine*'s mascot was, I always said, a dead ringer for Yves.

Dull, fat Yves. The Book shows me pensive and distracted. My thought bubble says: *Yves – I wonder where he ended up?*

I moved on; pictures, gorgeous pictures, everywhere! Blurgits and briffits, lucaflects and emanata! Hites and dites, burstlines and plewds! Our apartment's walls displayed class after peerless master-class in sequential art. Looking at them, I felt an old hunger gnaw. That's what great art does, of course; it disinters buried loves. So I went to the desk and opened the near-forgotten drawer. The one where my inks and papers, my brushes and paints lay neatly arranged, as they had done for years. I caressed the tools of my once and future trade, hoping for some muse, some divine spark, to take me by the hand, to set afire my creative fuel. And then I replaced them, these instruments of desire, in their allocated places, for me to fondle another time. One day I would draw again, perhaps; but not that day.

The knowledge of what I once was calmed me, somehow. I shoved a few shirts into the washing machine, added an unmeasured scoop of powder, and slammed the door shut. The machine shuddered and chuntered into its cycle, and was still grumbling to itself as I walked into the hallway. There, on the little table against the wall, I saw our wedding photograph: all awry, again! Marilyne must have nudged it *en passant*. Before repositioning it, I drank in the distant joy it framed. The way she stood next to me, her arm through mine, her fine, pale hair framing a face that some would murder for. Eyes like laughing African violets. The Bézier curves of her waist and hips, in and out, like sweet echoes of the first ellipse, a line drawn before Man's fall. All set off by that bouquet of roses, that heavenly yellow so bright against her bridal dress! She'd held the flowers low, that day, as though to hide her womb's secret, our hearts' joy. *I do,* we'd said; *I do, I do.*

I kissed the photo and replaced it. Then I left the apartment, snail-paced down the communal stairs of our apartment block (*when* would the landlord repaint the walls?), and pushed aside the door that opened onto the pavement. The traffic's snarl was immediate; I covered my ears, but could not exclude its aural carnage. Yet beneath it all, I still heard Marilyne, on that far-off day in Paris, saying, *I do.*

I believed you then, Marilyne. I believed you.

Chapter 3

In the Book, I see that I am wearing my loose-fitting, pale-blue suit, no tie, on that balmy day. Marilyne would have rolled her eyes (*You look like a slob, Philippe*) but I liked it – it always made me feel like the hero in Will Eisner's *Spirit* comics. In fact, it was a Will Eisner kind of morning altogether that day; the sunshine had washed all disguise from the city's faults, giving Geneva the grubby tawdriness of Eisner's New York. All outlines were sharpened somehow, all colours definite and discrete; each Genevoise was as clearly defined as a cardboard cut-out. But I hardly noticed any of that; my thoughts were elsewhere. Whatever indefinable irritation had been troubling me since I awoke troubled me still. A small, sharp concern; a little splinter of a worry, lodged under my mind's skin.

I scowled my way onto the tram; the Splinter worked its way deeper. I frowned through the tram's windows; the vehicle whirred and clinked from stop to stop. I alighted at the usual place. I stamped along the pavement to my shop and opened up. I sat down in front of my computer, but left it untouched while I gnawed at a hang-nail and stared through the door's dusty glazing. Another tram rattled sedately past, and I saw my shop-front in its windows: a semi-transparent reflection repeated sequentially, in each pane of glass in each successive carriage, as the tram clunked past en route to Cornavin station. The yellow lettering was reversed, of course, but I knew well enough what it said: *La Market Jaune*, in each reflection, in each window, one after the other: *La Market Jaune, La Market Jaune, La Market Jaune.* And underneath, in yellow capitals, there was written, I also knew, although I could not see it from where I sat: *Proprietor PHILIPPE FAVRIER.* And the proprietor must run his business, I thought, so go to it. Turn the computer on, and then make another coffee.

I hauled my despondent body from its chair; but before I could get to the back of the shop, where a tiny cubicle miraculously hid basin, kettle and mini-fridge, I heard – oh no! – the *tinkle-tink, tinkle-tink* of the shop door's broken bell. *Merde! Merde!* I turned, heart sinking, and saw a familiar figure. Long grey hair, pale blue eyes above a large, hooked nose. A three-quarter length liver-brown coat, unbuttoned as always; and, as always, thin, blue-grey cotton trousers, frayed and stained where the hems dragged against the ground at his heels. That obscene, unmistakable gait: bent backwards by some odd curvature of the spine, he was obliged to proceed waist-first, such that his groin preceded the rest of him by several inches. Truthfully, with his head thrown back and his feet trying to keep up, one would think a malicious angler had hooked Laurence's scrotum and now reeled him in.

Yes, Laurence. Always the morning, and always first thing in the morning, damn him; always telling me how to arrange my shop and what to put on the shelves. Why? Why me; why La Market Jaune?

"*Bonjour!*" he boomed.

I grabbed at my ears; the monstrous power of his basso profundo was perhaps the most bizarre of his attributes.

You could hear his mad bellows, aimed at nobody in particular, from streets away, even over the traffic. I sat down again, and peered over my computer screen, forcing a smile to my face.

"*Bonjour,* Laurence. A lovely morning."

"My friend!"

I flinched again; somehow, I was never prepared for such timbre and decibels. Extraordinary how one man could produce that volume without any apparent effort.

"How might we help you today, Laurence?"

"Crabs, my friend! With pincers of gold!" He pushed one hand into his trousers and scratched vigorously at his groin. It sounded as if he were digging in a bucket of wet sand.

"That is beyond my remit, Laurence. Perhaps a pharmacist—"

"*Putain!* I speak of Haddock, of Thomson, and, mark you, of Thompson!" His sneer was cosmic.

"Yes, I *did* understand the allusion, Laurence. I thought perhaps you were being euphemistic and, er, sensitive. Although you have always been endearingly explicit regarding your health in the past, of course."

But whatever Laurence was listening to now, it wasn't me. Head cocked, he followed something inaudible, surely, yet apparently as real as the tram's clank outside the shop door. At the same time, he made slow, elaborate gestures with both hands, as if kneading the air, or conducting an invisible orchestra. The act was so convincing, I swear I almost heard the string section myself. And as he followed these soundless sounds, he scanned my shelves: my pride, my joy. Stacked high with the brightest, glossiest covers in the history of the Ninth Art, my units tastefully displayed the zenith of graphic creativity, from the classics of the thirties and forties to the stars of today, from drama to wit, from tragedy to bawdy humour. All of human life was lived on the shelves of La Market Jaune. Laurence craned around, taking in each and every masterpiece, before turning back and pointing at me with both hands.

"You should replace all this rubbish. Particularly that which you display in your window, at the front." He gestured extravagantly behind him, without taking his eyes from me. "At present, you have only rubbish in the window. Nobody wants your rubbish, the things you put in the window. Put material of quality there instead. Not rubbish. Do you hear me?" His voice was now lowered to the pitch of a giant's bassoon; perhaps he thought it to be persuasive.

"I hear you."

"Replace the rubbish with *anything* – you know – but only material of quality."

"Mm-hm."

"Do it *now*." Laurence stared at me from behind his nose, blue eyes bulging. He was close enough to smell: unlaundered clothes, unwashed skin, unwiped arse. Did I want an argument with him? Not really. The Splinter had sapped my energy. Should I then choose the nuclear option, and phone the police? After all, they knew Laurence well; every now and then, when he became too much of a public nuisance, they picked him up and ferried him to the psychiatric section of the Hôpitaux Universitaires de Genève. I think they often twisted his arm a bit on the way, and maybe the orderlies held him down and gave him an injection when he got there, because he'd developed a violent aversion to arriving at the hospital by that route. (Although, oddly enough, he was happy enough to take himself there in his more lucid moments; more than once I'd seen him, sitting in the waiting room, sweet as Spidey's Aunt May.) Usually, I only had to mention *police* or *hospital* and – usually – off he'd go, wetting himself with alarm and shrieking at the world's injustice. But looking at him then, on that lovely day, I just didn't have the heart. But for the grace of God, I thought, there go I. Be kind.

"Okay, Laurence," I said. "Here you go. Look." I went to the *Tintin* shelf, got a couple of copies of *The Crab with the Golden Claws,* and carefully placed them in the window display. In fact, I placed them so that they covered up the last three Competition winners – or rather, *all* three winners, for I'd only started the monthly competition twelve weeks ago. Valiant but disappointingly derivative efforts along the lines of Jack Kirby, Art Spiegelman and Serge Pellé, respectively. Nobody would buy them, so hiding them hardly mattered. "How's that? Better?"

Apparently not: Laurence, radiant with a puce that suggested imminent infarction, raised his fingers to his mouth in horror. "*Pantoufle!*" he bellowed through grimy digits. "*Marchand de guano!*" He turned on his heel and opened the shop door. *Tinkle-tink.* "You haven't heard the last of this, *putain!*" The door shut behind his bellow. "*Iconoclaste! Hérétique!*" Curses reached me in diminuendo.

How much can one person take, on one sunny spring day? First Marilyne and her Post-it of Patronisation; next the Splinter of Worry, digging away at my drug-crippled memory; and finally, Laurence the Loudly Obscene, demanding that I rearrange perfectly arranged shelves.

And behind it all, the slow-grown ulcer of my resentment: the damned drug and what it did to me. *You must take your medicine, Philippe.* Okay, Marilyne; but why? Is it for others or for me?

The injustice of it! To sleep a small death each night, my dreams buried under drugs; to wake each morning, with nothing in my head but sticky darkness; unrested, thirsty, with a bursting bladder. The tedium! The intellectual rot! In the Book, I pull at my hair; I grasp my ears and crush them. As if such small pains could give my life back its lost colour, or retrieve the creativity amputated by pharmaceutical science, or even just stop that phantom limb itching and kicking. They could not, of course, and that was why my shop was so much more than just a place of work. As I'd often told Marilyne: until my shares, my inheritance, came to me, only La Market Jaune kept me sane. (Yes, we laughed; but what other word to use?).

La Market Jaune: Geneva's one and only independent outlet for *bandes dessinées*. The best, most unique BD shop in Switzerland. You'd have to be a sequential art aficionado to know the allusion – *La Marque Jaune* is the iconic book from Edgar Jacobs' *Blake and Mortimer* series. A work of sweet genius; I never understood why people read *Tintin* when they could have *Blake and Mortimer*. The Edgar Jacobs stories have far more depth and imagination than those of Hergé. Anyway, that was why I gave the shop the name I did. It also spoke to the kind of BDs I liked, on a personal level. Old school; quality not vulgarity. And finally, La Market Jaune allowed me to retain some small involvement in the only world where I did not feel foreign. If I could no longer create art – if the well-springs of inspiration had been capped by my father's chemical genius – at least I could gain some spurious pleasure from trading others' creations.

But on that particular day, the Ninth Art's salve gave no relief. The Splinter had gone too deep. What *was* it, that irked me so? Something Marilyne had said to me, or I to her, perhaps? I pushed at pharmacology's fog, but all I heard was Laurence's foghorn roar: *Replace the rubbish with anything – you know.*

Wait: there! Thank you, Laurence! This morning – she *had* said something; a slightly odd turn of phrase. *Don't forget* anything. *You know.*

Not 'don't forget this specific task' – for example, *Don't forget to take your pills, Philippe* – but *Don't forget* anything. *You know.* As in, *Don't forget about this thing, the slightly irritating thing I talked you into, which we are now not talking about. You know.*

Referring, of course, to the looming Normality of this Friday evening. An evening when I would have to smile politely while Georges Clooney kissed my wife; as Normal.

Oh God!

Chapter 4

"Do I *have* to go, Marilyne?"

"We've been through this, darling. Partners are invited, and you agreed to come. Everybody's expecting you."

"That was before I realised who was organising it!"

"Georges likes to manage these things, *cheri*, and he is good at it. Philippe, are you really wearing the same suit you wore this morning?"

"I like it. It's very Eisner. Anyway, I've had a shower and changed my shirt."

"As you wish."

We were in the bathroom; she was doing her makeup in front of the cabinet mirror while I kicked my heels by the window. Infelix twined his soft, black-furred warmth around my shins.

"What's the occasion, again?"

"My department has been awarded Centre of Excellence status for cardiac surgery. Cool, no?"

"Yes. I remember now. But what's that got to do with Clooney? Why does *Clooney* always need to trail after you?"

"Georges is a talented surgeon and a valued member of my team." She put away her lipstick, closed the cabinet door and picked up Yves' knife. "So the accolade belongs to him as well." She was silent a minute, sawing and dabbing at soft skin. Then, while I collected up bloodied tissues, she added, "Besides, I like him. You might, too, if you gave him a chance. He's not so different from you and I, you know. An outlier. One of us."

So that was it, right there. That was why I'd been in such a foul mood that lovely day; it was a hangover from the night before, when, as if by afterthought, Marilyne had disclosed that her most annoying colleague would be present at an evening already guaranteed to be tedious. I'd protested; she'd brushed me off; we'd argued and sniped without resolution. I'd listed Clooney's shortcomings, but nothing I said could make her accept that Clooney was what I, at least, could see him to be. A sneering, conceited *grande école* snob who believed himself to be the yardstick of all good taste. Not 'one of us' in any way. And so, what had begun as a minor contretemps had mutated into something altogether different. In fact, we hadn't argued so bitterly since Paris.

Yes, that was it: the Splinter in love's flesh had a name, and its name was Clooney. Real name, Georges Cuvier; known to all as Clooney, due to a striking resemblance to the actor in his younger days. Arrogant, pretty-boy Clooney . . .

In the Book's panels, I writhe: the Splinter twists and burrows.

I threw the red-stained, scrumpled tissues into the toilet and flushed them away. Then I picked up Yves' knife from the sink's edge, where Marilyne, untidy as ever, had left it. I was about to follow her out of the bathroom, but her voice trilled at me from the hallway.

"Take your medicine now, Philippe. You might forget later."

Yes, Marilyne. Whatever you say. I put the knife down and returned to the bathroom cabinet.

The pedestal mirror did not face the room. I saw no Inkling in its glass. Not that day.

It was all very Clooney. A restaurant I'd never heard of called La Salapanzay, an upstairs private room. English choral music bled from Bang & Olufsen boxes behind the bar. French philosophers sneered oil-painted sneers from the walls. Around and about, in twos and threes, standing and sitting, milled the great and the good of Swiss cardiosurgery and their simpering spouses. Between tables, waiters strutted in tight trousers; on their shirts, badges suggested that their names just happened to be Rousseau, Descartes, Voltaire, and Camus.

When we arrived, Marilyne headed straight to the ladies' – I guessed her cuts were still bleeding – and in her absence, Clooney pounced.

"Philippe! How kind of you to attend our little celebration." He looked me up and down, as though I were some kind of insect that was entertaining inasmuch as it was bizarre.

"Always a pleasure, Georges. Nice venue. You're a regular here, are you?"

"I reserve regularity for bowel movements, Philippe." Clooney always pulled out his toilet humour and waved it at me, every opportunity he had. He knew it annoyed me.

"You seem to know all the waiters."

"Only the philosophical ones." His perfect features arranged themselves into a sarcastic smirk. "But enough of me. And no shop-talk; I insist that we stray no closer to cardiosurgery than *this*." He presented me with a plate left by Descartes: small heart-shaped pastries. Delicate nibbles, the kind that fragmented in your hand. Something struck him. "At least, I say 'no shop-talk,' but I forget who you are! Tell me *your* news, Philippe. It is so rare that one may speak to a real shopkeeper, ah, a real *comic seller*." One corner of his mouth pulled downwards, making a half-smile that tugged at his cheek from nose to lip.

"Well," I said, "truthfully—" But Clooney was looking over my shoulder.

"Benoît," he called. "Benoît, you *must* come."

And Benoît, a balding, stork-like creature with rimless glasses, dutifully came.

"Philippe, allow me to introduce Benoît Egli. Benoît is our new Professor of Paediatric Cardiology. We knew each other at the Sorbonne, isn't that so, Benoît? Benoît stayed on in Paris, but Marilyne has now tempted the poor man away from that den of decadence. As she has tempted so many other men, of course. But Benoît, listen: Philippe is – can you believe it? – Philippe is a *comic* seller!"

"Ah?" Benoît, exuding polite confusion, proffered a handshake. I juggled the flaking canapé from right to left hand, while my glass of champagne tilted treacherously.

"Pleased to meet you," I said. "And while Georges' description of my occupation is highly amusing, in fact—"

"In *fact*, it is a little joke, Benoît, a poor one but mine own. Philippe trades in *bandes dessinées*, yes, he has a *shop,* yes," – Clooney could scarcely contain his laughter – "but there is nothing *comic* about him. He is, as you can see," – Clooney nodded at me, and suddenly my cherished Eisneresque suit felt ridiculous – "an *homme serieux*. Indeed, Philippe is our local arbiter of graphic tastes, our shrewd dealer in the – what is it? – of course, the, ah, Ninth Art."

"Really?" said Benoît. He pulled a tissue from his pocket and wiped at his hand. I looked at my own hand: the canapé's innards had leaked over my palm. Tuna, apparently.

"How interesting. But what is your connection with cardiology?"

"Well," I said, transferring champagne glass and canapé remnants to my right hand so I could search my pockets for tissues with my unsullied left hand, "actually—"

"He is Marilyne's *husband,* Benoît!" Georges' intonation trumpeted the hilarity of it all.

"Really?" said Benoît, again. His bemusement had gone up a notch. He blinked at me and examined his hand.

I knew what they were saying, or rather, *not* saying. And on one level, I couldn't blame them: to others, to Normals, Marilyne and I seemed like a mismatch. A high-flying, beautiful cardiosurgeon hitched to a funny-looking 'comic seller'. Glamorous Marilyne and jug-eared Philippe. Odd. Amusing. I understood all of that. But they didn't know the real Marilyne, nor what she sometimes did during her late evenings at the hospital, nor how we meshed like cogs that have worn each other's teeth into reciprocal shapes over the years. Nobody else, I told myself, could replicate the special mutuality by which Marilyne and I held this hard world at bay.

And there was something else these Swiss snobs didn't know: namely, my particular situation. Because I was going to be a lot wealthier than these up-themselves doctors. You don't get real money just by stitching hearts together. But I would be seriously wealthy just by being me – because of Favrier Pharma. Because of my shares. Thank you, Dad. I can't thank you for much else, but thank you for the shares. And when they vested, watch out world. There'd be some scores settled.

But until vesting day, Marilyne and I had to put up with Normals. People like Clooney.

"Is it not wonderful to meet people from outside our dull, cloistered world of medicine?" Georges' dark eyes glinted with faux good humour. "Tell me, Philippe, when might we see *Being and Nothingness* adapted to the *bande dessinée* format? I believe Sartre's existential musings would greatly benefit from being, ah, reduced to cartoons. Don't you?"

Talking to Clooney was like rolling naked in nettles. I forced a stupid smile to my face.

"Naturally, the Ninth Art is not for everyone, Georges. Taste is subjective. But graphic art does not *reduce,* as you put it, real life. It *emphasises* it. The power of the cartoon is a matter of record. To be mocked in a BD, to be lampooned in a line drawing – it is too much for some. Remember *Le Canard enchaîné* in France?"

And if Marilyne hadn't chosen that moment to come back from the ladies', I would have continued the theme. I would have been explicit about the dangers of the Ninth Art. I would have said something like: *If being mocked in a humorous cartoon can precipitate murder, who can seriously mock the cartoon's murderous power? Who? Well, Clooney?* And had I been more forthright at that point, perhaps Clooney would have backed off at later points. Perhaps he would have kept his big mouth shut at Café Titeuf. And then, perhaps, everything would have been different. But I'll never know, and the Book can't tell me, because the Book only shows what actually happened, not what might have been. And what happened was this: Marilyne came back and – just as I had foreseen, just as he did every time he saw her – Clooney was onto her like a leech. Kissing her. Kissing my wife.

Only on the cheeks, and he *was* a colleague of hers, but that wasn't the point. The point was, I hated it; the point was, he was deliberately baiting me. He looked at me over her shoulder while they hugged, and pursed his lips to show me that he was hiding a triumphant smile.

I wasn't about to give him the pleasure of knowing he'd got under my skin. I turned my back on him and made drab Normal conversation with Benoît's spouse: What-do-you-do-where-do-you-live-oh-how-interesting. Her efforts to escape were ineffectual, until my bladder (damn that drug!) forced a precipitate toilet visit; when I emerged, she was hiding behind Benoît in a gaggle of socially-gated snobs. Whispering shibboleths and giving me side-eyes.

My humiliation continued for the next three hours. Repeatedly, I attempted polite engagement with people who evidently considered me bizarre; repeatedly, I was barely tolerated until said people could flee back to their own kind. Why must I abase myself to my inferiors?

For Marilyne's sake, of course. For the sake of my lovely, strong wife, with that pale hair that fell about her face so in such delightful, errant strands; for my Marilyne with her Vitruvian proportions and effortless grace; for my Marilyne and all her horrible, hidden faults and fragilities. So I endured. And all the while, Marilyne circulated among her colleagues, effortlessly triumphant. Like a golden sun floating through the void, orbited by dull, lightless planets.

In the Book, my thought bubbles churn: *Oh Marilyne! Normality burns my soul, Marilyne, I hate it, but I do it for you. All for you. Clooney and the others, they are the monochrome background to our own bright pigments. We are 'we', Marilyne, forever, and only we can be we, and together we make a new colour that only we can make, that cannot fade. Promise me, Marilyne. Promise me.*

You *did* promise, Marilyne. I turn the Book's pages, memory after sweet-panelled memory, and something blurs my vision; if it has a colour, I cannot name it.

Chapter 5

The sunny weather of Friday continued into Saturday: a workday for me, but – for once – not for Marilyne. Her morning, apparently, was to be unashamedly domestic. By the time I'd had my shower and second coffee, she was in the kitchen surrounded by flour, sugar, eggs and mixing bowls. The mess was disastrous. But I let it pass; in marriage, one must go the extra mile. Also, she was making fairy cakes, which she often did when I was upset. I deduced that she was feeling guilty about making me go to her Clooney-infested work party. Good; yesterday's bruises still ached.

And yet their pain was soothed, or subsumed, just by being in the same room as Marilyne. Just by seeing her there, doing things, no matter what. Just by watching the rebellious hair that escaped its tie to tickle her cheek; the pensive frown as she checked a recipe; the absorption in something so simple and inconsequential, yet so pleasurable. I often thought that baking was a form of release for her. After heart surgery, it must be a joy to slap ingredients around in the knowledge that if things go a bit wrong, it really doesn't matter. I sat at the table and nibbled through breakfast while she beat eggs into froth. I thought of how she sometimes hugged me, and wondered how her arms could be so slim and yet so strong.

"New whisks?" I asked.

"Mm-hm. We didn't need them in the theatre anymore."

It took me a little while to process that, on a number of levels.

"You use *egg-whisks* in the operating theatre?"

"No, stupid. These are aortic rakes. But they make great whisks, look."

"Oh. Would I be correct in assuming aortic rakes are used to, um, rake aortas?"

"Mm-hm. Just to hold the major blood vessels aside. Gives us a bit more room to poke around."

"Okay. But – forgive me for being *stupid* – doesn't the hospital have a need for these aortic rakes?"

"Well, yes, but these are old models. They should have been replaced with an updated design months ago. I'm just helping the procurement department make the decision they should have already made."

"What! You mean they're not new? Those things have actually been in someone's *chest*? Jesus, Marilyne!"

"What?"

"You're making buns with them!"

"Oh, don't be stupid, Philippe. They have been autoclaved, you know. They're perfectly sterile."

We were silent for a little while. I glared at her; she winked saucily and poured the buttercup-yellow mixture into a bun tray.

"So, Philippe, for lunch, how about meeting up at Café Titeuf?"

And that's how I knew she was *really* feeling guilty. The Café Titeuf was her long-standing favourite, yes, but it was also where we'd go to make up after arguing. So, she knew she was in the wrong, for sure. Excellent.

"Of course, darling," I said. I kept my voice totally neutral. No triumphalism from Philippe. "Café Titeuf would be perfect. Come to the shop, about twelve."

Business was slow that morning. Laurence came and went (*Putain!*) without incident; my inbox filled with spam and phish; I logged a couple of internet orders. Time bled away in daydreams. In the Book, imagined joys form flowery clouds around my head. And the largest and most flowery is the Trustees' forthcoming release of the Favrier Pharma shares that had (nominally) passed to me after the passing of Favrier *père*. Briefly, my eyes are replaced with Scrooge McDuck dollar signs. But the dollar signs disappear as I am reminded that, right now, I must mark time in an impoverished Normality. A spurl of disappointment spirals above me as I consider the sacrifices I have made to accommodate this dulled existence, and those I make to comply with Marilyne's needs.

Infelix, for example.

He'd come with Marilyne, like a black, furry dowry, when we got married. I was fine with that: in Paris, we'd had a house with a garden and a cat-flapped door, and he went out when he needed to. No problem. When we moved to Geneva, however, Marilyne insisted we took an apartment on the top floor of a *fin de siècle* building, in the utterly unleafy Old City.

"It's very small," I'd said.

"Yes, but each flat has its own little cellar, in the basement beneath the apartment block. So there's more storage space than you think."

"There's no lift. Four flights of stairs, every day."

"But Philippe, it's so beautiful . . . I *love* the view over the old buildings, and we're so close to the hospital. And the lake . . ."

"The lake, *oui*. There will be gnats in the summer."

"Oh Philippe, don't be stupid."

"There's no garden. For the cat, I mean."

"There *are* such things as litter trays, darling."

Within a month, then, we'd rented a top-floor flat and bought a litter tray. And as Marilyne always left very early, and got back very late, dealing with the litter tray became my responsibility. Not a big deal; but the point is, it was never part of the deal. That wasn't what I signed up to when we got married. That's not what Favriers do.

So thank God for La Market Jaune. Because when Infelix infuriated me, and when the drug-smothered death of my creativity racked me, and when Marilyne's beauty tied me down and wounded me, and when the Clooneys of this world turned the ratchets and rubbed in the salt, only La Market Jaune brought splints and salve. It was my only refuge from a world – the Normal world – that did not understand me, and for which I had no map; my route out of a maze made for Normals, through which even Marilyne moved with unerring direction and matchless grace. It gave me light and warmth whenever I lost my way or got left out in the cold. It was my small candle of hope, and although the flame often wavered, it never quite went out.

That morning, without customers to serve or online orders to meet, I turned to the day's snail-mail. I began by sorting the post according to envelope size. The smaller items – bills, insurance offers and the like – I trapped beneath a gaudy Batman and Joker paperweight (a Comic Con freebie from DC Comics). Joker grinned in sadistic glee; I grinned back at him and turned to the larger envelopes. These – A4-sized, deliciously weighted packages in anonymous manila or presumptuous white – remained stacked neatly on my desk; delightful mysteries set aside for leisurely investigation. Why did I gloat over them so? Because they contained the little joys that had given me new purpose, new strength: the Competition entries.

The Competition! Eat your heart out, Amazon, and all you other internet giants; laugh at our archaic bricks and mortar as you will, but you'll never compete with we independents when it comes to local flavour. The artisan model, not the stack 'em high and sell 'em cheap model. People still want the personal touch, and they can't get that from the one-size-fits-all dot-com behemoths. With each Competition entry, Asterix thumbed his nose again at mighty Rome. As I read through the entries, the throb of yesterday's humiliations diminished; with each turned page, thoughts of Clooney sunk beneath memory's surface.

Of course, few of those submitting to the Competition were gifted artists, and fewer still could write captivating dialogue. None excelled in both word and image. But that didn't matter; they were all learning their craft, and I, Philippe Favrier, gave them an outlet for their ambitions. Some drew inspiration from Dave Gibbons or Brian Bolland; some from Hal Foster or Chester Brown; some from Tezuka or Toriyama. All were amateurish in different ways. But each was like an extended, open hand, a whisper saying: *You are not alone.* In the Book, I see my worries fade as I peruse these offerings, one after the other.

Although, now, as I read the Book carefully, I notice it has captured something of which I was unaware at the time. As I examine one particular entry, the light in La Market Jaune takes on a different quality: shadows deepen, colours take on the tones of twilight. The overall effect is close to chiaroscuro. Also, the point of view changes: I am seen from above, as though examined by some giant destiny that looms over me. I look bemused; my thought bubble has only a question mark (bold, italicised, Comic Pro). And now that I study this particular frame, I see that my profile has elements of what I shall see in the mirrored mirror that coming, fateful day; it is as if my physiognomy itself has a physical inkling of the Inkling to come.

I am reading, of course, the latest issue of *Madame Médecin*.

"How is business today, darling?"

"Pretty good. I'm getting the fourth-month entries now. Nothing outstanding yet, but early days."

Marilyne had stopped by La Market Jaune, and now we were walking towards the Café Titeuf. Her hip nudged softly at mine; her perfume teased me. In the Book, we pause briefly in front of Doré et Fils, art gallery and fine art auctioneer. Its window display is joyful: cubist angles meld with expressionist blurs and blazing acrylics. An explosion of art. But there is a gap in the display: a central hiatus where a picture has been removed – or where space has been made for a picture to be placed. The lacuna vomits a dark meaning.

"Fourth-month entries?"

"You know, for the Competition. I told you about it."

"Forgive me, Philippe – all the bureaucracy around applying for Centre of Excellence status has drained my mind. And now I've been roped into helping with the Cardiac Glycosides Symposium, so I'll have even less free time than usual. People think I've nothing better to do. So, just remind me, *cheri*. What competition?"

"It's a publicity thing. For La Market Jaune. I invite submissions of BDs from local artists, on a rolling basis. Each month, I pick the best entry from the previous tranche of submissions. I got way more entries than I expected the first month, and it just grew from there. And most of them are quite good. One or two odd ones, but that's to be expected."

"But does it cover its costs? The prize money, for example?"

"There are practically *no* costs, Marilyne – that's the joy of it! As for the prize – the winner gets a free BD of his choice, and the pride of seeing his or her entry prominently positioned in the shop window. That's it. No money changes hands."

"Truly?"

"Yup. I mean, I have to keep all entries displayed and available for purchase in La Market Jaune – that's why people enter the Competition, to be honest. But for that small inconvenience, I get publicity. And entry fees."

Indeed; each new entrant, another five francs. It all added up. In fact, last month the Competition income was the difference between making a loss and breaking even. But I didn't tell Marilyne that.

Anyway, it wasn't just the money; it's difficult working on your own, and the BD competition, in a way, had validated my existence. It put La Market Jaune on the map, and showed that people valued what I did. It demonstrated the strengths of the small bookseller. Most unexpectedly of all, it gave me, almost, a sense of *community*. Suddenly, thanks to the Competition, I no longer felt alone in snobby Geneva. Rather, I was confirmed as one of a tribe of confrères, part of an artistic movement that had its roots in Hogarth and Honoré Daumier; a movement that later bore such glorious fruit as America's Action Comics and Japan's Manga.

"And how will people find out about your Competition?"

"Well, word-of-mouth, I hope. But also, I got the *Tribune de Genève* to run a piece on it, so that should generate even more interest. Classic marketing strategy. It's out today, I think."

"That's wonderful, *cheri*! We'll get a copy now, and have a look."

Café Titeuf was quiet, and we took the pavement table we always used to take. Monsieur Titeuf (as we called him; we did not know his name, so we gave him one) greeted us with a reproachful air; *It's been a long time,* was the implicit message. He'd once charmed Marilyne, when she was having a *petit café* alone one day, by pinching the toe of her shoe while picking up a serviette that he'd dropped. This amused her, apparently, and thereafter she'd insisted that we visit the café once a fortnight or so. That was in the old days, the days of shared time, before she'd got so busy.

The days when we'd have a small strong coffee each, and an ice cream with a liqueur poured over it, and set the world to rights. The nice days.

Yes, Café Titeuf was our special place. It was so good to be back there again, with her. Even so, I had some things to say.

"I'm not happy, Marilyne."

"Oh, darling! What is it? How can I help?"

"Clooney."

"Georges? What about him?"

"He's an arrogant shit."

"He puts on an act, *cheri*."

"He's just bloody condescending. Like the rest of them."

"They are part of the Normal, *cheri*. We must accept it. For now."

She smiled at me, sly and elfin and charming, and I came close to drowning in the deep violet of her eyes, and had to look away fast. *Accept the Normal!* It was alright for her –

she'd always done the fitting-in thing, the pretending thing, the camouflage thing, better than I. And anyway, the accepting-and-fitting-in strategy had limits: consider Clooney. Consider his deliberate provocation, the ageless, eternal taunt between XY genotypes – *I am a better man than you; I could have your wife, and she would enjoy it.* That kind of baiting might well be Normal, but that didn't mean I should put up with it.

"You know that evening, in La Salapanzay?"

"Mm?"

"Clooney didn't bring a partner, did he?"

"No. He is unattached, at present."

"Seems a bit odd, doesn't it?"

"Why? Everyone is single sometimes."

"Maybe it suits him. Maybe it gives him more freedom to, you know, be free."

"Be free?"

"Sleep around."

"Philippe, who really cares? It's none of our business."

A moped droned past, engine straining. Marilyne yawned prettily. In my coffee cup, the dregs made a pattern that made a face that made a Clooney sneer. Monsieur Titeuf approached; I pushed the cup away. I could feel Marilyne looking at me, feel that look of exasperation mixed with worry that she used to such effect. Her eyes! Infinite violet, essence of blue, a hue that made indigo look insipid. But I refused to look. I wasn't in the mood to give in; I had been wronged, and she should acknowledge that.

I turned on my phone and swiped moodily at the screen. Alfred E. Neuman appeared. Marilyne craned closer.

"Who is that, Philippe?"

"You know who it is. Neuman. From *Mad Magazine*. Like in our pictures, in the kitchen and hall."

"Oh yes. I couldn't see properly, because of your thumb." She peered at the screen. "In a world where all are imbeciles, he is a kind of Everyman, no?"

"You know who I think he looks like? That guy who used to follow us around in Paris. When we were students."

Marilyne's forehead made soft, delicate furrows.

"You know," I said. "Yves."

"Yves? I don't really see the resemblance, Philippe."

"Oh, come on. Pudgy face, prominent ears, vacant expression, asymmetrical features. General dullness."

"I always thought he was sweet."

Indeed; she'd thought that ever since our Paris leaving party, when Yves presented her with his odd gift. The knife. He'd been so proud of it; apparently, it is difficult to 3D-print a sharp blade. Something to do with printer resolution, or the physical properties of printable plastic, or something. But Yves had managed it: a printed plastic knife with a heavy, ridged haft, a smooth, ovate pommel and ornate quillons. And a fine, serrated blade with a wickedly sharp edge. But why? It was wasted effort. You can get a knife at any DIY shop.

"Sweet and stupid," I said.

"Yves?" said Marilyne, gaping.

"Of course Yves. That's who we're talking about, remember?"

"Yves?"

I frowned at her. "Is there an echo here?"

"Yves? Yves! *Mon Dieu*! Yves!" She was standing up now, hand to her mouth to better project her voice. Monsieur Titeuf looked at her, arms akimbo, as disapproving as only a Swiss waiter can be, and then turned to follow her gaze.

And I did likewise. "Yves?" I said. "Yves! *Mon Dieu* . . ."

Chapter 6

In the Book, Yves is made conspicuous by the absences that trail him: the absence of bright colours, absence of dynamism, absence of expression. When illustrating Yves, the Book's artist is uncharacteristically parsimonious with colour and primitive with technique. Indeed, Yves is shown always tinted in sepia: skin, clothes and hair seem made of identical material; a dull, khaki-coloured mass. No gradations of tone give depth to Yves' chubby form; scratch Yves, the Book implies, and you will find nothing beneath. No lucaflects grace his environs; nothing, it seems, can shinc or gleam beside Yves' matt tedium. No blurgits or briffits follow his movements; speed, the Book's artist indicates, is to Yves as it is to a snail. Thus, when I saw him in the Café Titeuf that day, I saw only a slow, heavy vacuity; an emptiness standing before our table, sweating slightly, staring at Marilyne with pop-eyed hopefulness. In the Book, I look blankly from him to Marilyne and back again. Above my head is only a spurl of confusion. Marilyne's speech bubbles, by contrast, are full of delighted dialogue, dogged by hyperbole and tailed with exclamation marks:

"Yves! This is unbelievable!"

"We were just talking about you, weren't we, Philippe?"

"You're looking great, Yves! Isn't he, Philippe?"

I look again. Yves' belly fights his belt; his rucksack struggles with what it holds. Later, I would discover he always carried a jumble of 3D-printing paraphernalia: spare printer nozzles, plastic filaments of many colours, CAD print-outs for the little monsters he made, and prototypes of their tortured little limbs. But at the time, I thought he'd joined the legions of the homeless, and was wandering around Geneva with his life on his back.

"Yes, Yves," I say. "You *are* looking great."

Slow, dull Yves. How had we first made his acquaintance? I flick back through many pages of the Book, but find no clear answer. In Paris, Yves had been on Marilyne's medical course, but had dropped out after a year – his 'character was unsuited to medicine', apparently, and he ended up in biomedical engineering. I was following a Fine Art course; we only overlapped because I spent so much time with Marilyne and her medical chums, pretending to fit in. Yves trailed that bright caravan like a beggar. But he didn't even bother to pretend he belonged; he was just *there*. Always there, but without impact: human wallpaper. All I remembered of him was the tedium, the pain of attempting conversation only to be met with monosyllables. Yet Marilyne came to know him well, clearly . . .

Anyway, we pulled up a chair for him, that day, and Monsieur Titeuf flounced over with a menu, and then we had a chat, Yves and Marilyne and I, and filled in the gaps that the last few years had opened up. Or, at least, Marilyne filled them in:

"Philippe's business goes from strength to strength, Yves. He has started a monthly BD competition – have you seen the write-up in the *Tribune?* Look, it's here . . ."

"Do you hear that, Philippe? Yves has a flat in Les Pâquis – just around the corner from La Market Jaune."

"Yes, I am still cutting up patients, Yves! It's going well, but sometimes a little lonely, because, you know . . . I miss the old days, *hein*? But listen, even the world of cardiosurgery throws up a kindred spirit from time to time. Truly. And you will need some introductions, being in a new city. Leave it with me."

As for Yves, by painful questioning we established that he had moved to Geneva two or three months before to take up a job with one of the medtech companies that grow over Switzerland like mould on cheese. Something that used his 3D-printing and plastics engineering expertise: construction of personalised prostheses and similar items.

"It sounds perfect for you, Yves!" said Marilyne.

Yves thought about this for an age, and then said, "Yes."

"Look, I really need to get back to the shop," I said. "Busy, busy."

"And I to the gym," said Marilyne. "But we shall get together, all of us, as soon as possible." She pulled out her phone. "Saturday evenings are best for us, but I have been roped into a Symposium this month, and it runs over two successive weekends *and* the intervening week, can you believe it? . . . Let's see . . . How about this?" She showed him the electronic diary on her phone, and pointed to a date. "Does that work for you, Yves?"

It did. His slow, unsmiling nod indicated excited acceptance. "My place," he said.

"Great! Six p.m., then. We can't wait, can we, Philippe?"

"No, we can't," I said.

Later, after he had gone his way, I asked Marilyne if dinner with Yves was such a great idea. "I remember what he's like, even if you don't. He's needy. Very needy. Soon, he'll expect to accompany us wherever we go. You wait."

"Well, I don't remember Yves being like that at all. Anyway, he's new to Geneva, so we have to help him to settle in. We outliers must help each other; you of all people should understand that, Philippe!"

'We outliers': as if Yves were not just another Normal! As if he were *one of us* any more than Clooney!

Yves' arrival, and the silly fuss that Marilyne made of him, discomfited me: I shut up shop early that afternoon, and went to mooch around Carouge. With its Nice-style architecture and bohemian vibe, Carouge almost lets you forget how prim and ugly the rest of Geneva is. And if you find your way to the banks of the Arve – especially when it is in spate, such that its torrent's roar drowns the grumbling traffic – you almost forget you are in Geneva at all. It's not always easy to escape the pavements for the river, but it can be done. On one little street, for those who know, there is a place where the run of metal railings pauses, giving access to graffiti-smeared concrete steps leading steeply down from the pavement to the bank. Here is a part of the Arve that few visit: here are trees, and bushes with bird nests, and muddy, overgrown banks. Here is peace; usually.

But even the Arve's clean waters could not wash away my worries about Marilyne, nor my accumulating resentment. It was almost as if she was taking advantage of me. I sat on a dryish log and made a mental list:

We'd moved to Geneva to support her career; the impact on me, apparently, was unimportant.

We'd taken a top-floor flat, which meant Infelix needed a litter tray, which I had to clean out. Twice daily.

She demanded that I continue with the medicine she prescribed, despite its impact on my mental acuity and artistic creativity; despite it, even, slowly but surely, killing that part of me – that *creativity* – that linked Marilyne and I, that made us *we*.

She expected me to accompany her to her work-related events, and there endure the barbs of Clooney and his ilk.

She demanded that I put up with her perpetual acquisitions from the hospital. Not just the equipment she insisted on using when cooking, but also the other things she hid in the cellar.

Overall, her career had increasingly taken over her life, leaving little time for me. Nevertheless, she could find time for dinner with one such as Yves – and assumed I would accompany her!

Above all, above *all*, she was drifting further from me and closer to Clooney. Day by day. Clooney!

I threw pebbles into the river; I rocked back and forth on the log and hugged my own shoulders. Surely, surely there was something I could do to jolt her out of this rut she'd got into, in which Philippe was dragged along like unwanted baggage, getting skinned and bruised on the way. There had to be. I peeled bark from my impromptu seat, and scratched a heart in the wood with a sharp pebble. I chewed at my lower lip, and then scratched an *M* inside the heart. I stood up, kicked at the log and pushed it down the bank with my foot until it was in the water. Then I gave it a shove, and watched the current slowly catch it and take it downstream until it disappeared among the lucaflects of the water's surface. *Goodbye, M.*

Oddly – as though by pushing out the log I had nudged a reluctant Providence – I found the puppy almost as soon as I'd set off for home. I thought at first it was a bundle of discarded clothing washed up on the bank. Then I looked more closely: matted, sodden fur pushed up into little tufts, a belly swollen with the gases of death. One soft brown eye looked dully out at a world too cruel for little things; the other had been closed by the pressure of the ground against which it lay. In the same way, one side of its mouth had been pushed open to reveal china-white teeth while the lips on the other side of its muzzle remained politely closed. This gave it a schizophrenic air: one half squinted and snarled, the other remained calm and balanced. "You need the pills, my friend," I said to it, as I turned it this way and that with the toe of my boot.

And then, as immediate as a dropped vase, it struck me: how obvious! This, *this* could be what I needed. Like manna from heaven, the dead puppy could be the gift that gave new life.

A minute's scouting found me an empty plastic bag, caught in a bramble but reasonably intact. I put the little body in this and left for home.

When I arrived back at the apartment, Marilyne was in the shower. That was good. *Don't show your cards, Philippe!* That's what Dad always said: *Don't show your cards.* I dried the puppy with kitchen paper, wrapped the little body in cling-film and put it in the freezer. *Keep them close to your chest, Philippe!* Yes, Dad, I will. As for you, Marilyne, I thought, as I shut the freezer door – sorry, but you'll have to wait.

"I can't wait, Philippe!"

I spun round, jaw dangling. "Marilyne!" She was in the kitchen, wrapped in towels, damp and flushed. "Wait? Wait for what?" My voice had gone up an octave. I backed up against the freezer.

"For dinner with Yves, of course. It's so exciting – it'll be just like old times. Being able to act freely, chat *freely.* You know."

"Ah, yes. Dinner with Yves," I said. "Fantastic."

Chapter 7

"Putain!"

"Goodbye, Laurence."

Tinkle-tink.

A Monday morning like any other. Or almost like any other. On this particular Monday, the sweet solace of my shop was given added savour by the growing pile of Competition entries waiting for me to pass judgement. Topmost of which was the oddity that had bemused me on Saturday, just before we bumped into Yves: *Madame Médecin and the Virus*. It was awful, but it was strangely awful. In fact, reading it again, I got the impression it was *deliberately* awful. There was something mocking about it, and that irritated me.

At least, at the time, I thought that was why I was irritated; but now I think I was disturbed, on some subliminal level, and that imbalance manifested itself in irritation. But why did it disturb me? The artist clearly had ability; the drawings were quite good in a Robert Crumb-like way. Just like the first three issues of *Madame Médecin*. But perhaps the very Crumbiness itself – the tedious stereotyping – was part of the problem. Thus, the female superhero, Madame Médecin, was drawn with a Dan

DeCarlo- or Kurtzman-like, obsessively stylised, almost fetishistic female anatomy – *Little Annie Fanny* with a stethoscope. Yawn. Her arch-enemy, PseudoFifre (presumably a clumsy attempt at wordplay, *sous-fifre* being a byword for underling) was a small, balding, weasel-faced man; a stock criminal. Yawn again. But I'd seen worse work without it getting under my skin. Perhaps I was frustrated by the plot? It was, after all, tiresomely predictable: PseudoFifre has developed a weaponised virus, COVID-X98, that he plans to unleash on the world. Society will break down under the weight of the pandemic, enabling him to enrich himself by theft. But wait! Madame Médecin and her team of ace lab technicians invent a new vaccine in double-quick time. The world is saved. Yawn, yawn, yawn.

So, once again *Madame Médecin*'s creator had fallen back on a dull, unimaginative plot and risible stereotypes. It was as though the artist wasn't taking his art – or my Competition – seriously. Yes, *that* was what was irritating me. The implicit disrespect. I searched for a name, but – as always – the artist had left the work unsigned, without a covering letter. Stupid. But he or she had sent the five-franc entry fee, and that was the important thing. I put *Madame Médecin Issue #4* back on the pile.

Tinkle-tink.

A couple of thirty-somethings. I watched them meander among the shelves of classics old and new. I observed their confusion gestate, emerge and grow. I saw them find, at last, what they sought, in the corner of the shop where I had hidden it. *Tintin.* Confusion was replaced with relief; they brought their intended purchases to the counter.

"Thank you," I said. "A famous *oeuvre*. But the field has exploded since Hergé's time." I nodded at the bright, busy shelves all around my shop. "And if you really want old-school, try Edgar Jacobs. Much more depth and imaginative flair than *Tintin*."

"Pardon?" said one.

"Thank you," said the other.

Ah: non-francophones. Probably employees of one of the international organisations that infest Geneva – CERN or WHO or UN-something-something-something.

"You should try something else as well," I said, speaking slowly. "You'd be surprised."

"Is for learning French," said one.

"Is for friend," said the other.

Why do people find it necessary to provide an explanation – no, an excuse – for their BD purchase? 'It's for a friend'! Come on! Comics are an art-form, not a crime. You don't need an excuse to buy one. You don't.

You should, however, have a good excuse for choosing *Tintin* when there is so much else you could read. But *Tintin* was what they wanted, and in La Market Jaune *Tintin* is for sale, so I sold them *Tintin*. Goodbye, fools.

That gave me an idea. I had already pushed my *Tintin* stock into the least visible, least accessible corner of the shop, behind some tall aisle units. If I compressed all Hergé's work onto the bottom shelf in this corner, I would free the top shelf. Where better to store – I mean, 'display' – the Competition entries? After all, I was obliged to do so: "All entries will be displayed for sale in La Market Jaune," I had unwisely stipulated. That awkward, out-of-sight corner would be the ideal home for these unwanted orphans.

And if anyone knows about being orphanly and unwanted, the Book tells me, it is Philippe Favrier. I'd thought that old pain was over; after all, Marilyne had promised *I do* and so had I, and I'd forsaken all others including my muse, my art, just to keep her happy. So why did the old loneliness now snarl and whimper behind me, like a hungry, frightened dog?

Because of the Splinter, of course: because of the Clooney-shaped Splinter, which burrowed deeper into my flesh each day, incubating a pus of dead affections. That was the wound that drew the black dog on, snarling at betrayal's heel. There was something going on between Marilyne and Clooney – I could just *tell*. Soon after Yves' arrival, Marilyne had phoned him – I know, because when I came out of the shower, I heard her alto trill in the kitchen: "Bye, Georges, and thank you! See you in someone's chest!" What might that have been about, and why could it not have waited until they saw each other at the Hôpital?

Whatever it was, it had kicked off a trickle of correspondence between them: a message here (over Marilyne's shoulder, I see Clooney's smirking WhatsApp face), a call there (each time, Marilyne casually strolls back and forth, but always, it seems, moving away from my earshot). More and more, Clooney occupied her comments and, I guessed, her thoughts; some days it seemed like her fascination with the obnoxious snob could not end.

And I had no answer for it. When Marilyne told me of his effortless competence in the theatre, I smiled, but beneath my smile, my teeth ground. When she repeated some witticism or other of his, I laughed, but my fists clenched. It felt pointed, as though she were comparing us: *See? Is he not a better man than you?* It wore me down; the erosion was almost physical. Sometimes, I would look deeply into the mirror, turning my head from one side to another as if seeking an answer to some unformed, unspoken question. But the Book shows only blackness in the glass, as if to censor my reflection or mute whatever answer it might once have given.

A trying time indeed. Nevertheless, in La Market Jaune that day, as I stacked the Competition entries in Orphan's Corner, some small, rebellious part of me rose up and declared itself. I decided to fight, fight the Clooneys of this world. I really had no choice. Who other than Marilyne could ever understand me? Who else would ever have me? If Clooney stole her from me, there would be nothing for me in this world, ever again. After the annihilation of such a love, life would offer only ashes. I put the last Competition entry on the shelf, and nodded grimly. And then Favrier Pharma's medication asserted its explosive diuresis, and I scuttled to the smallest room.

The flushed toilet still gargled to itself as I texted Marilyne.

Am in love with someone. Let's go out for dinner tonight and I will tell you all. I was quite pleased with that: romantic, wistful, amusing. Guaranteed to tweak the heartstrings, surely.

I'm sure she's a very lucky girl! But I am on call tonight & working evenings this week! Sorry!!!! Oh, yes. Damn.

Ok. Saturday then?

That's when we are doing dinner with Yves! Really darling don't you listen!

I was a bit annoyed by that response; after all, my brain fog was the consequence of the pills she insisted I take. She could have been a little more sensitive. But I only sent a glum emoji. She texted back almost immediately.

But wld love to do a nice dinner with you sometime ASAP cheri. I will cook for us, okay? Like old times. Must get to theatre now!! xx

I was cheered by this, at first. The Book depicts a pink heart floating above my head; I have the wibbly-wobbly smile of a lovesick teenager. But as I read and re-read

Marilyne's text, the heart develops hairline fractures, and my mouth becomes neutrally horizontal. She'd love to do dinner *sometime*, she said. That could mean anything, couldn't it? Well, couldn't it? The heart cracks in two; my mouth turns down in glum disappointment.

Sometime. The classic non-specific, make-no-promises, don't-call-me-I'll-call-you hand-off.

It just wasn't good enough.

Damn Marilyne. Damn Clooney. Damn idiots who buy *Tintin* despite all other options.

At noon, stomach gnawing, I locked the door of La Market Jaune behind me and set off, past the tram stop, heading for the little supermarket on Rue Marie Bertrand. The pavements heaved; humanity swelled. I paused to give way to a young mother with a child in a push-chair. And where did *circumstance* dictate I should pause? Before the window of Doré et Fils, art dealer – naturally! Where else for circumstance to conspire?

The Book shows clearly what I saw that day. Within the art gallery's window it sits, centrally positioned; mounted but unframed, as if no boundary could contain its infinite joy. A sheet of paper with nine panels drawn in Chinese ink and graphite. On the lower right margin, outside the panels, I read a flowing, post-war cursive: *Planche 8 / Numero 8 / 1953*. That is, the eighth version of the eighth plate; created in 1953. An example of Edgar Jacobs' original line drawings of Blake and Mortimer, yes; but more extraordinary still, it is a page of artwork from *La Marque Jaune*, the first and most famous exemplar of the *Blake and Mortimer* BD series. The creation which had haunted my boyhood, the *oeuvre* after which my shop was named. A small piece of history right in front of me; a glowing gem of genius separated from me only by millimetres of glass.

I looked more closely; indeed, I could not look away. Blake and Mortimer, energetically posed in their nineteen-fifties suits, spouted squared speech bubbles, blank except for hand-written numbers – 14, 15, 16, and so on. In the Book, my face is equally blank, as though I cannot believe what lies before me. But belief soon came; and with it, desire. I wanted it, this reification of culture, with every fibre of my being, with a passion that gripped my heart and squeezed it dangerously tight. There was no price label, only a little sign. *Interested parties enquire within.*

I pushed open the gilded door of Doré et Fils. Their bell caressed my hearing: a melodious, tastefully understated chime. A bell that sang: *Reeeee.* The young woman behind the counter looked up: an impeccably dressed, flawlessly groomed, Slavic-cheeked beauty. If she had been a bell, she would have sung *Meeeee.* I glanced around the gallery. Down-lighters washed the walls' neutral white with a lambent radiance; a polished, onyx-black floor dared me to tread on it. Here and there, squared pillars grew from the floor to support this sculpture or that. But oh, the hung colours on those pale walls! The clamour and laugh of tints and tones! Each painting would hold the eye, tease it and spurn it; the eye would move on, dejected and downcast, only to be buoyed by the next gilt-framed delight. Their hues near paralysed me: my hands involuntarily rose towards my mouth, as if pulled by the spasms of a delightful tetanus. It had been too long since I'd lost myself in pigment; too long.

"*Bonjour,* M'sieu." Slavic cheeks dimpled.

Now that I was here, inside the gallery that actually possessed – that was *actually selling* – an original planche from *La Marque Jaune*, I found myself affected by a kind of paralysis. There were so many things I could say; so many approaches I could take. *The Jacobs piece: would you be so kind as to reserve it for me?* Or: *I am very interested in the graphic art in your window, from the* Blake and Mortimer *series: may I examine it more closely, if you please?* Or even: *Please, for the love of God and all his angels, let me take that sheet of sequential art immediately!* But if I was too keen, they'd hold out for a top price. I'd need to proceed cautiously.

"*Bonjour,* M'sieu?"

The dimples had gone. I realised I was staring; made a goggle-eyed buffoon by indecision.

"The piece in the window, Madame!"

"The Brauner self-portrait, M'sieu? A fine example of the surrealist movement—"

"No! And not the early Kandinsky, either! None of that rubbish! I'm talking about the *quality* item." I moved closer, and leant over the counter. Now I had her attention; she moved back slightly, as though to assure me she was listening. "The Jacobs. Do you hear? The Jacobs!"

"Ah, of course, M'sieu. The graphic art sample. Such items are rarely seen at auction, still less in galleries such as ours—"

"I know that! I want to buy it!"

She blinked at me in a 'does not compute' kind of way. What was wrong with her? Was this a gallery where art was sold, or was it not?

"We appreciate your interest, M'sieu. I must tell you that the vendor, for whom we are acting, wishes the item to remain on display until August. We are inviting offers throughout this period, but the sale will not be concluded till then."

"Fine. I am here to make an offer, so kindly tell the vendor—"

"M'sieu, there is, I regret, a process to follow. If you would like to register—" She started tapping away on her laptop. "Your name, please?"

"Philippe Favrier. But—"

"Philippe Fourier?"

"Favrier! But this is absurd! How can I know what price to offer?"

She gave a micro-shrug with one über-chic shoulder. "The vendor's instructions were precise, M'sieu. Your address, if you please?"

We went through her 'process'; at the end, she asked me what I would be prepared to offer, and I gave her a figure. It seemed generous to me, and she frowned in a way which could have meant she hadn't expected me to offer so much. Or maybe it meant she expected me to offer more; maybe she recognised the name, Philippe Favrier, as being linked to the Favrier Pharma fortune, and thought I would be more generous. I didn't know what it exactly meant, that frown, but I thought it was probably good whatever. After all, if she knew I was *that* Favrier, she'd come back to me if the offer wasn't high enough. I was sure of that. As I left Doré et Fils, Miss Slavic Cheekbones trilled, "*Au revoir.*" I gave her a look over my shoulder, just to let her know that I knew how things worked in the art world. The door closed behind me: *Reeee.* Outside, I pulled my mobile phone from a pocket and took a snapshot of that one-in-a-million quadrangle of inimitable culture, in that glorious window display, in that best of all art galleries. My heart kicked and punched and kicked again as I marched away, on that most wonderful of all days.

Chapter 8

Planche 8 charged the rest of that afternoon with its divine electricity. Colours hummed and glowed; pigments sang from pictures, and I sat on my deskchair in La Market Jaune like an anchorite blessed with an eternal happiness. Customers came and went, and I came very close to embracing each of them. When I returned home, I could do nothing except wait for Marilyne. I fidgeted and paced, hardly able to contain myself. Just think of her reaction when she heard the good news! She could not fail to be as excited as I; she would, perhaps, take a day off, or an hour at least, to come with me to Doré et Fils. To look at what, even now, I could hardly believe was there.

I thought of how happy Marilyne would look when I told her, and what she'd say. I made something to eat. I watched some television. I wondered where she was, and then remembered she'd said she would be working late this week. (When *wasn't* she working late?) Fatigue pulled at me; I made a coffee, and then another. The caffeine brought wakefulness, but also diuresis. I hopped from foot to foot, cursed, and eventually, inevitably, acceded to the drug's demands on my bladder. But even this iterated discomfort, this perpetual reminder of flesh made weak by pharmaceutical tyranny, could not dissipate the joy of Edgar Jacobs. I wondered where I would place Planche 8; perhaps, *here*, in the bathroom, on the wall next to the cabinet? As I pondered this, I detected, from the corner of my eye, a movement; a movement outside the window, behind the reversed shaving mirror. I looked; the shadow of a perky tail indicated that Infelix waited on the roof. I pressed my face to the rippled glass and mimicked his yowls. "You'll be fine out there for a while longer, Infelix," I said. But wait: what was that? Sounds in the corridor outside the apartment! A *clack* of heels and a scuffle of a bag placed on the floor. A grating and gripping of a key in the lock.

Marilyne!

It would never do for her to find out that Infelix spent all day on the rooftops. I opened the window, pulled him in, and ushered him out of the bathroom. He scampered to the kitchen, and I – all innocence and insouciance – went into the hallway. Marilyne was pushing aside the photo frame on the hall table to make room for her keys.

"Hello, darling!" she cooed.

The joy of Planche 8 was nudged aside by a small, but distinct, irritation. "Not there please, *cherie*," I said.

"Pardon?"

"Your keys. Please tidy them away. There's no room for them on the table." That was true. It was a small hallway with a correspondingly small table. It could only realistically accommodate the framed wedding photo, centrally positioned and facing the door.

"Oh, Philippe, don't be stupid. If I leave them anywhere else, I'll lose them. Don't fuss, darling, please." She planted a small kiss on my cheek on her way past. I picked up her keys, repositioned the photo frame and followed her into the kitchen. I carefully and pointedly placed the keys on the work surface, below the empty spice rack. She gave me that small, wicked smile of hers.

"Are you in a bad mood, dear-heart? You seem a little grumpy."

She handed me a white plastic bag and a sheaf of print-outs she was carrying, so that she could unbutton her coat. I put the bag on the table, next to my unread Competition entries; it was very light, and its contents clinked hollowly as they moved against each other. Next to the bag – after pushing Yves' knife aside – I dumped her papers. The top one, I noticed, was the draft of a publication, heavily edited and annotated in Marilyne's tiny hand-writing. *Title: Novel cardiac glycosides from Thevetia peruviana. Georges CUVIER and Marilyne FAVRIER. Presentation for Cardiac Glycosides Symposium.*

Clooney. Well, it would be, wouldn't it.

"Grumpy?" I pushed the Clooney-Marilyne endeavour to one side. "No. In fact, I have the most wonderful news."

"Really?" Her face lit up as only her face, of all faces, ever could or ever will. "Do tell!"

I told her. I sat back in quiet triumph and waited for her reaction.

"But don't you have enough art already, Philippe?"

"What? *What?*" Words failed me. "Marilyne, this is not just another addition to our collection –"

"*Your* collection."

"– this is an Edgar Jacobs! From *La Marque Jaune*!" I looked dumbly at her, my speech centres crippled by disbelief. She looked at her phone; a text had just pinged onto the screen.

"That's very nice, darling, and I know you like Edgar Jacobs . . ." – she paused to read the text – ". . . but we don't have the room. It's such a small flat . . ."

"*You* wanted this flat!"

She paused, her thumbs working at her phone. *Send.* ". . . so I don't see where it would go, Philippe . . . Anyway, how much is it?"

"Oh, as to that, they are inviting offers . . ." I didn't mention the figure I had given to Miss Slavic Cheekbones; no point in telling Marilyne I had already thrown my hat into the ring. One bridge at a time. "A bidding process, you see. A great opportunity to get a one-off creation for a good price."

"Mm. Or to pay too much for something which – like *all* art, Philippe – has no objective value. *Cheri*, I just need to make a call . . ."

And that was that. She started chatting to somebody; I thought I heard Clooney's pompous accents, made tinny by the phone's speaker. Planche 8 was forgotten; Philippe was forgotten. She just didn't understand, or care, about the significance to me – the almost religious significance – of *La Marque Jaune*. I didn't bother showing her the photo on my phone; what was the point? I decided I'd just buy Planche 8 myself, without discussing it further. Something black and weighty settled on my shoulder and crooned in my ear; I listened to it, and listened to it some more, and looked at Marilyne's draft publication. *Novel cardiac glycosides. Georges CUVIER and Marilyne FAVRIER.*

I picked up the paper. Just like the reading material my father used to bring home, all the time, when he was running Favrier Pharma. In the long, lonely dog-days of summer, I'd say, *Can we have a game of chess, Dad? Please?* And he'd say, *Just a minute, Philippe, just a little minute,* while he buried his face in some publication about some new drug. And we'd never have that game of chess, never.

"Philippe?"

"Sorry?"

"You were miles away. I said, is anything the matter?"

"The matter? Why don't *you* tell *me*? Or should I ask Clooney?"

"Clooney? What? What are you talking about?"

"You and Clooney. That's what I'm talking about."

"Oh Philippe . . ." Suddenly, she looked tired, and I almost felt sorry for her. "Please don't go this way again. Geneva was a new start, remember? And we've been good for nearly five years now, yes?"

"I admit that I may have got things wrong in Paris—"

"*May* have?"

"—but that doesn't mean I'm always wrong. I can see what Clooney's trying to do. I'm not stupid."

"Georges is *gay*. You must know that."

"Even if that's true, he's still trying it on. I can see it. And he's so arrogant – sometimes I just want to—"

I couldn't get the words out; my fists were clenched so tightly they hurt, and my heart was pumping, pumping, like a mad thing, chambers and valves, tubes and muscle, all clutching at my chest.

Marilyne sighed impatiently, but I noticed that she also looked troubled. "Georges is Georges. That's how he is. And he's one of my colleagues, so I have to work with him. That's how work is. Sometimes I think you've been shut away in your shop on your own for too long. You've forgotten what real employment is like."

"So my employment is not *real*?"

"Don't look for offence where none is intended, *cheri*, please. I know how well you've done. Five years next month, with the economy as it is, competing with the likes of Amazon. You have worked so hard. All I'm saying is that, for someone like *you* – you know – the lack of social interactions hasn't been good for you."

"What's not good for me is seeing you and Clooney getting all chummy." I prodded at her publication draft. "Good excuse, this. For late nights with Pretty-boy, I mean. Is that why you brought it back? As a kind of pre-emptive excuse-type thing?"

The expression went out of her face, and she looked at me carefully, neutrally, as though she was evaluating one of her patients: *I have given you a thorough examination, M. Favrier, and this is my diagnosis.*

"Philippe – now you *are* being stupid." And she sat down at the table, nose in her phone, fine hair veiling her face, her husband dismissed.

Stupid? I gave her a long, long stare; it was a wonder the hackles on the back of her neck didn't rise in warning and make her turn to me. But she just went on texting and scrolling, scrolling and texting. Such insensitivity. Eventually, I got up and went to the living room and turned on the TV. But every channel had Clooney on, and every time he spoke, he said, *Can you believe it? Marilyne's husband is – a comic seller!*

I was still angry an hour later when she poked her head around the door.

"Philippe? Are you coming to bed?"

I turned the TV volume up full. I didn't look at her, but I know there was an eye-roll. I saw it from the corner of my own eyes, it was that obvious. I would have stayed in the living room all evening, but I needed the toilet *again*. Unbelievable! You and your *bloody* drugs, Marilyne! First you cripple me with pharmacology, and then you run off with Clooney, leaving me to limp after you!

So I went to the bathroom. And yes, here it is, that grubby page in the Book, the page I have returned to so often, the page where the mirrored mirrors reveal to me a bloody Inkling of what sits upon my shoulders. Look. The Old City spreads out below, in three-point perspective. The bathroom dormer spills its light over the tiled roof. I throw the towel, it catches the pedestal mirror. I replace the mirror clumsily and incorrectly. I open the bathroom cabinet. Mirror sees mirror. The Inkling, the suspicion of what may be, shows itself on their silvered surfaces, as inevitable as death. Whispers grow. And grow.

Who was that in the mirror? Whose head was on my shoulders?

I think I knew, even then. But I pushed the unformed thought away; I shut it in the cabinet with the silvered glass. The correspondences were absurd, the implications unthinkable. This is real life, not a comic book; so I told myself.

Chapter 9

I woke up to silence, the morning after I first saw the Inkling's grimace, and an odd feeling inside, as though something within me had also been silenced, but in the way that a beaten dog is silenced. Perturbing, but I repressed it. I had more immediate concerns, after all: Georges Clooney was seducing my wife. And this knowledge chased me from bed that day.

In the kitchen, Infelix swarmed at my feet, begging; I took him to the bathroom and pushed him through the window. Then I put a hand to the bathroom cabinet, intending to get my pills – but stopped. Memories welled and writhed. If I opened the cabinet and exposed its mirror, what would I see? *Who* would I see? A small part of me was intrigued, in a small, shuddering kind of way, but my greater part revolted, and I could not proceed. Not for the life of me. Who hurries to look in a mirror where he'd last seen another's head where his own should be? I had no wish to revisit that stranger's profile, none. It was as if there were an echo of a whisper, a whisper that said: *Don't open that box of frogs.* I can't say I actually heard it; but if I had, I know that's what it would have said. *Don't open that box of frogs, Philippe. Just don't.* So I didn't touch the bathroom cabinet, except to push its door more firmly shut. Then I adjusted the shaving mirror so that it faced away from the room more definitively, and went to the kitchen, seeking breakfast. And I never took that pill.

Marilyne was long gone; nothing of her remained beyond a teasing perfume and a clutch of Post-its on the fridge. *Remember: working late tonight*, said one. Another said, *Hope you're in a better mood today! Love M.*

'Love M'. She always used to sign off with something like 'Loads of love', or 'Love you so much.' More recently, her affection had become abbreviated: 'Much love', for example. Now it was just 'Love'; soon, no doubt, that too would go.

I turned from the fridge and noticed, on the kitchen table, the draft of the scientific paper that Marilyne was writing with Clooney: *Novel cardiac glycosides from Thevetia peruviana*. Next to it was the bag that Marilyne had handed to me last night, while she removed her coat. An opaque white plastic bag, knotted at the handles. I prodded at it; the contents felt hard, but not heavy. What now? A Jarvik-7 prosthetic heart pulled from a patient that it couldn't save? A brace of second-hand stents furred with fat and platelets? I pulled at the knot; its tangled strength defeated me, so I tore a new mouth in the bag's side and – at arm's length – pulled apart its lips and peered in. Not too bad this time: not like the things she had arrayed in the cellar. Just a clutch of twenty or so little plastic tubes with screw-on caps. They were of the type used for urine or stool samples: clear plastic, adorned with a blank label, on which dotted lines waited for the patient's details. Each had a capacity of about thirty millilitres. Unused, true, but still: more medical *bric-a-brac* and *brocante*, brought home for no good reason. It made it so difficult to keep the place tidy.

I'd always put up with that particular habit of Marilyne's because it was part of our normal, or Marilyne's normal, and that was fine, but the truth was that I'd always found it annoying. The egg whisks, the things in the cellar. And, for God's sake, the sternal retractor – in the kitchen drawer! A piece of equipment normally used for keeping the two halves of a patient's chest apart while the surgeons dig and delve; so why should we want it in the kitchen? Marilyne had never provided an answer to that, and thus far it had found no purpose. Just more clutter.

And that, I realised, was yet another example of how Marilyne always, *always* got her own way, and how Philippe – soft, stupid Philippe – always gave in. My discontent grew, and took the form of a hunched, awkward thing which shoved Marilyne's sample tubes into the junk drawer and stamped around the flat.

Thus, the day continued, and thus, somehow, one day flowed into another. In the Book, this period appears chaotic: it is as though the panels have been randomly ordered, such that the narrative flow is disjointed, and successive scenes are unrelated. But oh, how bright the colours! One page is particularly vivid; its full-page panel bursts with colour and action. In this, I am centrally positioned. My hands extend towards the reader, my legs disappear into the background imagery. The exaggerated foreshortening of my limbs gives the impression that I am about to erupt from the page and grasp the reader by the throat – an impression strengthened by the fierce determination that pulls my brow into a frown and bares my gritted teeth. All around me, images seethe: Laurence, grimacing in pleasure or pain, with his hands inside his trousers; a small boy, wearing a T-shirt with a capital *A*, sitting in a corner, alone, weeping; Infelix snarling in foul triumph while voiding his bowels; Marilyne, in a black dress, lying on her side, one hand on her hip's gentle curve; Clooney, grinning like a carnivore, oozing with the triumph of a seducer; and throughout, writhing and puking and pulsing and dripping, tangled masses of sacs and tubes that are surely biological, but from what deviant life-form I cannot tell.

It is uncomfortable to read, that panel, almost nauseating; yet I find it difficult to look away. To turn the page is an effort of will. When I do so, I see that Marilyne and I are in the kitchen. I am sat at the table, brushing crumbs from its surface into my hand; she is standing and talking to me, arms akimbo, like a teacher.

"You were dreaming last night."

"I have not dreamed for years. You know that."

"Well, you were thrashing around and talking in your sleep."

"Nevertheless, there were no dreams."

"Are you sure?"

"I think I would know."

She hesitates; I feel the deep blue weight of her eyes.

"Are you taking your pills regularly?"

"Of course."

"Then how do you explain this?" She places the packet of Favrier Pharma pills in front of me. "I have counted them, Philippe. There are four more than there should be."

I gather the last of the crumbs, stand up and go to dispose of them in the kitchen bin. Behind me, I hear the snap and crinkle as she pushes a pill from its blister.

"Take it now, Philippe. Please."

I swallow; she leaves. As the door shuts behind her, the little pebble of drug makes its peristaltic way down my throat.

"I had no dreams," I say to the void she'd left behind. "None."

From here, the Book's colours become more muted once again; its panels describe my well-trodden routines. Infelix. La Market Jaune. Laurence. Art by proxy only, while my soul decays.

Thursday rolled around, then Friday, and with each day I sank more deeply into a profound emptiness. At home, I sat in the kitchen watching Swiss motes dance in Swiss sunbeams. In La Market Jaune, I sat at my desk listening to Swiss dust fall. Sometimes I felt as if I were the only living thing in Geneva, and that I was surrounded not by peers but by marionettes of string and painted wood, dancing their jerky, mindless dances. Doubtless Laurence would have disabused me of this, but it seemed that he had ceased his tedious visitations. I wondered if perhaps he'd finally succumbed to one of his many health issues. Perhaps he'd died?

I felt guilty as soon as my hope made itself known. But still, at least he wasn't here, driving me mad with his idiocies.

And yet, without Laurence, I felt unable to concentrate. Maybe it was because I was on edge, perpetually expecting a sudden bellow that would rupture my tympanic membranes. Maybe it was because his absence accentuated the absence of other customers, and reminded me of accounts that needed balancing, of commercial uncertainties, of my own terrifying uselessness. Whenever I stirred myself to do something constructive, my good intentions were displaced by something else. Often, the distracting element was a thought of Clooney – my mind's eye revealed him, in lurid three-strip Technicolor hues, in all kinds of tableaux in which Marilyne was a willing participant – but increasingly, I was also disturbed by a persistent irritation with *Madame Médecin*.

Two more issues had arrived, one after the other within a week; it seemed the artist was entering some kind of creative crisis, or submitting to some irresistible compulsion. I now had six stories from this anonymous fool's made world. Something of the artist's obsession transmitted itself to me, for I kept going back to the loathsome creations; kept taking them off their shelf and looking at the artwork and tutting at the dialogue. I could not help myself. There was something about them, something about both style and content, that niggled at me. Some kind of teasing, unseen meaning. I'd often take them home and study them, on the sofa or at the kitchen table. But whatever I was looking for in their pages, I did not find it. Not then.

So I replaced *Madame Médecin*'s adventures on their shelf in Orphan's Corner; the corner which said, *Steal me, or pay for me; but for God's sake just take me*. I left them there, that Saturday, and went home.

Even so, as I swallowed my Favrier Pharma pill that evening, the images from that anonymous creation still swarmed around me, and fragments of its absurd dialogue floated through the air. I pulled at my ears, but heard them still. I ran the bathroom tap; I turned on the shower; I flushed the toilet. Anything to drown out those idiot words that wormed their way through my brain. Nothing worked.

The Book shows me opening the bathroom cabinet, looking for earbuds, cotton wool, anything. And then: a knock at the door! Aghast, I look in the cabinet mirror, at the reflection of the bathroom door behind me. I see the door, yes, but oh God, who and what might be behind it? There is a whole world in the glass, a whole world! I hear the knocking. I watch the reflected handle turn. I watch the reflected door open.

"What *are* you doing, Philippe?" Marilyne waved an exasperated hand at the steam and turned off the tap. I slammed shut the bathroom cabinet and turned off the shower.

"Just having my pill, *cherie*. As you say I must."

"You appear to be having a sauna. If you've *quite* finished, I have to get ready."

She placed Yves' knife on the sill, prepared for the mortification of flesh, and took out her makeup. I sat on the edge of the bath and watched her. She turned the pedestal mirror to face the room and began to put on lipstick. Her reflection gazed back at her, its eyes saying "cut me" in violet entreaty; the Inkling grinned its looking-glass grin from my memories; I shuddered. What were we even keeping mirrors *for?* What was the point?

"Why don't you let *me* be your mirror, Marilyne? I'll tell you when your hair's right, and what clothes look good. I can even do your makeup for you."

Her mouth made a little red *o*; she continued reddening her lips.

"It can't be rocket-science," I said.

"Thank you, darling, but there are some things a girl needs to do for herself, you know?"

"It's just that . . ."

"Mmm?"

"The effect they have on you. The mirrors."

"Surely you are used to it by *now*, Philippe."

"The point is that *you're* not used to mirrors. Not really."

"Oh, but I am, *cheri*. I really am."

"Why don't we try an experiment? Get rid of the mirrors, all of them, and see how we go."

"Because then, Philippe, when your experiment generates the inevitable result, we would be subjected to the expense and inconvenience of purchasing mirrors all over again."

"We don't have to be all irrevocable about this. We can put them in the cellar, and bring them back if we really need them."

Marilyne was quiet for a moment; her reflection pursed its lips again. Such beauty. She reversed the mirror and picked up the knife.

"Let's just keep out of the cellar, okay, Philippe? It's already too crowded. Now, hurry and get changed, darling, or we will be late for Yves."

"What? Yves? *Yves?*"

"Please don't tell me you've forgotten about dinner, *cheri.*"

I do not know how Normals experience memory. But I do know that I can open my Book anywhere, this colourful parade of framed events, and find a painted recollection. For example, here: that first dinner with Yves. The artist has once more modulated his style to accommodate the dullness of our host. The Book's panels are cack-handedly inked, and the pages printed with a colour-off registration method, giving the look of a nineteen-fifties comic. The technique perfectly matches the clumsy decor and muted palette of Yves' apartment.

We are sitting at Yves' dining table, the three of us. All around – heaped in corners, sitting on shelves, hung by puppet strings from pelmets – are Yves' plastic, printed monsters. A bald, big-hipped woman with six breasts; a man with an arm instead of a penis (its little hand is extended like a beggar's); a rabbit with dog's teeth and owl's claws; a crab with three doll's heads (one large, two small) budding from its carapace; and so on. Marilyne is talking about their early days in medical school, the term before Yves dropped out.

"And do you remember, in that practical class, where we were measuring hormone levels in urine, and I had to provide a sample, everyone did, and then someone, I think it was Jean-Paul, you remember him, don't you Yves, he went into oncology, anyway he actually spilt my bottle of pee over himself, and I was so embarrassed, even though it wasn't my fault, because you still feel somehow responsible when someone is soaked in your pee, *n'est-ce-pas*?"

"Yes. . . I suppose so. . ." He was gazing fixedly at Marilyne, the fat dolt, stony-faced and unsmiling. I decided to contribute; *noblesse* must *oblige*, sometimes.

"Oh come on, Yves, when have you ever taken responsibility for peeing over somebody? You're just the pee and flee type, aren't you? Splish, splash, thanks and dash."

Yves glanced at me; a puzzled frown corrugated his oily brow. Then he turned back to Marilyne and directed his answer to her. "Actually, I've never done that. Never."

"And we're very relieved to hear it! Philippe, I don't know what you are talking about. He's disgusting, isn't he, Yves?" Her laugh, as always, sent little silvery ripples down my spine. I almost got up from my seat to kiss her.

Yves continued to goggle at Marilyne. "Yes . . . Ha ha ha." He laughed as though it were something he had learned to do. *Laughter signals amusement. When others laugh, I too must make this noise: Ha ha ha.*

"I dare to speak what others only think," I said. "And à propos of that, Yves, what were you thinking of when you bought that shirt?" I was being provocative, but really, somebody had to tell him.

"It's a Ralph Lauren shirt." He was still speaking to Marilyne.

"Yes, but it is a Ralph Lauren shirt in a very brave shade of yellow. You must be exceedingly comfortable in your own skin to wear something like that."

Marilyne rolled beautiful so-blue-they-are-violet eyes. "I think it's a lovely colour, and it suits you very well, Yves. As if Philippe knows anything about fashion. Or indeed, people."

"Have you tried wearing it with matching trousers? That might produce an interesting effect." I smirked, and emptied my glass. Surely, I thought, my incessant needling would provoke *some* reaction? Something to show that there is life inside Yves. But Yves didn't remove his eyes from Marilyne; it was as though he could not speak to me except through my wife.

"I wouldn't like matching trousers."

I ground my teeth. It was for *this* that I'd given up a Saturday evening? "Please pass the wine, Marilyne."

She passed the wine without looking at me; she was listening to Yves hold forth on novel polymers and prosthetic devices, while he scrolled through images of false limbs on his phone.

When we finally got back home, I was foul-tempered.

"I don't know why you're making such a fuss," Marilyne said. "It was a nice change. We hardly ever meet people who are, you know, like us, and Yves is very interesting, no?"

"When you say interesting, you must be referring to his detailed and lengthy exposition on the use of polypropylene in foot orthoses."

Marilyne frowned at me.

"Fabrication of personalised medical devices is not always trivial, Philippe, even with state of the art 3-D printers. We see this in the theatre all the time – made-to-measure stents that don't quite fit, for example. And Yves takes on all the really tricky jobs: intricately customised prostheses, resorbable scaffolds for growing artificial organs to precise dimensions, personalised neural implants. He gets client requests that verge on the outlandish, and, as far as I can tell, fulfils them excellently."

"Ah. So he is a competent technician."

"Don't be so snobby. There's far more to it than that. Didn't you see the pictures on his phone? Anyone else tasked with making a false leg would generate an ugly husk of smooth plastic – you know, those things that are supposed to be skin-coloured, but which don't match any skin, anywhere. But Yves pays as much attention to form as to function. He works out the physical parameters – strength, stiffness, length, width and weight – and then generates as much beauty as those constraints will hold. Abstract shapes, geometrical patterns, iridescent colours – really, he's a true artist. Don't roll your eyes, Philippe – an Yves prosthesis is as much a sculpture as any Henry Moore. His works will one day be seen in the best galleries. I'm convinced of it."

"His profession is one thing. His *real* interest, frankly, is just odd."

But she just laughed.

"Like drawing dreams and trading *bandes dessinées*? Or like collecting hearts? You see, he is not so different from us, Philippe. Beyond the Normal, as I keep telling you."

Here we go again, I thought: Marilyne attempting to compare Yves' clumsy infatuation with the artistic modalities wielded by Marilyne and I!

"I'm sorry, but his creations are just nauseating. Why does he need to have them in the dining room, of all places? And the decor – everything was brown!"

"Well, I thought his apartment was lovely."

Speechless, I looked around our Old City apartment, where our – *my* – collection of original BD artwork spread colour and burstlines on the walls, cheering one's every glance. Wordless, I remembered that we'd departed this elegant sanctuary, spent good money on a taxi to Les Pâquis – that province of whores and junkies near Cornavin station

– and bled away four hours of irreplaceable life in Yves' gloomy three-bedroom apartment.

"Lovely? His flat hasn't been decorated since the nineteen seventies." This was true: *chez* Yves, wallpaper of orange and brown flowers rubbed shoulders with highly varnished stained pine and dark brown carpets. "And it just *felt* dirty. It made my skin crawl." Indeed; Yves did not smoke, but the previous owners doubtless had, and anything that might once have been white in his kitchen or bathroom was now nicotine yellow. In Yves' flat, even the air seemed to have a tint of raw umber. I guess that suited him; to live in anything brighter would have been to slap his colourless personality each day.

"But it's comfortable, *cheri*. He's got so much more space than us."

"But look at what he *does* with the space, *cherie*." There was the rub: of what avail is space if every inch is taken up with the monstrous? In Yves' apartment, you couldn't get away from his ugly loves. Despite two of his three bedrooms being entirely dedicated to his infatuation, the results of his solitary labours infested every other room too – slumped on shelves, piled in corners, occupying armchairs.

"It takes a lot of expertise to 3D-print such complicated structures."

I thought about what Yves had made. A thing like a large maggot with the head of a pig. A four-armed monkey, its chest split by a huge vagina, its hairless visage leering with mutant lust. A face that grew other faces, with faces growing on those, like fractal, gurning warts. And so on, and on.

"But why *would* you? Anyway, we've done our duty to Yves now. Next Saturday, it's just us two. You said you'd cook, remember?"

"No, Philippe! Next weekend I will be at the conference in the Hotel de la Liberté. I've told you that several times.

I'm sorry, darling, but it's a very busy time right now. Our dinner will have to wait. And as for 'doing our duty' – I told Yves that we'd make it a regular thing. Once or twice a month."

"What! Marilyne, are you *trying* to provoke me?"

"Oh Philippe, don't be stupid."

"I am not, repeat not, dedicating an evening a month to sitting in Yves' flat, listening to Yves' anecdotes about plastic, and pretending to admire his disgusting handiwork!"

"At least Yves is doing *something* creative with his time, Philippe."

The injustice literally struck me speechless. I looked at her, mouth agape; she tapped at her phone, adrift in some oblivion that I could not understand.

It was *you* that prescribed me the Favrier Pharma pills, Marilyne. You know, the ones that stole my dreams, my art, my creativity. And it was you that kept insisting I take them, day after day, month after month. *You.*

But she hadn't finished, my lovely wife. She looked away from her phone, into the middle distance, and then – slowly, musingly, as though twisting Yves' knife deep into my broken soul – she said: "I bet Georges would like to come to dinner with Yves, you know."

"What! Clooney? *Clooney?*"

"Mmm." Something softened in her face. It was hard to define, something around the eyes and mouth. As if something invisible had nuzzled at her ear and aroused some old amity.

"That bastard!"

She frowned. "A little unkind, Philippe. Why do you say that?" The softness had gone; her cheeks seemed sculpted all of a sudden.

"He was mocking me, the other day! At La Salapanzay – mocking me!"

"Really? In what way, precisely, was he mocking you?"

"Don't patronise me! You were there! You saw it too!"

"Remind me of this supposed insult."

"He was laughing at my profession, and my Competition, and, and—" And I could not bring myself to show her the deepest cut of all: that Pretty-boy Clooney had laughed at the incongruity of one such as I – balding, bat-eared, weasel-faced Philippe – being married to someone like Marilyne. Because the thing about humiliations is that recounting them humiliates you all over again. Such hurts do not fade with time; they are forever, for their own memory refreshes them, and no span of time can dull their eternally resurrected pain. So I stopped midsentence; I hid my shame. But Marilyne's silence, her direct gaze, compelled me to say *something*. "And if he touches you again, Marilyne, I don't know what I'll do. I really don't."

"Oh, Philippe – don't be stupid." In the Book, she exudes tired contempt; her speech bubble sits between us like a tumour grown from words.

And had Marilyne been looking at me when she said that, rather than texting yet again, she would have seen a new Philippe, a different Philippe, a long-buried but revenant Philippe looking out at her from this Philippe's eyes, and she would have fallen to her knees and begged for mercy. But she was not looking; she did not see. She just swiped and thumbed at her phone. As though I were of no consequence and Clooney the source of all that mattered. As though my anger and pain were little, little things; as though I were an imp-child and Clooney a colossus that bestrode Marilyne's world, a divine and worshipful being.

Chapter 10

I sat at my desk. Another day yawned before me.

Outside, the tram chuntered past, transmitting its yellow message: *La Market Jaune, La Market Jaune, La Market Jaune.* Joker grinned his grin. My BDs waited, all agog. Nothing happened. Nothing. The Book shows a series of almost identical panels, like one of those spot the difference competitions; the small increments of change only accentuate the glacial flow of tedious hours. Look, they say: nothing, nothing, nothing.

If Marilyne were here, I thought, she would be continually active: making coffee, cleaning the shop's micro-kitchen, standing at the shop entrance and exchanging happy badinage with strangers as they passed by. Or even just texting somebody on her phone. Why couldn't I be like Marilyne?

I checked my phone. No texts. Would I hear the *ping* if one came through? I raised the ring volume and changed the ringtone to something more penetrating. I waited. Nothing, nothing, nothing.

I went through the saved messages and considered deleting all those from Marilyne that were over two years old, but could not bring myself to do so. I thumbed through the photo gallery – Marilyne asleep, mouth slightly open like a child; Marilyne holding her sternal retractor aloft in one hand, while raising a glass of champagne in the other; Marilyne's palm in close-up, a sewing needle pushed through the flesh between forefinger and thumb; and so on – until I came to the snapshot of Edgar Jacobs' Planche 8. Here I paused; such bittersweet joy, to know that this of all masterpieces was so close by, and yet not mine! I jettisoned my phone's usual wallpaper – Alfred E. Neuman – in favour of Planche 8, and checked my texts again. Still nothing. She texted Clooney all the time, but me? Never.

Loneliness sank into jealousy and slowly drowned. I slumped over my desk, hands to my ears; my mouth made a rictus of despair while seven imps from an emerald hell slowly tore my heart in two.

I was losing my beautiful wife.

And I could not stop it.

And I could not bear it.

I knuckled at my eyes. What next, in this shitty, shitty world?

Tinkle-tink.

"*Bonjour*!" On my desk, Comic Con Joker vibrated under sonic stress; the pile of unopened post threatened a slow, sideways collapse.

"Laurence!"

"My friend!" He marched up to the counter and assaulted me with breath like sublimed kryptonite.

"We've missed you, Laurence. Have you been away?"

Laurence placed both hands on the counter and leant closer. Cringing, head down, I pretended to read emails while he unsmilingly scrutinised me, as though reminding himself of my every mole and foible. After eyeballing me for a minute – truly, a whole minute – without saying anything, he decided to get something off his chest. Literally. He put paint-stained hands to his sternum, grasped two handfuls of cheap cotton and pulled in opposite directions. Somewhere, a seam gave way with a slow rip, closely followed by the scutter and ping of plastic buttons on floor and walls. He pulled again, until the flabby, fallen muscles and yellowed flesh of his torso, his curly white chest hairs and odd naevi, were fully exposed, from neck to navel. Like a mad parody of the iconic image from DC Comics, where Clark Kent rips open his shirt to reveal the Superman costume and *S* logo beneath.

"You see?" he roared. "You see this, my friend? Is it not a travesty? The bashi-bazouks, the *zouaves* at the hospital, it was they that did this to me!"

I looked. A twinned pattern of rosy-red, cross-hatched marks, a geometric Rorschach blot, had been scalded onto his pasty, sunken chest. The paddle burns of a defibrillator – I'd seen enough of them when I'd worked as a medical orderly in Paris, chasing Marilyne around ICUs and autopsy suites. So that was why he'd disappeared for a while. I pulled a sympathetic face.

"Have you been ill, Laurence? I am sorry—"

"*Je vous demande* – do you see my chest? Those *putains* at that *bordel* of a hospital grilled my nipples, I tell you! Like a pig on a spit!" He put two grubby fingers on the affected items, and rubbed them gingerly, groin thrust forth, while staring at me with a total lack of expression.

"They were only looking after you, I think."

"Like a pig on a spit!"

He desisted from comforting his teats, and tucked the loose ends of his shirt into his trousers, pulling the button-denuded hems across his front until he was semi-decent.

Then he pointed, first at one shelf and then at another; pointed with great emphasis, grunting as his finger stabbed the air, before turning his groin to me again.

"You have failed, my friend!"

"How so?"

"The Castafiore emeralds, the treasure of Rackham, the balls of crystal. Also, the secrets of the *Unicorn*." He winked grotesquely; it was like watching an ischaemic stroke slowly play out on his face. "You know whereof I speak."

"Mm-hm. The *Tintins* are in the corner, Laurence. Over there."

"Spread the jewels of wonder around your shelves, *putain!*"

"Maybe tomorrow."

Laurence didn't seem to expect this response, for he needed to give his reply deep thought. After perhaps thirty seconds of staring contemplation, he boomed, "Do it! Or I'll fucking *kill* you."

I just could not find it in me to put up with Laurence, not that day. I waved my phone at him. "If you talk like that, I'll call the police, and they'll take you to the hospital."

Laurence gaped at me, as though unable to conceive of such perfidy. Then he backed furiously out of the shop, one bony, white-knuckled fist raised in the air, belching decibels, his voice massacring the airwaves.

"Fuck you! Fuck you! Fuck the police! Fuck the doctors! Fuck the nurses!"

He stopped on the pavement just outside, and leered at me through the window, pushing out his tongue, grasping his ears between thumb and forefinger and pulling them out and down, making an absurd, crazy, goblin face, before striding away, groin-first, head held high.

The thing about Laurence's visitations was the unique quality of silence they left behind. It was as though the very molecules of the insubstantial air were setting themselves back into their proper orbits. It was like the relief of analgesia after the ripping of flesh. I drew a deep breath and let the glorious quiet enfold me. I looked around. All was well. Outside, the trams clunked past; within, my BDs spread colour across the shelves; before me, the post. The Competition entries. I picked up the topmost and opened it.

The Book shows my surprise turn to irritation and then anger. It shows me leaf through the entry, mouth downturned and pulled to one side to expose gritted teeth. It shows the title of what I read: *Issue #7: Madame Médecin and the Implants of Youth.*

Another one! Already! Again, unsigned and anonymous, yet with the correct entry fee. Again, crude, derivative, stereotyped and unimaginative. I slapped it back on the desk, snorted with contempt, and turned to the remaining envelopes.

But I could not focus on them. I found that my eyes were following the pictures and reading the words, yet nothing was being processed. It was as though my brain were going through the motions, on autopilot, while my mind was elsewhere, mulling over other things. Obsessing, in fact, on *Madame Médecin and the Implants of Youth.* I returned to the abomination. What *was* it, that demanded my attention so? It was as if there were some message there, hiding at the edge of understanding; a face in the shadows, mouthing silent words. I read it a third time: was there, in fact, something here of value? No, it was nonsense, an absurdity, fatuous and dull beyond imagining! And yet . . .

Stop, I told myself. I was going round in circles; I needed to clear my mind. Think more coolly, more logically. I covered my face with my hands and shook my head as if to dislodge an accretion of unwanted thought. When I looked up, there was a dark silhouette just outside the shop door. A customer?

No. Laurence was back, peering through the glass frontage. His palms made a peaked sunshield above his eyes.

Again? Now what?

Tinkle-tink. He stood on the doormat, one hand keeping the door open, the other extended towards me, a skinny index finger channelling all his warped discontent in my direction. With a twinge of pity, I noticed a spreading dark patch on the crotch of his trousers.

"You haven't heard the last of this, my friend!" he roared. "Indeed you have not! *Putain!* I know what you are!"

A couple of girls on the pavement squealed and trip-trapped past him, school rucksacks bouncing. I reached for the phone, but Laurence had already turned his concave back on me and exited. His mad bellow – "I know what you are!" – reached me from somewhere near the tram stop.

And it was true. He did know what I was, the bastard. He knew exactly what I was.

Chapter 11

Normally, I can manage Laurence with little disturbance to my equanimity. But my day had already been blackened and spiked by thoughts of Marilyne and Clooney, and I was, I guess, pre-disposed to be pulled into Laurence's head. Why not? I thought. Why *not* stride around Geneva in urine-soaked pants, bellowing at strangers? What's the difference between that and selling comics, or working in a bank, or developing pharmaceuticals? What's the difference? There *is* no difference, none at all. They're all just things that you do. Such was Laurence's siren call. And truthfully, for a small second, I wondered what it would be like to rush out of La Market Jaune to join him; in the Book, I see that I caper from side to side in front of the shop counter, pointing a finger at my empty chair and bellowing, *"Putain!"*

Tempting indeed; but such self-indulgence would not endear me to my one and only love, who was a little more distant each day. No; better to clear my head, to get out and feel the sun, to breathe the breeze that falls from the Alps and tugs waves across Lac Léman. So, with the bundle of Competition entries under my arm and a packet of sandwiches in my hand, I locked up the shop and set forth.

The Book shows me grim-faced; my thought bubble is a scribble cloud.

I had no firm plan, no direction; I let my feet lead me. I'd vaguely intended to go to the Île Rousseau, the charming little island just off the Pont des Bergues, but instead I wandered erratically, this way and that, eating my sandwiches on the hoof. Perhaps the gorgeous weather made me forgetful of time, or reckless in its use; whose mind cannot wander on a fine day? By chance, I passed Doré et Fils. From the gallery window, Planche 8 displayed its mesmeric images; I bathed in their effulgence. And then – and I don't know how or from where the feeling came – I just knew that somehow, sometime, Planche 8 would be mine. The certainty was uplifting. My cares receded; It was almost as though the very prospect of Planche 8 was somehow extracting the Splinter and relegating Clooney to his proper sphere, that of the dull and the Normal.

I could have turned around at that point. I could have gone back to La Market Jaune. Perhaps, had I retraced my steps, all would have been different in the Book; but I did not. I continued walking, through panel after pixellated panel, towards fate's dark-inked outline.

I do believe there is a perverse attraction that operates in the sphere of human life and death. A kind of gravity that draws us to that which we would rather avoid. Sometimes the consequences are trivial: the cyclist who rides straight into the rut he saw five metres away. And sometimes the consequences crack open destiny's shell to permit the hunched egress of some new devil bent on tormenting one's every waking minute. I don't know why such disaster-lusts arise, nor why we submit to them. But I do know that, for whatever reason, on that day – strangely, fatefully, *inevitably* – I found myself drawn to the Café Titeuf. Our special place.

The Book's dyes suddenly darken. Emanata, the stock comic-book symbol of surprise, radiate from my head. My legs bend at the knee, my feet leave the ground in shock; my face is comically aghast. Within me, I feel the Splinter – for it had *not* been pulled, no, not at all – move deeper, and its surrounding abscess swell more tightly with unexpelled rage. Betrayal's shadow darkens the sunny day. I felt like I'd walked into my own life as an observer; one who sees, but is powerless to affect, the vindictive machinations of his enemies and their gradual destruction of his life and soul. Events or people? Both conspire, I tell you; both of them; all of them! Look: there is Marilyne, sitting at the table – *our* table – by the pavement. She is laughing, the way she used to laugh with me, at that table, in that café. And there is a man, sitting in my place, in front of my wife, with his back to me. I have to do a double-take, because he should have been me, but he is not. The Book's artist is unambiguous: he is better-dressed, taller, better-looking.

It was Clooney.

Again, I could have turned around. I could have gone back to the shop. I could have asked her later, at home, about her little liaison. But I did not.

As I walked closer, I heard the tail-end of a conversation.

"One has to make allowances . . . You know he's on the spectrum, of course?"

"Of course, Marilyne. But that changes nothing. Nothing at all."

I slapped my half-dozen Competition entries down on their table – *our* table, damn it! – and sat down casually, as though nothing was wrong.

"Room for a third?" I said, with a friendly smile.

"Philippe!"

"Ah – *le critique d'art*, himself! *Bonjour!*" Clooney half-stood and tried to crush my hand, but I crushed back, and we sent little messages of hate through our eyes. He had a small yellow rose in his lapel. As usual, his sartorial perfection made me feel shabby.

"I like the flower," I said, nodding at his lapel. "Nice touch."

He smirked his customary smirk, but remained silent, as if waiting for Marilyne to speak. And Marilyne, usually unflappable, for once had no ready words. One hand had gone to her throat; the other re-arranged the empty coffee mugs on the table, as though to make room for me. She batted her eyelids at me, sending Morse-coded dots and dashes of confusion in sweetest, deepest violet.

"Are you not working in your shop today, *cheri*?"

"I popped out for lunch. Are you not working in the hospital today? *Either* of you?" I looked at Clooney, searching for some give-away sign.

"We're at the Cardiac Glycosides Symposium. At the Hotel de la Liberté." Marilyne pointed a delicate chin down the road, and made that beautiful little frown that I always wanted to kiss away. "I *told* you about that."

"Oh, really?" I said. But then I noticed the delegate's lanyard around her neck, and felt stupid. Gorgeous Georges had one too. He smirked again, reading every aspect of the situation, and delighting in it.

"As a captain of commerce, Philippe is occupied with far loftier matters than the dull routine of cardiac medicine," he said. "Such different spheres can never collide, *n'est-ce-pas*?"

"We're all busy," I began, with the kind of world-weary shrug that invites complicity. I was about to continue, to say something like *You know how it is*, to invite him into a camaraderie of the heavy-laden, to offer an olive branch; but Clooney just had to interrupt.

"Busy, indeed, since you are working even over lunch. You see this, Marilyne? Does it not make you feel ashamed to be idly drinking coffee . . . May I?" And he leant forward and snatched up the Competition entry from the top of the pile I'd thrown on the table.

"Wait—" I said, feebly, but he was already talking over me.

"And what *chef d'oeuvre* is this? *Madame Médecin and the Implants of Youth,* no less! Extraordinary!"

"I get all sorts of—"

"Have you seen, Marilyne? Titanium hip replacements used as bludgeons, and operating theatre *décolletage* – is that not a precise and complete description of the orthopaedic world? But wait – no – this is extraordinary!" He mimed amazed disbelief, looking from the BD to me and back again, mouth agape, before bursting into peals of false, loud laughter. "Marilyne? Did you know about this?" He pointed at one of the panels on the page he was holding, while Marilyne inclined her head towards him, half-smiling, half-frowning. She was gently tapping the heart-shaped Tissot watch I'd given her on our first anniversary.

"I will take that back now, thank you," I said, holding out my hand. Enough was enough. Clooney extended *Madame Médecin* towards me, but agonisingly slowly, keeping it face-up in front of Marilyne.

"You see?" he said. "You see the advantages of the *bandes dessinées?* You and I, Marilyne, we simply offer individuals the temporary stay of an inevitable death – but Philippe deals in *immortality!*"

"I'm glad you recognise that my art will outlive yours, Georges . . ." I leaned forward and took the BD from him, while he looked at me exultantly. I didn't want to rise to the bait, but I just couldn't help glancing down at the *Madame Médecin* page he'd been showing to Marilyne. What the hell was he going on about? It was only the usual odd nonsense. Marilyne had again placed that small, kissable frown on her forehead; obviously she was as puzzled as me.

"Ah, medicine once was an art, but today is only dull science." Clooney pulled a mock-sad face. "We must sully our hands repairing broken bodies, little more than technicians, while you exist on an ethereal plane where all is beauty – I imagine. As I said, such different worlds cannot overlap." He heaved a sigh, pretending to look desolated.

I decided to ignore him, to cut him out of the conversation; to bring Marilyne back to the realm where Philippe Favrier reigned.

"Marilyne – while you are here, why don't you stop by Doré et Fils?" I nodded back in the direction of the art gallery. "To look at Planche 8. You remember – the sheet of Jacobs' original *Blake and Mortimer* artwork, from *La Marque Jaune*!" I held out my phone to her; Planche 8 glowed on its screen.

"*Cheri* – how exciting!" She said the right words, of course – she always did – but she was looking at her watch again.

"*Extraordinarily* exciting." This, dry as drug powder, from Clooney.

"We must go and look at it, together, Philippe, sometime – but perhaps not today, *hein*?" She looked over her shoulder, towards the hotel and her conference.

"Look at it? *Look* at it? We must – I must buy it! You hardly ever see such things, Marilyne – I simply *cannot* miss this opportunity! We discussed this!"

"And in our discussion, you mentioned that Doré et Fils were inviting offers – somewhat *elevated* offers, as I recall."

"The price will fairly reflect the nature of the item, obviously. They are not fools, Doré et Fils. In any case, Marilyne, that particular concern is increasingly irrelevant." I nodded at her, meaningfully; I did not want to discuss my inheritance, the forthcoming Favrier Pharma share bonanza, in front of Clooney, but I knew she would know what I meant. Hardly a week went by without us sharing our impatient anticipation.

"That particular concern, Philippe, is *always* concerning. Life in Geneva sucks up all my income." Really! As if my income was of no importance! Usually, I *at least* covered my own costs. Clooney, of course, missed nothing.

"Oh, to be a kept man," he said. "And oh, to be kept by one so beautiful."

"Don't be ridiculous! I pay my fair share!"

"Forgive me, Philippe. I meant nothing by it." His grin made a lie of his words. "I simply assumed that a cardiac surgeon earns more than a comic seller. I do not say it is right; I only say that it is the way of the world. Perhaps it is because the world values the work we do. Certainly, our patients are pleased when we delay that final rendezvous which awaits us all."

Marilyne's frown had grown, and she tapped at her watch again. She opened her mouth to speak, but I had something to say to Clooney. In fact, to *both* of them.

"But that's not quite true, is it, Georges? Not *every* patient values your efforts."

"Really? This is your evidence-based opinion? Do share the grounds for your assertion. *If* you please."

"Well, as a matter of fact," I said, with a self-deprecatory chuckle – the kind that warns of an anecdote which will paint a good picture of the teller. "I had to mollify one of your dischargees only today . . ."

Clooney raised a supercilious eyebrow. "Fascinating! How so?"

I wasn't quite sure how to play this. Should I tell of a dangerous psychotic, tipped over the edge by the Universitaire cardiac team – a lunatic who started taking his clothes off in my shop before I talked sense into him with quick-thinking, firm authority? Or should the angle be that of a poor patient who comes to heal his scars – scars caused by the Universitaire cardiac team – in my establishment, where he is assured of sympathetic company? In the end, I went for the former.

"One of my regulars, who has a suite of health issues, poor soul, felt compelled to show me his defibrillator burns in the shop. From the look of them, I'd say someone at the Hôpitaux was a *little* over-enthusiastic—"

Clooney snorted, and Marilyne looked pained. I ignored them.

"—but in any case, the man was grotesquely over-excited, and potentially violent, so the situation was, shall we say, a little fragile. He almost burst my ear-drums with his yelling, but I calmed him with some judicious words, and dissuaded him from removing the rest of his clothes. People in that state respond best to quiet authority. Not a skill that is taught in medical school, perhaps."

I mirrored the expression of tired contempt that Clooney had smeared onto his face. But Marilyne was looking puzzled.

"Wait," she said. "Do you mean *Laurence?* Roaring Laurence?"

"Eh? You *know* him?" Damn!

Clooney bellowed with baritone laughter; when the effluvium of false hilarity had dissipated, Marilyne continued.

"*Cheri*, everybody knows Laurence. Especially at the hospital. With a voice like that, how could we not? He has an intermittent, but long-term, *torsades de pointes*-type arrhythmia problem, which we have to monitor. But I must say, I don't really recognise your description of him as dangerous. He can be a little erratic, yes, but he's safe enough when he's medicated. Just a little unruly."

Clooney laughed again. "'Unruly' – ha! Once, he decided one of our nurses looked like Bianca Castafiore, and chased her around the ward with a giant erection, declaring his undying love. We had to sedate him with extreme prejudice." He laughed yet again, and yet again too loudly.

"Georges, *please*," said Marilyne. "Some anecdotes are better left untold, *n'est-ce-pas*?"

"The giant erection does not please you?"

Why was Clooney always so vulgar? It was just unnecessary. I jumped at the chance to change the subject. "I'm impressed you should know who Bianca Castafiore is, Georges," I said, sweetly. "Perhaps you dip into *Tintin and King Ottokar's Sceptre* from time to time? Between chapters from *Being and Nothingness*, of course."

But Clooney didn't drop his grin by a nanometre, and if Marilyne noticed my put-down, she didn't show it. She turned over one slim wrist to again show her watch. "Georges, the afternoon session will be starting in fifteen minutes, and given that I am chairing it – and you are opening it with a most excellent paper on the potential utility of yellow oleander glycosides in ventricular fibrillation – I think we should be leaving, *non*?"

"*Bien sûr*," said Clooney, getting up. While Marilyne fished for some change to tip Monsieur Titeuf, he leaned towards me. "Pseudo . . . Fifre . . ." he said, in a low voice, playing out the words slowly, with a delighted, cruel grin. "*Deathlessly* funny!"

PseudoFifre? What of him?

I watched them walk away, along the pavement to the pedestrian crossing; and as the light turned from standing red to walking green, Clooney put one proprietorial hand to my wife's arm, as though to guide her across. As if she needed guidance at all, let alone from him; she was his boss, for Christ's sake!

I watched them all the way across the road and along the pavement on the other side. Then I got up and followed them, just to make sure they really were going back to the conference in the Hotel de la Liberté. I watched them pause in front of Doré et Fils, and have a brief, animated discussion in front of the window, punctuated by Clooney's extravagant gestures and Marilyne nodding. They were too far away for me to see clearly, but I thought she had a mocking smile on her face. They continued walking, deep in conversation; I continued following. They stopped at the hotel entrance, where a cluster of people waited by the revolving door. I wasn't sure, but it looked like Clooney's hand might have moved to the small of her back.

I stood there for long seconds, just observing, thinking about things, thinking about Clooney. And I could not escape the feeling that I was looking at some unbalanced world where all was wrong, as I watched Gorgeous Georges and Marilyne walk into the Cardiac Glycosides Symposium at the Hotel de la Liberté; as my wife moved further and further away from me.

My thought bubbles are clear: *I swear to God, Marilyne, if Clooney is trying what I think he is trying and if you let him, then I will react. You know I will, Marilyne. You know I will.*

Chapter 12

Coffee cooled, untasted. Infelix scrabbled in his litter-tray. Marilyne buttoned up her coat. Its tailoring accentuated her figure; its granite-grey set off the straw tones of her hair.

"Why so glum, *cheri*?"

"Am I glum, Marilyne? *Am* I?"

"Mm-hm. And irritable."

"Well, have a guess *why*, Doctor Wonderful. Make a diagnosis." Go on, Marilyne. Make your excuses about Clooney. Let's hear them.

"Is your Competition not going as it should?"

"Actually, it's going fine. Except for that stupid *Madame Médecin* thing."

"Why have you turned it into a *bête noir*, darling? It is only an amateur cartoon strip. If it displeases you, dispose of it."

"There's more to it, Marilyne. It is a *deliberate* provocation. I'm convinced of it."

"Listen to yourself, Philippe."

"No, *you* listen to me! These entries are not like the others! There's something familiar about the images and dialogue, something weird, but also – and get this, Marilyne – whoever is behind them *doesn't want to win!* They enter regularly, they pay each time, but they never provide an address, or even a name! It's like they're mocking the Competition, or like they don't want their name associated with it."

"If they want to conceal their identity, that's okay, isn't it? Who cares?"

"There's more to it than that! It's *intended* to irritate – can't you see? But anyway, as I said, there's no problem with the Competition, as such. That's not why I'm annoyed."

"Mm-hm. And must I guess what discomposes you, or will you tell me?"

I shrugged my shoulders; Marilyne rolled her eyes.

"Okay – my guess is that you still wish to be difficult about Yves. Correct?"

"Difficult? About Yves? *Me?*" This was not only unexpected – I hadn't been thinking about dinner with Yves at all – but also was such a perversion of the truth that I found myself struggling for words.

"I'm right, aren't I?"

"Marilyne, it is absurd to accuse *me* of being difficult because *Yves'* company is difficult to endure! Even *you –* "

"Philippe, you have made your views abundantly plain. Repeatedly. And I'm sorry you don't appreciate Yves – yet – but if that's the way it is, we just have to change things."

I goggled at her; could it be this easy? "Really, Marilyne? You'd do this?"

She nodded. "Of course, *cheri*. I want you to enjoy dinner *chez* Yves as much as Yves and I. So next time, Georges will be coming along too."

"What!" In the Book, my head radiates jagged exclamation marks and dark spurls.

"Yes! Did I not tell you that I introduced them? They got on tremendously well. So Yves is more than happy for Georges to join us. Isn't it wonderful?"

"Marilyne—"

"You know how Georges can always think of something amusing to say. The ambience will be of a different quality. That is what you want, no?"

"No! I mean, yes, but not Clooney! I want the company of *like* minds, Marilyne. That's all."

"And that is precisely why I am suggesting this little change, *cheri*."

"Don't be ridiculous! Clooney is even less one of us than Yves."

"You'd be surprised, you know. About both of them."

"What do you mean?"

"If we do dinner, the four of us, you'll see."

"I categorically refuse."

"Why?"

"Why do you think!"

"Please don't be difficult, Philippe. This is for your benefit as much as mine. We both need an outlet where we can be *what we are*. And, frankly, so do Yves and Georges."

The Book shows my reaction in a quarter-page panel. I glare at Marilyne, arms folded; she glares back, but my speech bubble spells my insurrection without ambiguity. The font is boldly rebellious, my profanity obscured with a grawlix: "I'm damned if I go to another @*?X$&*! dinner with Yves!"

Clooney sat in my thoughts like a mocking incubus all morning; I could not escape his image. It was as if La Market Jaune had been infected by his smug eidolon. Clooney the playboy, Clooney the hunk; Clooney who always had everything go right for him. *PseudoFifre – deathlessly funny.* What could he have meant? I re-arranged shelves of perfectly arranged BDs. I squared up stacks of imported American comics that needed no squaring. I did some filing. All to no avail. I felt jittery, unable to concentrate, vaguely nauseous, infinitely dissatisfied. Was I to fail at everything? No! Planche 8, at least, would be mine. But others were doubtless lusting after it, perhaps even negotiating with the art gallery at this very moment. Do something, Philippe! I speed-dialled a number on my phone; a female voice answered.

"Doré et Fils, good morning."

"This is Philippe Favrier."

"Fourier?"

"Favrier!"

"Of course. May I help you, M'sieu Favrier?" Miss Slavic Cheekbones, without a doubt.

"I just wanted to expedite matters,"

"M'sieu?"

"Regarding the Edgar Jacobs piece. I'd like to discuss how we might speed up the transaction."

"Ah! You wish to bid—"

"No! I have already made an offer! I am here to complete the purchase."

"Complete –? M'sieu Favrier, permit me to be definitive. Offers are invited until August sixteenth. That timeline cannot be compressed. But decisions will be very rapid thereafter. The successful bidder will be informed on the following Saturday, if not before."

"Permit *me* to be definitive. I am in a position to purchase now, and I wish to proceed as soon as possible."

"Your position is appreciated, M'sieu. The vendor also abhors delay."

"Mm. Then we understand each other."

"I am pleased to hear that, M'sieu."

"But do let the vendor know who it is that wishes to purchase the item, *hein?* Favrier. Philippe Favrier. Understand?"

"We will pass on all pertinent information, M'sieu, I assure you."

"Mm."

I hung up. Something about Miss Slavic Cheekbones was unconvincing; I didn't trust her. I looked again at the photo of Planche 8 on my phone, and was reminded of Clooney at Café Titeuf. *PseudoFifre – deathlessly funny!* Yet again I looked for meaning in what he had said, and yet again failed. I wondered if he was alluding to some comment I had made and forgotten, or some event that I could not recall. I considered scouring the Book for clues and indications. But no; I had better things to do than hunt for double-entendres in Clooney's provocative asides. Far better things to do than to brood on Clooney . . .

Who hasn't scoured the online world for details of a love-rival? This kind of masochism is universal; I was only being Normal. Paperweight Joker grinned his agreement as I started Googling.

But the search was not straightforward; surprisingly, Pretty-boy Clooney was little seen on social media. He used neither Instagram nor Twitter, as far as I could tell. His public Facebook profile was limited, and I was hardly about to send him an FB friend request just to see what photos he shared. On LinkedIn he was dully professional. It was as if he were deliberately hiding. Even Clooney's curriculum vitae on the Hôpitaux website gave little information on Clooney the man; beneath his self-satisfied mugshot smirk was only the expected list of achievements and appointments, culminating in his recruitment by Marilyne. It listed no hobbies or interests beyond medicine. I did, however, find one little red flag: shortly before joining Marilyne's team in Geneva, he'd been training in the Department of

Cardiovascular Surgery at the Hôpital Européen Georges-Pompidou.

And *that* fine institute is in Paris, so Clooney had been in the City of Light – the City of *Love* – at the same time as Marilyne and I. Both of them doing cardiology in the same city, at the same time? They would have *had* to have known each other. Yet she'd never mentioned him.

I thought I heard a warning bell at that point, just a whispered chime; almost inaudible, but a clear alarm, nevertheless. *Tinnngggg,* it went; *tinnngggle-tingggg.* My heart sunk; my hackles raised. I thought of Clooney and Marilyne, and wondered if she'd turned to him when things went so, so wrong for us in Paris. After Antoine. Or even – bile rose in my throat – even *before* Antoine! My hands white-knuckled on the desk's edge.

I continued my research; indeed, I could not stop. The plethora of results pertaining to Georges Cuvier, 18th Century French naturalist, hindered me, however; it was like looking for a Splinter in a heap of kindling. But eventually I found, posted on the internet, an old issue of a school magazine from about fifteen years ago; and there, on the page listing that year's leavers, was Pretty-boy, his adolescent portrait as smug as the adult it presaged. Apparently, he had been voted Most Likely to Win Nobel Prize in Medicine by his sycophantic peers. Beneath that absurd prediction, a 'How I See My Future' sentence by Clooney himself: *My sights may be set on the science of healing, but I remain an amateur of art both fine and coarse; convention shall not restrict my passion.*

An amateur of art both fine and coarse – how very Clooney! I looked through the rest of the magazine: acned class-mates, sports results, exam results, a self-congratulatory message from the headmaster, changes to the teaching staff. Nothing else that pertained to Georges.

Convention shall not restrict my passion. Typically conceited and self-regarding. I printed a screenshot of the adolescent Clooney and his pretentious assertion; I placed it centrally on my desk, this evidence, for close examination at a later date. My black mood lightened slightly; I felt, at last, that I was making progress. I had information about Clooney that neither he nor Marilyne knew I had, and this small fact warmed my soul. It was symbolic, but not in the sense of superficiality or cipher; rather, it was symbolic of greater, more significant changes to come. Like a small eddy signalling that a huge water had ceased its ebb, and was about to wash again long-abandoned sands. Go with the flow, Philippe! I thought. There is a tide in the affairs of men . . . let it take you!

But take me in what direction? In the Book, my head is cocked, listening. The shop swells with a heavy silence; presently, this is replaced by a thin, high clamour, as if of some distant, tormented soul.

I read the print-out again. *Convention shall not restrict my passion.* Inspiration failed. I sought help from the stacked shelves of La Market Jaune.

"My friends! He has followed Marilyne and I, this Clooney, this snob, this wife-stealer, since Paris! I know it!" The Book shows me throwing out my arms in rhetorical gestures; my words are capitalised, the font heavily bold. "I cannot remain passive in this matter, my friends! Action must be taken!" I nod vigorously. "The question is: *what* action?"

And just as I posed this question, my faculties, for once, broke through the drug's handicap. My thoughts were as precise and unimpeded as they had been in childhood. Maybe it was because I had been spared Laurence's early morning visit that day (though I still heard – or imagined I heard

– the suspicion of his boom and bellow over the Geneva traffic). Maybe that freedom from interruption had enabled me to see the key issue with greater clarity.

Or maybe I hadn't, in fact, taken my pill again? I wasn't sure; I can't be sure, for the Book does not specify. But it is certain that the world was more sharply focused that day. And the key focal point was this: if I kept raising the matter of Clooney with Marilyne, she would keep denying that Clooney mattered. The only way forward, therefore, was to gather incontrovertible evidence of their adultery, and present it to her. I mused; the logical Favrier brain, inherited from Dad, whirred into action. Before long, it had produced its conclusion: *Search among her possessions, during the day, when she is at work.* And then, at my ear, from the dark Inkling that sat upon my shoulder, a dark whisper: *Now. Do it now.*

Indeed: the shop was empty of customers; my accounts were up to date; I'd left all the Competition entries, including the latest *Madame Médecin*, at home – so what better time than *now* to start my investigations?

Back in the apartment, I set to work. I'd shut up shop early, and Marilyne wouldn't return until late – *Conference dinner. Love M.,* said the Post-it – so I had plenty of time. A shadow at the bathroom window begged for ingress, but I was in no mood for Infelix and his insistent complaints. So long as he was in by the time Marilyne returned, all would be well. No hurry.

I started in that end of the fitted wardrobe where Marilyne kept her clothes. As I slid the door along its tracks, the old net curtain – doubled over and pinned to the wardrobe frame so that it obscured the full-length mirror – trembled, threatening to let slip hidden reflections. I went through each pocket of every coat. I carefully emptied each shoe box and looked inside every shoe. I opened each compartment of all her assorted handbags. I searched her overnight bag. Everything I touched or opened released a delicate fragrance; it was as though her sweet-scented avatar stood by my shoulder, whispering, *What are you doing, Philippe? What are you doing with my things?* I found nothing of interest: just old tissues, small change, used plane tickets, last season's ski pass.

Almost as if she'd had a clear-out, just in case. As if she suspected I suspected. The feeling grew upon me that some disastrous truth, deeply hidden, was soon to be exposed.

I moved on to her chest of drawers. Underwear, T-shirts, tights, socks. A box of dress jewellery. A smaller box containing earrings I'd bought her from Maison Adler. Combs, brushes, hair gadgets, makeup. Perfume. Again, nothing that pointed to any Clooney liaison. Just like that old adage – I think I first read it in one of my 1950s *Rookie Cop* issues (artist, Dick Giordano) – that finding *no* fingerprints can be suspicious in itself. Who wipes their glass clean after drinking? I was onto something; I was sure of it.

I'd turned almost the whole apartment upside down, for no real gain, before I realised how stupid I was being. If she wanted to hide something, she wouldn't hide it here, in this tiny apartment where we tripped over each other all the time. No. There was only one place it could be – in the little cellar allocated for our use beneath the apartment block. We'd hardly entered it since our move from Paris, when we bundled into it everything that we couldn't fit into the flat. I yanked open the junk drawer in the kitchen, scrabbled aside Marilyne's plastic sample tubes that I'd tidied away last week, and dug out the cellar key. Then I left the flat and ran down the stairs, two by two. On the wall, my hand snagged peeling paint and dislodged thin scabs of magnolia.

Our cellar, as damp and dark and cobwebbed as such places always are, leaked silence and misplaced memories. Suitcases, all empty. Cardboard storage cartons, used in our house move, now flat-packed to save space. Two bikes, gathering dust since our arrival in Geneva (who'd cycle in this city's traffic?). A box of books we'd set aside to give away. Another box, containing toys and similar oddments for a baby or very young child. One of the soft toys still had a gift tag: *For Antoine: Welcome!* This box was fuller than I remembered, and had items that I didn't recognise. Clearly Marilyne had been thieving again. At my feet, a rolled-up rug. At the back, the locked steel cabinets with their bubble-wrapped jars full (I knew) of Marilyne's surreptitious autopsy acquisitions: spleens, bladders, glands, and odd fatty masses of obscure provenance, all drowned in gin-clear preservative. After Antoine, I'd never wanted to see another autopsy suite, but Marilyne remained unable to cease her illicit visits. And finally, success: there, in the corner, on top of the cabinets and pushed back into the darkness, a package. Something rectangular, about the size of a sofa cushion; wrapped in the old paint-stained curtain I used to wipe my brushes on, back when I made pictures. Nothing else had been dust-proofed, only this.

The cloth unfolded easily; its surfaces rubbed softly against each other, forcing revenant whispers from crusts of dead paint. *Philippe . . . Listen to our rainbow tones . . . Titanium white, napthol red, manganese blue!* Where are you now, my pretty things? But that way lay a dangerous kind of memory, something that murmured and hissed, so

I stopped my ears for a little minute, and then pushed aside the shroud of many colours to reveal what it had covered.

A small leather case: a thing from the last century, with reinforced corners and two brass catches. Old stickers on its surface, of the kind a teenage girl might once have favoured; old scuffs on its edges, from much fond use. It was Marilyne's, of course, a legacy from her grandmother; I recognised it. I picked it up, weighing its secret heft. I rocked it from side to side and its contents slid and chinked. I put it down and pressed my thumbs against the sliding buttons on either side of the brass catches. For a second I thought it was locked, but it was only stiff; the buttons gave, and the catches flipped open. I pushed the lid back to its fullest extent and looked inside.

At first, I saw only cardiosurgical paraphernalia. A large steel syringe, a bundle of scalpel handles held together by a rubber band, packets of unused scalpel blades in their safety sheaths, scissors, forceps, retractors, needle holders. A broken teaching model of the heart (some vessels in blue plastic, and some in red; some muscle in yellow plastic, and some in white). The broken pedestal for above teaching model. Catheters, heavy-duty surgical gloves, and a rolled-up item which I found to be a disposable apron. And beneath such impedimenta, as if deliberately hidden, a cardboard document folder. I grasped it by its corner; I pulled upwards, angling it so that the surgical instruments on top of it slid back into the case; I took it out and opened it.

What does the Book show? Pictures. Pictures of Marilyne, naked, her body delicately outlined in expert strokes of charcoal or graphite, her curves given seductive body by shading. Dozens of pictures. Some are just pencilled outlines, as if studies for a later, slower composition. Others are daubed with brilliant hues in oil pastel or acrylic: in these, the cuts on her hips or stomach are redly inflamed or ochreously scabbed according to their stage of healing. Here she lies on a bed, gazing at the artist with impossibly violet eyes. Here she reclines on a sofa, looking away through the window of our Paris apartment. Here she stands by the same window, looking back into the room. On the sill is a vase of miniature roses; their bright yellow bursts from the paper like a flame. And here, here, she sits on a chair, facing the painter and smiling with some secret joy, while her hands caress and support the rondure of her stomach. Oh Marilyne. Oh Antoine.

The paintings and charcoal studies were signed with two letters in the same singing yellow that gave the roses life: *PF*. Exactly the way I used to sign my work; exactly the same. But the uncoloured, pencil sketches – these were unsigned.

Chapter 13

In the sitting room, I moved the armchairs back and spread the pictures over the floor. I phoned Marilyne, and kept phoning, once every five minutes, until she picked up.

"Philippe?"

"You took your time."

"The last session has only just ended, *cheri*. It over-ran a little. I am just catching up with colleagues before we all head off to the conference dinner."

I thought I detected a micro-hesitation before *colleagues*. As though she'd been about to say *Clooney*, but had reconsidered.

"Very nice, I'm sure."

"Philippe? Are you all right?"

"Why do you ask? Should I not be?"

"You sound out of breath."

"I've just run up from the cellar." In fact, that was nearly an hour ago, but every time I looked at the pictures of Marilyne, and thought about the implications, my pulse rate soared and my breath came in short gasps.

"We have to be careful, darling, because your medicine *can* have cardiotoxic side-effects, and the first sign of that can be breathlessness. Maybe we should get you in for a check-up—"

"I'm fine!"

"Just think about it, Philippe, please. Anyway, what were you doing in the cellar? Please don't tell me you're thinking of cycling."

"I was just poking around. Looking for a book."

"What book?"

"It doesn't matter! The point is, I found something. Some things. And I want an explanation – I *demand* an explanation!"

"From me? Of course, dear heart." She sounded amused. "What are these things that I must explain?"

"I found them in your case. The little leather one, from your grandmother. Pictures."

"What pictures, *cheri*?"

"Pictures of *you*, Marilyne! You were naked. And it was in our place in Paris. And – oh, Marilyne – some of them were just before Antoine!" In one hand, my phone was warm and smooth; in the other, nails dug into my palm. "Who was it, Marilyne, that did them? Was it Clooney, even then? Will you just tell me, Marilyne? Please?"

She was silent; I could hear background chatter and laughter. "Wait one second, Philippe, please." I listened to background sounds: her heels going *tic-toc, tic-toc* on some hard floor, conference chatter fading. "Okay. Now. You are talking about the sketches, yes? The charcoal sketches of me?"

"Yes –"

"The charcoal sketches of me that *you* did, Philippe! You!"

"But *did* I, Marilyne? *All* of them?"

"Surely you would know, *cheri*?" She sounded almost pleading, as though suddenly scared that some secret were about to be finally revealed.

"Some of them may be mine, yes. Some of them may be artful copies of my style, even down to the signature. But some of them, Marilyne, are *not* mine and not even similar."

"I can tell you that nobody other than you has ever drawn pictures of me, Philippe, and certainly not that kind of picture." There was steel behind her voice; the hard, honed core of Marilyne that sometimes scared me.

"And I can tell you that I have never, never neglected to add pigment to my work. You know how important colour is to me."

"Oh – wait! You're talking about the *pencil* drawings, now? Just outlines, and always from behind?"

"Yes!"

"They were *mine*, stupid! Don't you remember? We had to set up some mirrors so I could draw myself, without, you know . . ."

Without Marilyne seeing her own reflected face, she meant. From behind, it seemed she could pretend that the woman in the mirror was someone unrelated, some anonymous life model. When I'd done a few drawings of her, she'd announced that she wanted to have a go. And, as with everything, she turned out to have a natural talent. Very different from me in style, but definitely talented.

"Do you really not remember, *cheri*?"

"Actually, I *do* remember something like that. But I don't remember you doing so many pictures. And some of the angles would have been quite awkward to set up with just two mirrors."

"Look, it was a while ago, darling. I can't recall every detail, but as you know, I was quite taken with the whole life-drawing thing for a little while. I did a few more while you were away at Comic Con in America. I'm sure I would have shared them on Instagram or something. But you may not have ever seen the originals, because while you were away, things went, you know, wrong . . ."

She meant Antoine, of course. Bless his seven days.

"But in any case, Philippe, *please* let us discuss this another time. I must get to the conference dinner now – people will be wondering where I am. Colleagues. See you tonight, dear! But it will be *very* late – you don't need to stay up. Love you!"

C-c-colleagues . . . Like C-C-Clooney.

I gathered the pictures and took them to the kitchen. I looked through them again, one by one, while I ate. I poked at some with Yves' knife; its tip punched delicate isosceles triangles in the paper. Finally, I returned to the sitting room and lay on the sofa, determined to wait up for Marilyne. And then I fell asleep. Usually, my naps would be interrupted by the urinary side-effects of the famous Favrier pill – but not that evening. (*Did* I take the pill?) I woke only when Marilyne came back, just after midnight.

I lay in the darkness of the sitting room, listening to her move around in the kitchen: the clink of a mug, the muted roar of the kettle, the soft scrape of chair legs on tiles. Something else; an occasional rustle, quiet and stealthy. Silent as Infelix stalking a squab, I inched off the sofa and ninja-stepped to the kitchen door. Marilyne was sitting at the table, with her back to me. She wore the black dress that she saved for formal occasions; her hair was up, revealing the wispy hairs – so fine they seemed colourless – on the back of her neck. As I moved forward, pace by cautious pace, she continued her nocturnal activity. The pictures; she was examining them, one by one. Each was picked up by its very edges, inspected minutely, and set aside. Most went into a neat pile at arm's length, weighed down by Yves' knife, but two she kept in front of her. One of those appeared to be mine – at least, it could have been mine, but I had no recollection of doing it – and the other was a monochrome outline of the type that Marilyne claimed to be hers. This she bent over, as though to inhale its memory. I moved closer, and just slightly to one side; now, I could see the delicate whorls of an ear, the corner of her mouth where lip met lip – just by that place where her skin always held the memory of a dimple – and her perfect throat, where the jugular's soft ridge stood sweetly. And now I was close enough for her scent to reach me and awaken something primeval in some ancient, pre-human part of my being. *C-c-c-Clooney.* How could she? And these pictures, that she now sighed over, tracing her own divine, unclothed outlines with one elegant finger, were they his work?

"They bring back such memories, do they not, Philippe?"

For a second I stood motionless, as if surprised into indecision by a choice I did not know I had. But then, still without looking, she reached behind her with one hand, unhesitatingly found mine – as if she had known exactly where I was at every point – and pulled me towards her, only releasing my hand to hug my legs.

"Such memories," she continued, "such unhealed pain. As if people like us do not suffer enough."

I saw that both of the pictures she had kept aside must have been done at a very similar time; in each, her belly's gentle swell was clear. The monochrome sketch showed her from behind, sitting with her legs tucked under her, leaning on her left hand, with her right hand beneath her stomach. She is turned ever so slightly to the right, so that the viewer sees the hint of a profile and the start of her stomach's curve. The other picture, done in my own style, is the one where she sits on a chair, smiling at the artist, with both hands holding – no, *presenting* – her stomach's curve.

I folded my arms to my chest. The pressure of her one-armed hug around my thighs was irritating; I felt trapped. And yet it was also enticing, heart-breakingly so; it spoke of the old days, of warm embraces unsullied by infidelity. Of love. And then I saw the print-out of her scientific paper, still on the kitchen table: *Novel cardiac glycosides . . . Georges CUVIER and Marilyne FAVRIER.*

"People like us," I repeated. "That includes Clooney, doesn't it? 'He's not so different from you and me.' That's what you said to me the other day. 'An outlier,' you said. About Clooney. Well, go on. Tell me how he's not so different. Tell me the details."

She didn't turn to me, but her head drooped a little, and she released my legs from her hug. I took a half-step back.

"Is it that he is made like us, Marilyne? Tip-toeing between his real nature and the nature demanded by stupid Normals? I hardly think so. Or is it just that he likes to make pictures, Marilyne? Pictures of you. Is that what you meant?"

"Philippe —"

"I *know*, Marilyne! Look!" I delved in one pocket, and then another, and finally found the print-out. I unfolded it in front of her. "From Pretty-boy's school days. *An amateur of art both fine and coarse.* Is this what he meant by coarse art, I wonder?" I flicked at the pencilled curve of Marilyne's bare buttocks; she flinched as though I'd hit her actual flesh. "And as for Antoine – well." I traced, as she had done, her belly's roundness in each picture. "It seems Pretty-boy was in Paris at the same time as us. Training in cardiosurgery. At the Georges-Pompidou. You knew him then, didn't you? So perhaps he was also an *amateur* of Marilyne, *hein*? All this time —"

But Marilyne had stood, and turned to face me. I'd hoped she would slap me; I wanted something physical.

Instead, she just looked at me, deep, deep into my eyes, as though she could see every working of my poor, unwinding heart.

"Okay," she said. "Shut up, Philippe. And listen to me while I point out how you are being stupid."

"Fine! Go for it." I pulled out a chair and sat down, as if in readiness for a show. Marilyne, looking down at me, raised a finger.

"Firstly, the Francophone cardiosurgery world is not big. Everyone knows everyone, everyone collaborates, everyone visits each other's institutes. It would have been more surprising if Georges and I had *not* overlapped during our years of training or soon after. Understand?"

I opened my mouth to respond, but she carried straight on.

"Secondly, that Georges is an art enthusiast is hardly news. Yes, he holds forth on fine art. He also has opinions on opera, *haute cuisine*, literature and philosophy. What do you expect? This is *Georges*. For all his good qualities, his non-Normal qualities – and he *does* have some, Philippe, though you are determined to overlook them – he is, nevertheless, a cultural snob."

"My point was—"

"Your point, if that is what you call it, Philippe, regarded Antoine. Now . . ." She reached down, grasped the hem of her dress, and slowly raised it above her waist, stopping just below her breasts. She held it there with one hand, and with the other reached across for Yves' knife, placed on the discarded artwork. "Look, Philippe." I looked at the cuts on her midriff: new skin, all pink and shiny, smiled gaily where brown scabs had fallen away. She held the knife to her lower belly, where the smooth flesh was unscored. "Perhaps you'll be able to read the truth cut into my womb,

Philippe. Perhaps it is written in words that will help you understand. Shall we see? Look." I watched, transfixed, as she pushed the knife's tip into the soft skin above her groin and pulled it upwards and to one side; a long, shallow cut which barely missed her navel. Dermis parted; blood welled. She put the point of the knife back into the initial site of insertion, pushed again – harder this time – and again pulled upwards, along the same trajectory. The red beads swelled. "We can continue, Philippe, deeper and deeper, until we expose the truth. Is that what you want?" Her voice was soft, almost amorous. "Because deep within me, Philippe, too deep to ever be excised, is the truth that you are trying to twist. The truth about Antoine." She brought back the blade to the cut's beginning. "You know I'll keep on, Philippe. Until we find the truth." The blood was running with some freedom now, making bright blooms on her cotton underwear. "That's what you want, isn't it? The truth? The very *deepest* truth?" She braced for another push, but I caught her hand and pulled it away.

"Stop," I said. "Just stop." I prised her fingers away from the knife; I took it from her and lay it on the table. The violet-blue of her eyes held me still; her mouth crooked into a half-smile. She kept her dress raised up. I remained seated, my arguments forgotten.

"Have we been stupid, Philippe?"

I leant forward and pressed my face to her belly; the heat of her fresh-cut flesh warmed my cheek, and the scent of her skin intoxicated me.

"Yes," I said.

"Go and wash, Philippe. You have blood on your face."

And that is what I did. And if there was a scrabbling at the bathroom window at that time, well, my mind was elsewhere; and if I forgot to take my pill again, well, Marilyne did not remind me; and in neither case can I bear full responsibility for the consequences.

I thought I'd never sleep that night, and indeed it seemed that I lay awake for an eternity of nights; yet sleep I did, and when I did, I dreamed – for the first time in years – and dreamed horribly. Marilyne sat astride me, rocking gently with the rhythm of a heartbeat, and smiling so sweetly. But there was something wrong, I could feel it – a sharp pain, like a splinter, but in some undefined part of me. Marilyne gave a little frown, and said, *We need to give you a very thorough examination, M'sieu Favrier.* She reached down with both hands, tore my torso open from top to bottom, and winched apart my ribcage with the sternal retractor from the kitchen. It was agony, but I could neither move nor speak. I lay there, paralysed, while she dug around inside me. Soon she was in me up to her elbows; I could feel her rooting around in my viscera, pushing aside lungs and liver and spleen, all the while with the pensive frown that made me want to kiss her. Finally, she pulled out my wretched, flopping heart, like a fat red fish. *It's all right, Philippe,* she said, as it gasped and spasmed in her hands, *it's perfectly sterile.* But then, with a puzzled expression, she raised the poor twitching thing to her ear. *Listen,* she said. And I heard it: *tinkle-tink*, it went, very quietly; *tinkle-tink, tinkle-tink.*

Chapter 14

I woke, gasping for breath. Marilyne's hand was on my chest; her nails were digging in. It hurt. She was fully dressed, sitting on the edge of the bed, and had a cold, hard look in her eye; a look I hadn't seen for a long time. Frosted violets.

"Philippe."

"Mmm?" I rubbed my chest. What the hell did she think she was doing?

"Philippe, where is Infelix?"

"Could be anywhere. In his basket, in the clean laundry, under the bed, on the sofa. How would I know?"

"I am asking you where Infelix *is,* not where he *could* be, in some theoretical world."

"I don't know! Aren't you going to be late for work?"

"He is not anywhere in the flat. Could he then be somewhere outside?" Her voice was low, and a bit shaky, like somebody trying not to lose it.

"The window was open for a while yesterday, so he might have gone—"

"He does not 'go' through the window, Philippe. Not unless he is *put* through the window." She was definitely losing it a bit now. Not like Marilyne.

"Well, let's just *open* the window and—"

"I've done that! He's not there! He could have fallen off the roof and *died*!"

"*Cherie*, cats do not fall from roofs. They may be pushed, but—"

"Don't you *dare* try to be funny! Just tell me: *Where is he?*"

"Marilyne, there are hectares of roofs out there, covering dozens of apartments. If he's not curled up next to some chimney, he will have gone through somebody else's window—"

"Then *you* can go around all the Old City top-floor flats and ask if they have my cat! By the way, what did he eat yesterday?"

"Well, I believe it was the normal arrangement—"

"You mean I gave him breakfast, and you didn't bother giving him dinner."

"You give him so much, it was hardly necessary—"

"No *wonder* he's not come back! He's looking for food! How could you be so *stupid*?"

She said more, much more. When the door slammed behind her, I lay in bed for a while grasping the pillow to my face. And that, I believe, was when I really became aware of the impact of yesterday's holiday from the Favrier drug. I had no urgent, bursting bladder to deal with, just a natural desire. For the first time for so, so long.

In the bathroom, I called through the window: "Infelix!" Of course, he appeared almost immediately. Usually, I'd give him a cuddle, but the world was my enemy that day, and I had no affection in me, no, not for anyone or anything. I held him in front of me, head-high. Beneath my fingers, I felt the fragility of his small life. I could have crushed him, crushed him. But I only dropped him to the floor and watched him run out in search of food. Then I paused, my attention taken by that most precious of hearts, suspended in its broad jar. I pushed it from side to side on the sill, sliding its weight across the painted wood. I ran my fingers over the paper label glued to the jar's side, as if to follow the curlicues and flourishes of Marilyne's neat writing. In the Book, my thought bubble says, *Such memories*, as I knuckle at an eye. *Such unhealed pain.* A small whim took hold of me, and I placed the jar on the open window's ledge. Just a small push, and it would career down the tiles and smash into a thousand shards in some stranger's courtyard. Just a small push, and Marilyne's life and mine would be shattered beyond repair.

I replaced the jar on the sill, and shut the window.

I let Infelix stay in that day. Not because I felt sorry for him, nor because Marilyne would have wanted it, but because I lacked the energy to put him out. Whenever Marilyne was angry with me, my will eroded; I would sink into an enervation that felt one step from death. To stir myself into any kind of action that day, was almost beyond me. But I had to go to work – what else could I do? – and in any case, I thought, perhaps La Market Jaune would soothe me with its magic, as it so often did.

The Book shows a cat's-eye view – from a point adjacent to Infelix's food bowl – of me leaving the flat. And then it shows me slouching along the pavement: slumped shoulders and bowed head, eyes downcast and arms hanging slackly at my sides. I am so hunched over that my hands almost touch the floor. At first, instead of a thought bubble, a dark grey rain-cloud hovers above me, but the rain resolves itself into letters in the next panel. *She loves me, she loves me not* . . . Comic Pro.

Tinkle-tink. I shut the shop door behind me. I didn't bother firing up the computer to check for internet orders and new publications; I didn't bother retrieving the mail; I just sat. Outside, trams clutched at the untidy wires criss-crossing above the road and glinted out their endless, mocking message: *La Market Jaune, La Market Jaune, La Market Jaune.* Around me, I saw the results of five years of effort and sacrifice. My carefully stacked merchandise no longer seemed consoling and cheerful; the colours had grown garish, their glowing pigments signals not of delight but of danger, like the warning colourations of venomous things – wasps and coral snakes. They pulsed at me, but slowly, as though breathing. Somewhere a soft voice spoke:

You are losing her, Philippe. You are losing your only friend in this world.

"I don't care," I said. "I don't care. Anyway, it is she who is losing me."

Clooney is taking her, you seller of comics.

"It would have been surprising if they *hadn't* overlapped in Paris. Anyway, he's gay. Everyone knows that."

Everyone knows he saves more lives in one day than you shall in your entire life.

"I never wanted to be a doctor! Despite Dad! Art is what interested me, always; art is forever."

Your cartoons are deathless, yes: deathlessly funny.

"It is the Ninth Art! It needs no defence from me!"

And if it did? Doubtless you would guard it as capably as you keep your wife.

"Oh, Marilyne!"

Within an hour, I'd locked up the shop again – *tinkle-tink* – and walked out blindly into the city. Indeed, I was almost literally blind; I could not stop my eyes from welling up. I paced the leafy avenues of the Parc des Bastions, aimlessly, and yet in search of something. I circuited the grassy park of Plainpalais, again and again, but found no relief. I took the tram to the Jardin Botanique, but its clipped lawns and carefully cultured trees and bushes, beautiful as ever, gave me no respite. Finally, I ended up pacing the shores of Lac Léman; its deep, clean currents, I thought, would buoy my drowning soul. But they did not. At times like that, slow-flowing waters are not enough; one needs friends.

And there it was: after relocating to a new city, followed by five years of single-minded focus on La Market Jaune, I had no friends. Indeed, I had scarcely any acquaintances. Except Yves.

I picked up a stone and threw it into the lake; a mallard took clumsy flight.

Yves. I *could* have a couple of beers with him. Why not?

But then again – Yves! Dear God! Could I really be contemplating this? *Yves has no conversation*, I reminded myself. He would speak only in response to another's gambits, and then only by way of closure, not contribution. *Yves has no humour*. The finest rapier wit would have its point turned on his dull hide, and leave him stony-faced. *Yves never laughs*. He would acknowledge amusement only by a false smile, forced through his gloomy carapace, as though levity somehow intimidated him. *Yves, in short, is dull, dull, dull.*

I walked along the lake's shore a little further, until the brutal edifices of Geneva's financial quarter loomed too close. I sat down on a smooth rock and looked out over the water, towards the rocky slopes of the Salève. No, I thought. There are limits. You'd have to be truly desperate to go drinking with Yves.

"Hello?" Yves' monotone flatlined from my phone.

"Yves! Philippe here. How are you?"

"Okay."

"Made any more little plastic monsters?"

"I don't make little plastic monsters."

"I meant your 3D-printer creations. The mini-golems. The dolls with mixed-up bodies and things."

"Yes, I know what you meant. But they're art. Not monsters."

"Okay, okay. It's all subjective. Anyway, I was wondering if you'd like to go out for a drink tonight? I'm at a bit of a loose end, because Marilyne's at this conference, and she's not getting back until late, so I thought why not paint the town red with Yves?"

"I can't tonight. I'm busy."

"Oh? You've managed to persuade a nice young lady to kill some time with you?" Jeez! It'd be a case of first torturing time and *then* killing it!

"No. I've got to work on a project tonight. An art project. It's in my diary."

"Wow! It's great that you're really going for it like this. What are you doing now? Something tasteful, I hope?"

"I don't want to tell people what it is, yet. But I might be able to show it to you, at some point. If it gets close to what I want it to be. In fact, I'd like to see if you can guess what it is. At some point."

"Sounds great, Yves! I look forward to the great unveiling. But listen, I don't suppose you might consider working on your project *tomorrow* and coming out for a little drink *tonight*?"

"No. It's in my diary for tonight. But I *can* come out for a drink this weekend. Saturday."

"What! Are you sure there isn't anything in your diary for a Saturday, of all evenings?" My sarcasm zipped over his head.

"Yes, I'm sure. I just checked it." My sarcasm returned, whooshing beneath his dull radar, to crash at my feet.

So we agreed to meet at the Chat Noir on Saturday evening. And it was okay, I thought. It really was okay. It didn't mean I was desperate, because the fact was that Marilyne and Yves liked each other, and although that was a bit bizarre, it also gave me a tremendous opportunity. Yves and Marilyne were friends; therefore, Yves might know something about Marilyne and Clooney. The right questions, subtly put, could – once and for all – reveal everything. In brief, I wasn't going drinking with Yves because I had nobody else to go drinking with, I was going drinking with Yves to gather intelligence. Just like Francis Blake would have done in any *Blake and Mortimer* adventure.

But, oh, if only I had a Mortimer by my side!

In the Book, I am shown with head angled and gaze unfocused, as if listening; as if, somewhere, a violin has lost itself in a high yellow vibrato and I am trying to trace its origin. From somewhere closer, the sounds of Geneva's crowds and commerce reach me dully. And everywhere, everywhere, just beyond the edge of hearing, are whispers.

Chapter 15

The Book shows a topsy-turvy afternoon: its colours are by turns muted (as if the prospect of drinking with Yves has painted all existence in dull sepia) and garishly intense (as though thoughts of Clooney and Marilyne have sprayed all life with pigments of sepsis yellow and gangrene black).

My attention was correspondingly erratic. I poked and fiddled at the empty spice rack that I'd promised Marilyne I'd sort out, but did nothing with it. I thought about returning to the Competition entries that still waited, on the kitchen table, for me to decide upon this month's winner, but I hadn't the stomach for it. I mused on my Favrier Pharma shares and longed for the freedom my inheritance would give me, freedom to leave that tiny Swiss apartment, to take Marilyne to somewhere remote and unpeopled: the cold wilds of Quebec, perhaps, or the lonely uplands of France's Massif Central. Somewhere far away from Clooney and his like, where I could keep Marilyne for myself and nobody, nobody else.

This gnawing dissatisfaction drove me to seek comfort in the usual way; I opened a bottle of wine and put my feet up on the sofa. And within an hour, I had reached the introspective state that often follows too much alcohol and too little food. Infelix, my insults forgotten, lay across my legs while I rubbed his ears and teased his fur. The heating was on. I was physically comfortable, yes; but my mind spun and fought itself. Clooney and Marilyne. Clooney and Marilyne. Time passed.

The door slammed; the framed wedding photo scraped across polished wood; keys were dumped on the hall table. My teeth ground of their own volition, but I said nothing; I could fight that battle another day. Saving my marriage was more urgent than addressing Marilyne's untidiness. Because some part of me still clung to the hope that none of it was true, that there had been some ridiculous misunderstanding, that Marilyne and I were still okay, that she loved me and only me. I guess that's why I tried so hard to please her that evening, why I fussed after her like a moonstruck teenager.

"Where is Infelix?"

"Marilyne, he turned up five minutes after you left this morning. Safe and sound – here – you see?" I pointed to his recumbent form. She walked past me – no kiss, nothing – picked him up and nuzzled his fur. He looked sleepily about, spotted me and winked at me over her shoulder, the swine. "There was nothing to worry about," I added.

"If you *really* think that leaving a cat out all night on the roof of a five-storey apartment block is an entirely worry-free course of action, then you are an idiot." Normally, when Marilyne is angry she blazes and spits like burning pine, but on that evening she was cold, cold. In the Book, little Frigidaire fumetti – the icicles of comic book art – form on the lower boundary of her speech bubbles.

She walked slowly around the sofa, cradling Infelix to her breast, her head bent over him so that her pale hair tickled his ears and made him shake his head in irritation. Such love! Indeed, there was something about her of a Madonna and Child, when she held Infelix so. And yet: How long would it be before his heart, too, was crucified on a piece of white card and drowned in isopropanol?

"Stupid," she added. "Completely stupid."

"That's not fair, *cherie*." But there I was stuck. To explain to her that the reason I knew there was nothing to worry about was because putting Infelix onto a five-storey roof had been my daily habit for months – that would be unwise. Her rage would be of cosmic proportions. And she was already looking at me suspiciously, as though some Inkling of her own had darkened her thoughts. I continued hurriedly. "It's not as though he had to spend hours balancing atop a pillar like some feline stylite. Remember, our apartment roof is contiguous with the roofs of much of the Old City. So he had a playground of acres. He had no need to approach the edges at all."

"Don't be ridiculous. Suppose he chased a bird and a tile gave way, or there were a sudden gust of wind. Anything might have happened. Just *never* do that again, Philippe. Okay?"

"Darling —"

"Never!" She stamped out to the kitchen. I heard the rattle of cat biscuits falling into a cat bowl.

I shuffled after her. Marilyne was sitting at the table, watching Infelix eat; her head was down, and she was playing with Yves' printed knife. First she would hold it in her left hand and gently run the tip under each fingernail of her right hand, as though to clean them; then she would pass the knife to the right hand and do likewise to the nails of her left.

"Would you like a drink, darling?"

"No. It's late and I'm tired. I'm going to have a shower and get to bed." She glanced up at me with a frown of genuine irritation. "Why are you still up, anyway?"

"If you can manage late nights and early starts, Marilyne, I think I can too. Anyway, I may well simply take the day off tomorrow. Why not?"

"Because if you don't open your shop, you won't sell anything. Unless your online sales have taken off."

"If you took the day off, too, we could go somewhere. Do something."

"Please, Philippe! You *know* I am at the conference all this week."

"How about Saturday or Sunday?" Hard to believe how plaintive I sounded. Like a child.

"For Christ's sake – I am at the symposium over the weekend, too. Honestly, Philippe, how many times do I need to tell you?" Her voice, all of a sudden, was inexpressibly weary.

"But that was the weekend just gone!"

"It takes up both weekends. Really, it's two conferences, Clinical and Research, that they've run together."

"But on the weekends!"

"Medical conferences *always* run over weekends. It's to minimise disruption to clinics. Surely you've worked that out by now."

I sat down at the other side of the table, opposite her. She really was being very insensitive. I bet she never spoke to Clooney like this. Infelix finished off his food and retreated a couple of paces to lick face and paws.

"You left your paper here."

"What?"

"Your journal paper. The one you're writing with – with Clooney. Novel cardiac glycosides."

"I'll get to it over the weekend."

Silence grew. I tried again. "I'm going to sort out that spice rack. I've got ideas for it."

"At last."

Sometimes, Marilyne could be so stony-hard. I hated it. I didn't know what to say. I'd tried to offer an olive branch, but she'd been entirely refractory. Anyway, I thought, who cares if she's going to be at her precious conference that just has to run over successive weekends? If that's the way it was, fine, because I would be going out drinking with Yves that very weekend. I'd have cancelled it if Marilyne had deigned to make herself available, but she hadn't, so *fine*, I'd do my own thing. I turned on my heel and went to brush my teeth.

I took my time in the bathroom. In fact, I didn't really want to leave; suddenly, it felt like a sanctuary for lonely, unwanted Philippe. I reached out to that little heart we loved. I picked up the jar and cradled it, taking care not to make the preserving liquid slosh around in case it broke the delicate vessels. I put it back, oh so carefully, and kissed the paper label: *Antoine*.

When I came out, I heard noises in the kitchen. It was Marilyne. And she was laughing.

I hadn't heard her laugh – really, spontaneously laugh – for so long that at first I thought she was crying, and I went into the kitchen with that sick fear you get when someone you love is in distress and you can only watch helplessly. But she was indeed laughing, doubled-up, almost incapacitated with mirth. I found myself smiling, too, as my fear ebbed away and was replaced with puzzlement. I also felt an indefinable lightening of mood; it had been so long since Marilyne and I had laughed together.

"What's up?" I said. "Are you really smiling, or is it just wind?"

"It's this, you idiot! Did you do this?" She was sitting in front of the pile of Competition entries. "Oh Philippe – are you *drawing* again?" And she collapsed into giggles for a second time, waving my anonymous friend's latest *oeuvre* at me: *Madame Médecin and the Implants of Youth*.

In this adventure, as Clooney had joyfully discovered, Madame Médecin – appalled at PseudoFifre's metastasising empire – develops a new type of hip implant which both repairs the joint and rejuvenates the patient. Her intent is to address the epidemic of failing hips among the ageing Swiss while also giving them new youth and energy. At one point – apparently, it was rather hot in the theatre – she had to rip off her surgical gown and finish a hip replacement operation wearing only latex gloves and underwear, the very image of a medical heroine from a teenager's dream, all perspiration-beaded *embonpoint* and damp, swelling curves. As always, her efforts are outstandingly successful: soon, an army of rejuvenated geriatrics apply their new-found vigour and mobility to fight the PseudoFifre-instigated crime wave on the streets of Geneva. Vanquished PseudoFifre fulminates as these vigorous pensioners, waving femoral implants like tactical batons, overwhelm his empire of evil. Bravo for Madame Médecin. You couldn't make it up, I thought; but somebody did. And you couldn't possibly find it entertaining, I thought; but Marilyne did. Apparently.

Which was actually disappointing. Of course, I wanted her to share my pleasures, including the Competition; equally, I wanted her to disdain work that was of no value. Literature wasn't Marilyne's *metier*, but she was no intellectual slouch; surely she could see that *Madame Médecin* was the lowest dross imaginable? Risible, perhaps, but not *funny*. My spirits, which had started to rise at her laughter, sank back with a little sigh. It was as though a starving man had had bread offered to him and then taken away, leaving nothing but the smell of fresh baking. And she was still reading and giggling.

"I certainly did not produce that thing," I said. "And I resent the imputation that I might have created something so ridiculous. Why would you imagine that this nonsense had anything to do with me?"

"Because . . . because . . ." She became speechless with laughter again. "Because, oh, can't you see? I didn't look at it when we were at the café, but now that I do, I understand why Georges was so amused! PseudoFifre! *Deathlessly* funny!"

"What? Give that to me!"

I still don't know why she found it entertaining; to me it was hurtful. Yet I stood there, smiling with forced good humour, while she delightedly ticked off all the features which, it seemed, I shared with the abominable PseudoFifre.

The initials: PseudoFifre, Philippe Favrier.

The outward appearance: apparently we are both big-eared, balding and skinny, with a hungry, discontented expression.

Key relationship: we both are linked to a more successful and intelligent female doctor – PseudoFifre and Madame Médecin, me and Marilyne Favrier. Well, okay, Marilyne didn't actually say 'more successful and intelligent', but I could tell that's what she was thinking.

I'd have accepted all that, had it been accurate – but it just wasn't true! Yes, Marilyne was clever, and yes, she saved lives while I 'sold comics', but that didn't make me stupid. And as for 'more successful', what does that mean? How do you define success? I was doing what I wanted to do, and it was making me happy, kind of. At least, I wouldn't have been happy doing anything else – isn't that a component of success? And yes, I know many people use that logic as an excuse for monumental failure, and it's true I didn't earn much, and if I depended solely on the income from my shop, then yes, I'd have been the first to admit failure, on one level. But my poverty was temporary; when my shares vested, Marilyne's salary would be an irrelevance, *and she knew that*. And on that evening, she was getting so annoying that I was about to remind her of all this, just to put her in her place, when she set off laughing again.

"But look," she said, "there's more! Look here!" She pointed to another page from *Madame Médecin* and again collapsed into laughter.

I looked; nothing I hadn't seen before. I waited for her hysterics to cease. Yves' knife was on the table still; I flicked the end of its handle. Round and round, it spun. Round and round.

"Look," Marilyne said, finally, "where the granny is braining the last of the bad guys with a titanium femur, and PseudoFifre recognises his scheme has failed, and he is trying to think of a new plot . . . *here* . . . don't you see?"

I looked. The little goblin clutched at the air with one hand, while the other tore at the side of his own head. I shrugged.

"Don't you see?" she repeated. "He's pulling at his ear! That's what you do! You're always doing it! Especially when you're annoyed, or trying to think!"

For me, the clumsy contortions of an evil gnome in an absurd BD, for her, an excuse to suggest another spurious point of correspondence between her husband and a cartoon bad guy. Tiresome. Anyway, it seemed that one can always learn something new about oneself. Apparently, I pull at my ears, especially when I am thinking. Or, as Marilyne said, "*trying* to think." Whatever.

But then, on reflection, actually, no, *not* 'whatever.' 'Whatever' implies it didn't matter, or I didn't care. But I did care. I hated it when she acted as though I was stupid. And I think it was that condescension of hers, that implicit belief in her own superiority, that made me lose it a little.

"Oh really?" I said. "Let me try to think about *this*!" I grabbed the scientific paper she had brought home, the one she was writing with Pretty-boy Clooney, and read from it in a silly falsetto voice.

"Here we report the purification of a novel cardiac glycoside, 5',3'-O-dimethylevomonoside, from the plant *Thevetia peruviana*, yellow oleander, also known as the suicide tree. The toxin is unusual both in its potency (LD50 <1 ng/kg in rats) and in its mechanism of action, which is reflected in the unusual presentation of total neuromuscular blockade, starting with paralysis of skeletal musculature and progressing to terminal interruption of function in smooth muscle and cardiac muscle."

I paused, and started tugging at my earlobe like it was the emergency brake for my runaway marriage. "Oh, wait, wait, I'm *trying* to think! Let me see, I think you've just spent a shed-load of public money, with months of unpaid overtime, for what? To find a new poison, I think! Oh, well done you, I think! How clever must you be, I think, to invent new ways of poisoning things! Isn't that just what we need – I *think!* Or have you in fact just been spending all this time mincing around with lover-boy Clooney – isn't that nice, I *think*!"

I was going to continue, but Marilyne had put on her grim face, and snatched the paper back.

"Don't be so stupid," she said. "All drugs are poisons on some level. And really, Philippe, how do you think Clooney and I can present our research without attending the same conference? I could just stop *working*, of course – but who then pays the rent?" She gave me a withering look. "You didn't *think* of that, did you?" And she stamped off to have her end-of-day shower.

My hand felt sore, and when I looked at it, I saw blood coming thinly from a razor-straight cut just where the thumb met the palm. It must have happened when Marilyne grabbed her research article from me.

"Hey," I shouted. "You gave me a paper cut!" But she didn't hear me; or if she did, she didn't answer.

I put a plaster over the cut. I left the wrapper, including the little white peel-off bits that keep the plaster sticky, on the chest of drawers outside the bathroom. I placed them next to her mobile phone, which she had put on the chest, and which she always brought to her bedside table before going to sleep. Then I lay in bed with my injured hand on top of the duvet, the plaster clearly and obviously visible. But when she came in, she just plugged in her phone to recharge, turned out her light, and burrowed under the bedding. She noticed nothing, and was asleep almost immediately. One minute, *maximum*, that's all it took. How could she do that? Even when I'm calm, I can't fall asleep that quickly, and at that point, I was seething.

And that's how I stayed – awake and bruised and cut and angry – for at least two hours, until I remembered that I'd not taken that evening's little yellow tablet, my 2.5 mg of anti-whisper drug. So I went to the bathroom and opened the cabinet. And then – call it bravado, call it recklessness, call it disaster-lust, call it what you like; and yes, maybe, maybe I just wanted to get back at Marilyne by opening up that damned *box of frogs* – whatever the reason, I held open the bathroom cabinet so that the mirror on the inside of its door faced the windowsill. I watched my reflection's arm reach back to the sill, past the jar containing that most special of all hearts, and turn the shaving mirror around. I looked again in the mirrored mirror; I saw that unmistakable profile, and this time, this time I knew what I was.

Yes: I at last understood. Mirrors cannot lie.

According to the Book, I never took my pill at all that evening; and who could blame me? The Understanding shattered me; not just the Understanding of what I was, but the Understanding that *Clooney* (Clooney! – and how many others?) had known it before me. It was as if one had been walking on a busy street, self-assured and proud, nodding to friends and colleagues, only to discover that one was naked, and the smiles one received were contemptuous leers or disgusted grimaces, not signals of amity.

So I took no Favrier drug that evening. I walked back to bed with bile in my throat and a plaster on my cut thumb and something hard and weighty in my chest. Because now, at last, I understood: *I* was the anti-hero in my own life's story.

I was PseudoFifre, and PseudoFifre was me.

That night, I had another dream. Or rather, a variant of the dream I'd had a few nights before. Marilyne was sitting astride me, as before. But again, something was wrong; she slowed; she stopped; something troubled her, some indefinable concern. She put both hands to her chest, dug her nails into her sternum, split it down the middle and swung the two halves of her ribcage back, as though her torso were a bathroom cabinet. Clooney's head burst out of her opened chest, and he stared at me with manic joy. *PseudoFifre!* he shrieked. *That's the diagnosis! PseudoFifre!* And when I looked in the mirrors mounted on the inside of Marilyne's ribcage, instead of Clooney's profile I saw my own, and understood again what I was. So did Marilyne; she pointed at me with a cruel smile and bellowed with Laurence's voice: *I know what you are!* Then she reached down, plunged her hand into my chest, grasped my heart and crushed it.

Chapter 16

Riiiing . . .

The sound of my phone alarm woke me, that morning, but it did not pull me from the bed.

Marilyne had left, early as ever; I remained beneath the duvet, contemplating my situation. The Understanding had changed everything. For if I was ugly PseudoFifre, someone must have made me so. Someone who knew me well enough to draw a cruelly recognisable caricature. Someone who hated me enough to cowardly lampoon my life; to mock my very real marital tensions by representing Marilyne as PseudoFifre's cartoon nemesis, Madame Médecin. That was the real Understanding: not just that PseudoFifre was I, and I, PseudoFifre, but that I had an enemy or enemies in Geneva. That he, or she, or he *and* she, was or were very close by. The only questions were, who, and how close?

In the bathroom, I pulled at the plaster on my thumb, and then stuck it back down. I dropped my pill into the basin and marvelled at how easily the water's vortex swallowed it. *Who*, and *how* close? The answer had to lie, I thought, in La Market Jaune; specifically, in Orphan's Corner, among the unwanted issues of *Madame Médecin.*

The anonymous artist's identity must be, could only be, revealed by examining his creation. To work, then!

They were all there still, the seven previous entries, on the Orphan shelves; nobody had bought a single copy. I flicked through them, and as I mused on those dull magazines with their dull dialogue, I felt once more their odd attraction; like the force that draws together the opposing polarities of magnets, something unseen held me to their pages. It was as though they had some glimpsed familiarity, something that I could not quite define, but that nevertheless connected I and them as surely as genes link siblings. I racked my brains; I gripped and tore at my ears; I gnawed at the problem like a rat at a pantry door. The more I considered it, the more I was convinced that I actually *knew* the author; *Madame Médecin* could not, I was sure, be the work of a stranger, spying on my life. But if not a stranger, then who? Given the level of spite implicit in a protracted campaign of anonymous lampoons, I was inclined to suspect Clooney. And now that I came to think of it, Marilyne had never actually *denied* she was having an affair with Clooney. Not in as many words. She'd just deflected the question by applying Yves' knife to her soft flesh and letting memories of Antoine bleed between us. Talk about below the belt. On my shoulders, the Inkling squirms in excitement; it whispers at me.

Clooney? Absurd, on the face of it. But it would explain some of *Madame Médecin*'s idiosyncracies. Firstly, the anonymity of the entries, and their cruel, mocking intent (*PseudoFifre . . . Deathlessly funny!*). Secondly, the unvaryingly medical nature of the plots; Clooney probably had no other source of inspiration to draw upon. So: Clooney was back in the picture. More accurately, he'd never left it. Perhaps he'd dreamed up *Madame Médecin* as a device to drive a wedge between Marilyne and I? Feasible, certainly. After all, Clooney's off-the-cuff reference to Bianca Castafiore suggested that he was familiar at least with Hergé's *Tintin*, and therefore that he had some knowledge of the tropes and techniques of sequential art . . . That said, there was something childishly simplistic about the *Madame Médecin* dialogue which didn't quite fit with Clooney's *modus operandi* – he'd find it hard to resist a clever-clever *grande école* quip here and there. More problematic still, however, was this: *Madame Médecin*'s creator was undoubtedly an *artist*. Not a great artist, perhaps, but evidently one of some ability. You can't fake that kind of skill; you can't acquire it from the internet. And while Clooney *might* have that talent hidden away, I'd never seen a hint of it. That, I decided, would be the killer clue: if Clooney could draw, then I had my man – my enemy.

What had Google told me, the other day? I pulled the folded paper from my pocket: *An amateur of art both fine and coarse.* So, even if he was not responsible for the pictures I'd found in the cellar – and I was keeping an open mind on *that* – it was still possible that he drew. Very possible. I would have to examine this further during my forthcoming evening with Yves. And when would that be? Why, *this* evening! Yes, I was going drinking with Yves that very night!

Correctly interrogated, Yves would, I was certain, be an excellent source of information. Of course, I would have to bleed him of evidence without raising his suspicions. Otherwise, he'd run straight to Marilyne. Or Clooney. So I'd need to plan the questions carefully. This would be part of a campaign, not just a conversation. And if I could prove that Clooney was behind this backstabbing *bande dessinée*, then maybe, just maybe, that would make the scales fall from Marilyne's eyes and she would see him for what he was. Yes, the next step was clear; I would go back to the apartment and plan my questioning of Yves.

Thus, a strategy fell into my hands like a gift. In retrospect, it was as if the heavens conspired. That should have made me suspicious, perhaps, but I paid it no attention. I simply did what I have always done throughout my life: walked from one panel into the next, according to the artist's whim.

As I shut up my shop, I felt eyes on my back; that feeling which bypasses conscious thought and goes straight to the most primitive parts of the brain. To turn and look for the threat was involuntary and immediate, and my gaze was drawn to the other side of the road. A woman: blonde, svelte, elegant. Walking fast, but with her head turned towards me. As our eyes met, she looked quickly away. Too late! I caught you, Miss Slavic Cheekbones! I caught you watching me!

I thought about running after her, about demanding that she provide a status report on the Planche 8 negotiations. Perhaps I should have. But the fact is that a tram chose that moment to clunk by, so I could not cross the road, and when the tram had gone, she had too, doubtless en route to Cornavin to catch a train to wherever she lived. And in any case, I needed to get home and make plans.

To draw up a campaign, I needed pen and paper. So once in the apartment, I went directly to the drawer where I kept my art materials.

It's odd to see it now, in the Book, but it was as though my subliminal self knew something was amiss the second I touched the drawer handle; my cartoon face looks at it askance, and my other hand is half-raised as if in defence against some anticipated threat. But it was not until I pulled at the drawer – until the rub of its runners made a susurration that turned into a whisper – that I became consciously aware of some perturbation to life's proper order. *Well now,* said the whisper, *who might have done this, I wonder?* For the drawer's contents were all awry; not badly so, not in a way that damaged a single brush or pen or creased a single piece of paper, but just enough to show that someone had been through the contents. *Who, I wonder?* An artist's pen displaced here, a mis-aligned paper there. *Who?* Either Marilyne or I, obviously. Unless another had been in our apartment. *I wonder.*

But I put it aside, that little puzzle, I left it alone; for now I had to prepare for Yves. I put some paper before me and picked up a biro; at the top of the blank sheet, I wrote *Questions for Y.* Beneath this heading, I wrote the following:

1. *Is Clooncy an artist? Can he draw?*
2. *Is Clooney exclusively gay?*
3. *(Provisional) What is Marilyne saying about me?*

Only three questions, but their answers would cover everything. Question One: If Clooney had any artistic talent, then he must be the author of *Madame Médecin.* There would no longer be any room for doubt; to believe otherwise would be to accept a coincidence so improbable as to be utterly preposterous. Question Two: This was the second part of my pincer approach. Because if Clooney *wasn't* gay, or if he was bisexual (is that what he meant by 'unrestricted' passions?) then *obviously* he and Marilyne were having an affair, and that too would strongly suggest he was the perpetrator of *Madame Médecin.* It was the improbable coincidence argument again: How likely was it that I would be persecuted by two unconnected individuals at the same time? The only thing that could convince me he was *not* having an affair with Marilyne would be independent confirmation that he was exclusively homosexual. Finally, if the answers to Questions One and Two were respectively no and yes, then I could consider – *maybe* – the possibility of reconciliation between Marilyne and I – *depending* on the answer to Question Three. And then, then we could investigate the mystery of *Madame Médecin* together, my wife and I, or even just ignore it. Because if Marilyne still loved me, PseudoFifre could go hang; he just wouldn't matter anymore.

That was the campaign in outline: three simple points. But its execution would require the questions to be subtly put, such that Yves was hardly aware they were being posed. I looked over the questions again; they satisfied me, but there was something missing. And that primitive, pre-verbal part of the brain, that part which has no need of language, which whispers not in words but in visions and pictures, knew what it was. Under its instructions, I retrieved my brushes and paints from the drawer and underlined each word of the three questions: Question One in acidic yellow, Question Two in leaf green, Question Three in heart-muscle red. The colours sang to me – oh, how they sang! Their tones caressed my mind, tinting it with this hue, then with that. They washed me with their radiant notes, and covered me with bright effulgent harmonies. They displaced the very air; I drowned in them. And I drowned willingly.

Time slipped; walls bled hues; all still objects – cushions, curtains, tables, chairs – ballooned with slow inhalations and languidly deflated again. The air was full of murmurings. Before me, pigment lay across paper in glorious, heavenly excess.

Riiiing . . .

"Philippe?"

I held the dream of a voice to my ear; if I cut its warm flesh, what then?

"Philippe?"

"This is Philippe."

"*Cheri*, I tried you at La Market Jaune, but clearly you were serious about taking the day off today! Anyway, just to remind you of a couple of things. First of all – *please* don't forget to feed Infelix! Okay? Philippe? Hello? The signal is bad . . . Are you there?"

"Philippe is here."

"The third person does not become you, darling, however amusing you find it. Anyway, the second thing is, I'm going to try and get away in good time, today. Because, you know what, I want a nice domestic evening – a meal with my husband, and an early night. How about you?"

I looked at my cellphone. The wallpaper sprang forth, without compromise: Edgar Jacobs, Planche 8.

"*La Marque Jaune.*"

"Don't be stupid, Philippe. You've decided to take the day off, so take it off. And we need to spend more time together – we've both been getting a little irritable recently, I think. So let's make it a super-quality evening, *hein?* It's the only chance we'll get for a little while. Philippe?"

"Oh, Marilyne!"

"Philippe? Is everything alright?"

Somehow, I was in the bathroom. I reached out to the jar on the sill.

"Antoine, Marilyne. What happened with Antoine. It split my heart in two. The *very* heart of me, Marilyne. My soul. It tore my soul apart."

I heard her silence; I felt the weight of it; I knew I should not have said what I said. But dreams do not lie.

"Philippe – Antoine is gone, now. And he left scars on both of us, *cheri*, you know that. But we have other scars, you and I, and we are still here. So continue. Okay? Continue."

"Will there ever be another Antoine?"

"Philippe – I need you to be strong. Take your medicine, if you haven't already."

I don't know whether it was me who cut the call, then, or Marilyne; the Book only shows my phone on the windowsill beside that precious jar, and me with my hands inside the bathroom cabinet. I do not look at its exposed mirror; I keep my eyes on the cabinet contents. I find the Favrier pills, and press one from its little blister, and swallow it.

Later, when the flat was silent and its bright colours dulled, and my bladder protested its sudden volume, I remembered again my investigative duty: my drinking date with Yves. The Book details my single-minded determination. To ensure that all went to plan, I left the apartment early, well before Marilyne might return, and took the tram to Carouge. Then I paced the pavement outside the Chat Noir until it opened. I left nothing to chance; I could not miss this vital exercise in intelligence gathering.

And quite definitely, I am sure, although the Book does not show it, I am sure that I left a note for Marilyne, to say that I would be going out with Yves. A little Post-it stuck on the fridge. Yes, I am sure of it; that the Book has no record of it is of no importance, for what artist can capture every truth? In any case, it does show this: my mobile phone, still on the bathroom sill, while in the next panel, I am exiting the flat on the way to my rendezvous with Yves.

I don't know why I left my phone behind; it was very unlike me. A tiny oversight, a minimal indiscretion; but an event that would conspire with other events. Again.

Chapter 17

Anywhere else in Europe, the Chat Noir would be a squalid, tacky-floored, stale-aired venue for life's losers, somewhere for them to escape their own squalid, tacky, lost lives: twenty-something men with bruised knuckles chasing twenty-something women with bruised pasts, while drug dealers circle like hyenas, looking for those who tire first. But this is Switzerland, and the club manages to be safe and civilised. You get the feeling that the clientele would wipe their feet before dancing on the tables.

That evening, I took a seat in the ground-floor bar; no point going downstairs, as there would be a band on later, and conversation would be impossible. A sign by the beer taps promoted a brand of Belgian Dark Ale: *Brewed with Chocolate*, it said. Nevertheless, it was smoothly drinkable and disappeared within minutes, so I ordered another. Perhaps I was being unwise; the ale was very strong and I'd not eaten since lunch. By the time Yves arrived I'd drunk most of the second bottle, and had developed that dangerous, false good humour that starts at the base of the skull and wraps itself around the brain, and which can turn in an instant to drunken rage. I watched him waddle through the door: chubby, moon-faced, forgettable, a walking nonentity.

"Hi Yves!" I said, brightly.

He nodded at me, smiling with only one half of his mouth, as though complete pleasure were beyond him.

"*Salut*," he said.

We looked at each other in silence for perhaps five seconds. I turned to the barman – a straw to grasp in a suddenly swelling ocean of boredom.

"Monsieur? Two beers, if you please. The Belgian Chocolate." Yves looked at me expressionlessly.

"You've hurt your hand," he said.

I drew back in mock amazement, covering the plaster with my fingers while holding my hands to my chest like a woman shielding her cleavage. "How could you possibly have known that? Are you a new Sherlock Holmes, another Rouletabille? Can *no* secrets hide from your deductive capabilities?" I made a gaping face at him.

Yves looked puzzled. "There's a plaster on it," he said, with a sideways, pop-eyed glance.

I sighed inwardly. This could be a long evening, I thought. Behind Yves, through the Chat Noir's window, I could see the ornate iron street-lights of Carouge glowing warmly in the night. *Come outside,* they said, *we'll keep the darkness down, and light your way home.* No; I had questions, and I needed answers. A cautious approach, however, would be essential, even with Yves. I decided to ease into my interrogation with some neutral topic. And somehow, I don't know why – I guess I was still hurting that evening, still bruised by the Understanding – I found myself talking about Marilyne.

"She's never at home any more. Always working late. I can't remember the last time we spent an evening together. A proper evening, I mean, not twenty minutes just before bed. It's like she only thinks of her job. Never of *me*."

Perhaps some expression passed across Yves' face; perhaps I missed it through blinking. In any case, I continued.

"Of course, we've been married seven years now. That's when the 'itch' starts, they say. Thing is, Yves, I've never had any such itch. Never. And that makes it all the more painful, you know . . .?"

Yves took a slow sip of beer and looked at me with dull eyes.

"Sometimes, I wonder if we should have married at all . . ."

Yves considered the matter like a cow with its cud, before – finally! – providing a slow opinion.

"You're lucky to have Marilyne."

"But do I actually *have* her, Yves? That's the question, isn't it?"

"She's beautiful. And so talented."

"I know. And that is part of the problem, you see. Because other people think so too."

"Yes. We could tell, all of us, back in Paris. Everyone could."

"Tell what?"

"That she was special. That she would go places. You're very lucky."

"Yes, yes, okay. But it's not a one-way thing, you know? Maybe *I* had certain attributes that *she* found attractive."

"And she's so caring. She'd help anybody."

"For example, not everyone could set up and make a success of their own business. Not when you have to compete with Amazon."

"Everybody loves her. Everybody."

"Five years, I've been running La Market Jaune. Most businesses collapse in their first year."

"Her patients worship her, apparently. And her colleagues."

"The number and quality of entrants for my BD competition is rising, month by month. The *Tribune de Genève* ran a piece on it a few weeks ago."

"And having a high-flying partner must take the pressure off you."

"What the hell do you mean?"

"Financially. That's what I mean."

Sometimes it was difficult to work out whether Yves was just dim or whether he was deliberately attempting to provoke.

"You think I need Marilyne's income? You think I'm a kept man? Some kind of *underling?* For Christ's sake, Yves – you work in biotech, don't you, kind of? How much do you think a ten percent holding in Favrier Pharma would be worth?"

"I don't know. Why?"

How could he not have known about the Favrier bequest? Everyone back in Paris knew; I'd had gold-diggers queuing up, in the old days.

"Favrier Pharma! The clue is in the name, Yves! My Dad set it up. I've got a whole bunch of shares. They're tied up in a trust fund right now, but not for much longer."

I waited for a suitable reaction, but Yves only sat there, drink in hand, looking at the table.

"So maybe it's *my* assets that take the pressure off Marilyne and allow *her* to pursue *her* career in the way she thinks fit. You didn't think of that, did you?"

Yves nodded slowly. "That's good. You should look after Marilyne. She's very special. You're lucky. She could have married anyone she wanted. So you're *very* lucky."

I took a deep breath, shifted in my chair, exhaled slowly, took a careful mouthful of beer. Remember, I thought. Remember the three questions. Remember the whole point of this crappy evening. Question One: Is Clooney an artist?

"So," I said, "I gather Clooney is to be the next happy attendee at dinner *chez* Yves?"

"Georges said he'd love to come."

"But do you think he's ready for your beautiful monsters? Your 3D-printer art, I mean. Because Clooney himself doesn't have any artistic background, does he? He just won't get your brand of surreal horror. Dolls giving birth to other dolls. He'll go away thinking we're all a bit weird."

"I don't think he'll do that."

"Really? Then he *does* have an arts background?" My heart hammered; this was too easy.

"No. I just don't think he'll think it's weird, that's all."

"Oh! But I wonder if that means he has some kind of innate artistic ability? In order to appreciate it, I mean. Perhaps he does sketching or painting in his spare time? I can just see that, you know. I can just see Clooney with pencil and paper . . . running off a few cartoons, perhaps . . ."

"Really?"

"Well, can't you?"

"No. Georges is terrible at drawing."

Something about that comment made me suspicious. It was too glib, almost pre-prepared.

"You seem to know Clooney quite well."

Yves didn't answer immediately; he just raised one shoulder in a kind of half-shrug, and looked around the bar shiftily, like a liar caught in a lie. I stayed silent, and he eventually found a response.

"I've seen quite a lot of him, since Marilyne introduced us."

"Really? So, now you just keep bumping into each other? Where? In the cardiac ward? At one of his hundred-francs-a-ticket wine-tasting evenings?" It did sound ridiculous, on the face of it.

"I think that's too much for a wine-tasting evening. You can get a whole bottle for twenty francs."

"So where *have* you seen him?"

"Well. At the Jardin Botanique, for example. He goes there to collect cuttings from that plant. The one with yellow flowers. You know."

"The dwarf rose?"

"No."

"Are you sure it was Clooney? He doesn't strike me as being a gardener. Anyway, it's not like him to get his hands dirty."

"Yes, I'm sure. And he's not a gardener. And he didn't get his hands dirty. He knows the people at the Jardin. They helped him."

Like every conversation with Yves, this one was going nowhere. I made a mental note of the Jardin Botanique episode (Clooney? Plants? Seemed unlikely, somehow), and decided to move on. Question Two: Is Clooney really gay?

"Anyway, since you know him so well, what's all this I hear about him swinging both ways? It's like being gay is just a fashionable coat for our Clooney. Sometimes he wears it, and sometimes he doesn't. And when he doesn't, he starts pestering the girls. That's what I've heard."

Yves goggled at me. "Where did you hear that?"

"It doesn't matter. The point is, he's not really gay. That's what I think. What do *you* think, Yves?"

"I don't think he has any interest in women, at all."

"But you can't *know* that."

"I suppose not."

"After all, who knows what he gets up to in his personal life? None of us really know him that well – except *Marilyne*, maybe."

I watched him closely, looking for any tell-tale glimmer of understanding, waiting for a give-away comment. Nothing.

"And I've often thought he seems very fond of Marilyne, don't you, Yves?" I wondered for a minute if I'd gone too far, made it too obvious. But no; Yves just nodded, unsmilingly.

"Everybody loves Marilyne," he said. "I already told you that."

It was true in a way; certainly, everybody loved the persona Marilyne projected, the mask she wore for the world. But who could lift the mask and still love the Marilyne underneath? Who would kiss her *real* face? Only me.

"How well do you think Clooney *really* knows Marilyne, though?"

Yves was silent. Because he didn't understand the question? Or because he didn't want to answer it? I ploughed on.

"True, they've known each other since Paris . . . but knowing someone for a long time is not the same as knowing them *well* . . . is it?"

"No, it isn't the same at all."

"Perhaps they got to know each other *really well* in Paris . . . I think that's possible. Don't you?"

"Of course it's possible. But it's not what Georges says."

"Really? What does Georges say?"

"He said that he'd known who Marilyne was, back in Paris, but had hardly spoken to her until she began recruiting a team for her move to Geneva. And he said that she is a truly special person. 'Far outside the normal distribution of dull humanity.' That's what he said."

It certainly sounded like something Clooney would say. But it also sounded a bit like something Marilyne might say. I didn't know what to think. I tried one last time, throwing any attempt at subtlety to the winds.

"It's like he has a crush on Marilyne – how childish!"

Yves smiled for the first time; though at what, I wasn't quite sure.

"Oh no," he said. "No, he doesn't at all. He's really not interested in women."

"You mean, you *think* he's really not interested in women."

"Yes."

Okay; time to give up on Question Two, I thought. One more to go. But I'd reached a point where I needed refreshment, so I bought another two beers, and two whiskies to chase them, even though Yves still had two-thirds of his first beer left. When I came back from the bar, I found that a couple of bikers – almost caricatures of themselves, like characters from *Mammouth et Piston* – had occupied the adjacent table. The fug of their filterless cigarettes precipitated on my throat's lining, but Yves seemed unaffected; he was gazing at the wall as if some riveting film were playing out on its blank surface. I put Yves' drinks in front of him, downed half of my beer in one, and felt myself sliding further into drunkenness. In the downstairs bar, the band had started. Tedious, unsophisticated rhythms pulsed through the floor. *Biff-biff Baff. Biff-biff Baff.* Anyway, time for Question Three: What is Marilyne saying about me?

"Here's a question for you, Yves. Quasi-philosophical. So, each of us goes through life with our own point of view, right? Trundling along in a little body-shaped box, looking out at the world. And we have this idea of what we are like, and we think that our self-image corresponds – at least partly – to how others see us. The question is, how close is that correspondence really? If we could see ourselves as others *actually* see us, would we even recognise ourselves? Or would it be like, oh, who's that, I'm sure I've seen them before – and then, *Oh no!* as you understand that *that* is what you are really like, how the *world* experiences you." Beer made me giggle foolishly. Yves nodded without smiling.

"Yes. Like seeing yourself on CCTV from an angle that you wouldn't normally see yourself from." *Biff-biff Baff.*

"Exactly! Exactly, Yves!" The delight of him providing an answer that went beyond yes or no went to my head, and I reached over the table to grasp his shoulder with a brotherly hand. He flinched, but smiled and pursued the theme as I downed the whisky chaser.

"Or like seeing yourself in two mirrors."

Biff-biff Baff. Per the Book, it seems that this was where my nausea began; from here, the artist shows my skin taking on a progressively greener hue, while my speech becomes increasingly slurred. Stock markers of inebriation scatter the panels: here a *hic*, there a red and swollen nose, there a finger raised in the didactic certainty of the toper. The bikers were chain-smoking, and the bar was now filling up rapidly; it had become hot and noisy. *Biff-biff Baff.*

"Yes, Yves! Two mirrors!" I paused; my train of thought had entered a dark tunnel. Get it together, Philippe. Question Three. "Different angles. Different points of view. So my question, Yves – my *question* – is" – I raised an imperious finger – "how might one's other half see one? The person who loves you more than any other. The person who you *thought* loves you. What's *her* point of view? What's *her* angle? Eh, Yves?"

Yves frowned. "If they love you, the angle doesn't matter. They love you. That's it. No matter how you seem to others, no matter what angle *they* take, your partner just loves you." He nodded.

"But . . ." Damn. The thought train had stopped at some unlit station. I filled the gap by drinking Yves' whisky chaser. New thoughts aboard, the train set off again. "But it's important to know which angles the other half finds more appealing, no? So one can improve. And I do so want to improve for Marilyne, Yves! I really, really do!"

Yes, I had reached the weeping honesty stage of drunkenness; like an open wound, I would now ooze wet truths at Yves.

"What does she *really* think of me, Yves? That's what I need to know. Do you see?" *Biff-biff Baff.* One of the bikers caught my eye and grinned at me through his beard, his eyes narrowed against the smoke.

"I don't know. But she must love you. Or she wouldn't stay with you." Good old, child-like Yves. For him, life really was that simple.

"Truthfully, Yves, I don't know whether she *will* stay with me. We've had some arguments . . ." I waved a hand at the world's sorrows. "The cat got locked out. And . . . things. She keeps getting angry with me, Yves. Sometimes it's like she's a stranger who just *looks* like Marilyne. I don't know what to do, don't know who to ask. I mean, what would you do, if you were me, Yves?"

I meant of course, *Who would you ask for advice?* not *What would your advice be?* Obviously; who would ask *Yves* for advice on such a matter? But, typically, he took it the wrong way.

"You should make it up with her. Apologise."

"Oh, really? *Really*?"

"And do something for her that she'd really appreciate. Something nobody else would do."

"This is your considered, expert opinion?"

"When you've been with somebody a while, you know things about them that nobody else does. So you can do things for them that nobody else would think of doing."

It was my turn to gape like a dolt, and that's what I did. What surreal turn of events was this? Yves – *Yves,* mark you! – was giving me pointers on relationship management!

"So that's what I think you should do," he concluded. "You need to think about other people a bit more. Try to see things from their *angle*." He nodded sagely, and then, as if to impart a secret known only to the Illuminati, leaned forward and lowered his voice. Next to us, the bikers also leant forward, as if in sympathy. "*I* find that kind of thing really difficult too," he said. *Biff-biff Baff.*

Getting marital advice from a flabby bachelor with the personal charm of a *bien coulant* cheese – it was too much! I flipped. I can't remember my exact words (the Book doesn't quote me), but I know I pointed out some home truths to Yves. In particular, I drew attention to aspects of his appearance and personality that contributed to his unattached status. But it was like punching a cushion. He just soaked it up, with no apparent effect; a flaccid volume that slowly flowed back to its previous shape. All he said was, with an odd semi-smirk, "You'd be surprised." Yes, Yves, I would be surprised; but not as surprised as you'd be if any woman let *you* touch her. I said all that, and more besides, the last fusillade delivered over my shoulder when I got up at my bladder's desperate insistence. The bikers gave me a chorus of "*Oooo*-oooh!" as I stumbled away, but I didn't care. I'd drunk Yves' second beer as well, and I was beyond help.

As I stood in the gent's loo, however, trying to focus on the graffiti and the little notice urging the clientele to stand closer (*C'est plus petit que tu ne pense* – it's smaller than you might think), I had a feeling that maybe I had indeed gone too far, said things that were unnecessarily cruel, maybe even untrue. And indeed, Yves was no longer there when I returned. The bikers had been joined by other bikers, who had taken over the table where Yves and I were sitting, and I was getting looks from the bar staff, so I concluded that the evening, for me, was over. I meandered out of the Chat Noir and headed for home, trying to walk off the alcohol, feeling ill and unsteady.

On the way back I crossed the Pont de Carouge, and leant over the parapet to look at the Arve flowing beneath me. Alpine air, cooled and agitated by the river, washed over my skin. The hand-rail was cold under my fingers; I stroked it with my palms, feeling its irregularities catch on the plaster at the base of my thumb. The cut was still sore; absurd, for such a small thing.

If only Marilyne had said sorry. If only there was no Clooney. No PseudoFifre.

I closed my eyes, trying to will away the spinning sensation in my head, the nausea threatening to erupt from my stomach. I was dimly aware of somebody walking towards me, but was too sick to care. I only looked up when a familiar howitzer of a voice assaulted my eardrums.

"*Bonsoir*, my friend!"

I looked around, shakily, almost losing my balance. It was difficult to focus on him; the outlines of his face seemed to undulate. I quickly looked away. Then, suddenly feeling very ill indeed, bent my head down so that my forehead rested on the cool railing.

"*Bonsoir,* Laurence," I said.

He had walked close to me, very close; too close. If I'd been less drunk, I would have been frightened; it wouldn't have been hard for him to tip me over the railing and into the Arve, ice-cold still at this time of year. But I was beyond caring.

"You have cancer, my friend!" he howled delightedly. "You will die in agony, do you hear? The growth will eat at your nerves! The pain is extraordinary!" He bent forward so that his mouth was next to my ear. "Furthermore, you will become constipated by the opioids! A prolapse is inevitable! Your bowels will emerge from your anus and hang down behind like a dog's tail! Do you hear me?"

Even through the drink I could feel that my eardrum had been traumatised by Laurence's close-range exposition of symptoms and sequelae. But I had more pressing concerns.

"And furthermore . . ." I turned to face him, and found my face perhaps a centimetre away from his, the stench of his breath suddenly overwhelming. "And furthermore, I am going to be sick." I leant over the railing and vomited, hugely and extravagantly, into the rushing, forgiving Arve. I wiped my mouth on my sleeve, and turned back to him. "You didn't think of that, did you?"

Laurence looked at me, stony-faced. "Disgusting!" he bellowed. "*Bougre de faux jeton à la sauce tartare! Grotesque polichinelle!*"

He marched off, bellowing Captain Haddock insults into the Geneva night: "*Marchand de guano! Espèce de porc-épic mal embouché! Jus de réglisse! Capitaine de bateau lavoir!*" And, in a final roar that set curtains twitching and brought faces to windows: "I know what you are, my friend!"

Chapter 18

Hangovers operate on two levels. Most obvious is the physical component. A tongue like a stiffened rag cleaves to a palate of rotten biltong; a breakbone ague tears at joints and muscles; horned imps peel back the brain's lining to pummel and gnaw at frontal lobes; gummed eyes squint disbelievingly at this new world of pain. That's unpleasant, every part of it, and I don't want to belittle it. But worse by far, in my opinion, is the knowledge of what drink led one to *do*, only a few hours before. And what *had* I done? My outburst at Yves, however justified, was embarrassing; but only slightly so. After all, I cared little for his opinion. And for Laurence to see me incontinently drunk was even less of an issue; even Laurence doesn't care what Laurence thinks. More concerning was what had happened in the apartment when I got home. Which was what?

I rubbed sleep-grit from my eyelids and blinked at my surroundings. In front of me, the lounge table; from beneath it, Infelix regarded me with yellow eyes. Clearly, I had slept on the sofa. Of course; Marilyne had been angry with me. She'd taken issue with a number of things. The state of me, for one – stinking of beer and urine and vomit, she said, and I'm sure she was right. Another point she'd raised, quite forcefully, was that I hadn't told her I was going out with Yves that night. Moreover, I hadn't taken my mobile, so she hadn't been able to get in touch and find out where I was. She'd come home expecting an evening of domestic bliss, and found only an empty apartment, with no explanation. I might have been anywhere; anything could have happened. Her critique of my behaviour had been icily contemptuous; fragments of the conversation floated to the scum-filmed surface of my memory.

"Of course I was worried about you! For all I knew, you'd had an adverse reaction to the medication, or some kind of *crise des nerfs,* and were wandering around on the train tracks! I might have called the *police,* Philippe! But you didn't *think* of that, did you?"

[. . .]

"What I find remarkable, Philippe, is that you see no contradiction between, on the one hand, insisting that you will be damned if you ever go to 'another *fucking* dinner with Yves,' and on the other, spending all night drinking with Yves on your own."

[. . .]

"Whether Clooney is there or not is utterly irrelevant. Why should Yves not invite others? Why should it be only us?"

[. . .]

"I have told you a thousand times, Philippe, Clooney is gay. It's time to stop this self-indulgent nonsense, now. Remember Paris."

[. . .]

"And why could you have not just told me – when I phoned you to say that I was looking forward to an evening in, with *you* – why could you not have simply *told* me that you had planned an evening out? Why let me hurry home in expectation of an evening that was never going to happen?

Why let me spend an hour cooking something nice for us both when you had no intention of coming home to eat?" And here, the memory of the hurt and anger in her voice returned to whip me with barbed thongs.

[. . .]

"Well, when you suddenly realised that you'd been out longer than you intended, and that you would not be able to get back to have dinner with your wife, and that you had inadvertently neglected to bring your mobile phone with you, why did you simply not borrow Yves' phone? Something else that you *didn't think of,* perhaps!"

[. . .]

"Just stay on the sofa tonight, Philippe. You are in a disgusting mess. But first, for God's sake brush your teeth. Here – I will turn on the taps for you. And before you forget, take this." She'd handed me the Favrier pill for the evening.

Yes, memories are the worst part of any hangover. And, by extension, I would assert that memories are the worst part of life. If only we could proceed in our poor realities, each of us, in a little bubble that comprised only the present and the very immediate past; if only our minds continually erased our histories and presented us each day with the sweetness of a blank slate. In other words, and from a personal perspective: if only there were no Book. No intangible but indestructible record of Philippe, of all the filth and guilt that encrusts him, all the shame that has grown on him each day of his stupid, worthless life.

Oh, to burn the Book! To baptise its reader in fire, to make him born again. To let him fly again on unsullied phoenix wings.

But such daydreams are childish, of course. One cannot choose to forget; one can only choose whether and how to live with the memory of one's actions. And the recollections made hard reading that morning. I tried to return to sleep, to find a merciful oblivion, but memory's images ran past my closed eyes continually, panel by panel, from the life-changing to the trivial. Paris. Antoine. Le Chat Noir. Soon, the blinding headache left by yesterday's evening was joined by the discomfort of a distended bladder, and I was forced to make my crooked way to the bathroom, geriatrically bent, while Infelix pounced on my feet. After doing the necessary, I drank about a litre of cold water straight from the tap, brushed my teeth, and stood under the shower. I stood there for a long, long time, running the water first as hot as I could bear, and then as cold. And eventually, a small flame ignited in the heart of me; the candle that I'd once lit for Marilyne, and that had been all but extinguished, now popped back into wavering life. I'd behaved badly last night; I could see that now. The hurt in her voice came back to me again and again; remorse sunk its talons into my liver and my soul. I had misjudged her. The discussion with Yves had made it abundantly clear that Clooney could neither create art nor appreciate the opposite sex. Clooney was no more than a colleague, at most a friend. I had, therefore, unjustly accused my wife. I was reprehensible, shameful. I was *stupid*.

I would make it up to her. I would start immediately. First, I would take the medicine that she insisted was for our mutual benefit – the Book shows the convulsive bobbing of my laryngeal prominence – and then, once dried and dressed, I would plan my Campaign to Please Marilyne.

My drawer of art material was in a sorry state. All items disarrayed. Never mind; tidying could wait, for I had other fish to fry. I took pen and paper and sat at the kitchen table.

Strange thing: while jotting down bulleted ideas, something Yves had said last night kept returning to me.

Do something for her that she'd really appreciate. Something nobody else would do. Indeed; but what might that be? What was Philippe Favrier's unique competence vis-a-vis the lovely Marilyne? Try as I might, I could think of nothing that could not be better done by another. Once, I would have made a picture for her, a cartoon, perhaps, or a still life in acrylics; but that was impossible while the creativity of Favrier *fils* was buried under the creativity of Favrier *père*. What then? I simply did not know, but I knew that I had to do what I could.

I began by tidying the kitchen. I took Marilyne's animal hearts from the shelf and wiped down the dusty jars until each glinted like the twinkle-toothed smile of a manga heartthrob. I emptied and refilled the dishwasher. And then (in the Book, a light bulb flashes above my head) inspiration! While putting away Yves' knife in the junk drawer, I saw again the biopsy tubes that Marilyne had pilfered from the hospital. I paused. I looked up, and there, on the work surface, was the empty wooden rack that I'd promised to modify so that it could hold our herbs and spices. Could it be . . .? Yes, it could! Remarkably, as if ordained by some household god, the sample tubes not only fitted perfectly into the retention holes on the rack, but also were sufficient in number to fill every such space.

I set to work immediately. I gathered together all our little cardboard packets of dried herbs and lined them up on the kitchen table, each next to a biopsy tube. On the blank label of each tube I wrote, in careful calligraphy, the name of the given condiment, and then I poured the spices into the relevant container. Finally, I arrayed the tubes alphabetically – *aneth, anis, basilic* – in the oak rack. Only two tubes remained empty, and on the blank label of each I drew a little heart, with an *M* in one and a *P* in the other.

One I placed just before *marjolaine*, and the other just before *piment*.

Yes, I did all that, and more, over the following days: I wrote micro love-letters on Post-its and stuck them on the fridge in a heart shape; I set up a weekly order of the little yellow roses Marilyne liked so much; I fed Infelix regularly, and *never* put him out onto the roof. But it made no difference. Marilyne's disappointment and anger were less evident, in that they were concealed beneath silky politeness, but they were no less massive, and their gravity dragged me after her in a miserable orbit, desperately hoping for a smile or a nod or some other kind signal. It seemed that nothing I did could touch her, nothing. In the Book, a curtain of Frigidaire fumetti hangs from her speech bubble, and when she looks at me her face shows the downturned mouth and narrowed eyes of an Archie Comics snob: the privileged Cheryl Blossom presented with odd, quirky Jughead Jones.

Eventually, I got so low that I even eschewed La Market Jaune. Instead, I wandered around Geneva like a tourist: I criss-crossed the lake on the yellow *mouettes*; I walked over the French border to ride the cable-car up the Salève; I visited museums. In particular, I spent a lot of time in the Jardin Botanique, where I would lie on the grass and watch the slow evolution of clouds.

Oddly, I kept spotting Laurence on my excursions. Once, from a distance, I saw him standing close to the Jet d'Eau where it powered into the sky, his arms spread out as though he hoped to be crucified by the fine spray that fell back to earth. Another day, I spied him, coffee in hand, remonstrating with M. Titeuf. And another time, much closer, I saw him striding down the Rue du Rhône, lecturing passers-by on haemorrhoids and shingles. I turned into Place des Bergues that day, to avoid being seen, but his boom and bellow seemed to follow me: "Faecal suppositories, my friends! A cure for all our problems, I tell you, a veritable panacea! Do you hear me? Faecal suppositories will renew us all!" I walked more quickly, and his echoes faded.

But on this occasion, Laurence's repulsive effect proved beneficial. To ensure our paths did not cross, I reconsidered my intended route along the lake's shore and past La Plage, where Marilyne and I used to watch the boats nudge each other and listen to the whisper and flap of their furled sails. Instead, I tramped off to an area I had not been for months: La Pointe de la Jonction.

Jonction is a weird corner of the city. It's where the Arve and the Rhône meet; a spear of land juts out into the water, with a viewing platform at the spear's tip, so you can look over and along the conjoined river's majestic flow. It's an odd, schizophrenic place: the two rivers have different natures, and rather than mixing at the point of confluence, they flow on side by side, one brown, one blue, reluctant to meld. You can actually see this: the blue Rhône and the straw-yellow, silty Arve marching along next to each other, two waters in one river. It ought to be one of the prettiest parts of Geneva, but somehow Jonction ended up ugly. Its banks support a thin ribbon of trees and bushes; the rest of the peninsula is taken up by modern apartment blocks and industrial warehouses surrounded by walls covered in tags and murals. Outside these walls collect the homeless and the troubled: addicts, criminals, illegal immigrants, and the mentally ill; those who find it hard to live, and those easing their way into death. The detritus of their lost lives litters the ground: needles, bottles, discarded clothing, plastic bags. It's not a place one goes without reason; yet I went there, that day, without any reason that I could recognise.

I followed the river's edge, forcing my way through brambles, my feet sinking into soft mud or sliding on wet stones. At one point, the path, such as it was, dipped towards the water before climbing again over exposed roots smoothed by years of seasons. To reach the first foothold on the upward path was awkward; my progress was impeded by a graffitoed log that the river had deposited on the narrow shoreline. I pushed it aside with my foot.

No. Not graffitoed. Scratched. There, in the pale wood, where a patch of bark was missing, somebody had scratched a heart. A heart, yes, and within the heart, a single letter: *M*.

Circumstances and conspiracies! Sometimes they work for good. That the log I'd sat on and carved at with a sharp pebble a couple of kilometres upstream had washed up here, in this very place; that it had remained here waiting for me to walk by it, on this very day of all days; this *could not* be meaningless. In fact, this was proof, surely, that some benevolent, unseen Advisor walked alongside me, nudging me towards the answers I so desperately needed. For what had I found on the Arve's shore, weeks ago, the day I cut a heart into the log and set it free? What had I brought home and carefully hidden, like a trump card I'd yet to play? The puppy!

Of course! The puppy. It was in the freezer still, but the day was young, and warm; ample time for the little body to thaw. All was *not* lost; no, not at all. I picked up the log, that wooden message from Providence, and placed it reverentially by a bush above the high-water line. Then I turned and ran for the nearest tram stop.

When Marilyne came home that night, late as ever (where do you go, Marilyne, during these long evenings, and who are you with?), I was already in bed. Her heels went *toc-toc* in the hallway, until a paired clatter told me she had kicked them off. An unoiled hinge betrayed her entry into the kitchen. A pause; an intake of breath; and then, very quietly: *Oh!*

I remained still, breathing slow and shallow so I could hear everything: the unfolding of newspaper, the gentle clink and tap as she collected her tools, the hushed glug of some chemical being poured into some container. I fell asleep to such noises and slept beatifically, as I had not done since the first days, back in Paris.

When I woke the next morning, Marilyne had of course already left. Now that I was back on the medication, my bladder was bursting under pharmacology's pressure, but I ignored the discomfort and hobbled to the kitchen; I just had to see. The puppy lay on the newspaper-covered kitchen table, its chest cavity cruelly exposed by a sternal retractor designed for larger anatomies. The excised heart bobbed in a jar of isopropanol. Gobbets of congealed blood, made black as tar by putrefaction, lay on the paper, which was corrugated and stained by what had leaked from the pup. It made me so happy, I don't mind saying I almost cried. Marilyne, my Marilyne – the warm, smiling, dissecting Marilyne – surely she was back!

Chapter 19

Galvanised by this small success, I redoubled my efforts to retrieve Marilyne. I would win her heart again, said I to Infelix, whatever it took. I cleared up after her dissection and washed her sternal retractor. I tidied the kitchen. I took my medicine as prescribed. I continued to ignore the call of La Market Jaune (but have patience, all you bright BDs, I shall return!) so that I could repeatedly clean the flat from top to bottom. I replenished the flower vases with water daily, so that the roses stayed fresh and bright. I even – and nobody can know how much this cost me – phoned up Yves and apologised.

"Hello, this is Yves."

"Yves? Philippe here."

"Philippe."

"I just wanted to talk, you know, about the other night. I think I might have been a bit rude?"

"Are you asking me a question? If so, then yes, you were rude." Yves! What's come over you?

"Sorry, Yves. It was the drink talking. And I wasn't very happy, because Marilyne and I, we, um, we'd been having problems. But great news, Yves, they're all over now, the problems, it's all okay between Marilyne and I now. At last."

"Really?" He sounded almost disappointed, the idiot!

"Yes, *really*. And you know what, I owe you a debt of gratitude. Because it was something you said that helped me patch things up. You said: Do something for her that nobody else would do. So I did. And it worked." I let it hang, waiting for Yves, with bated breath, to ask: *What was it, Philippe? What did you do?*

"Oh. Good."

"Er, yes. It worked really well."

"Good."

The trouble with Yves, I thought, was that it was so difficult to tell whether he was annoyed or just being his usual monosyllabic self. But on this occasion, I thought there was a strong chance he was still offended. I decided to go the extra mile.

"So, um, listen, Yves, I was wondering when our next little get-together might be?"

"Get-together?"

"You know. Dinner."

"Oh, dinner."

"Yes. Marilyne and I were talking about it just the other day."

"Um."

"She loved that evening. So – can I give her a date, something for us to work towards?"

"Hang on. I'll open up the diary." I heard a keyboard clack-clacking in the background. I suddenly realised I'd been hasty, far too hasty. There were limits.

"But Yves, we were thinking, Marilyne and I, that it might be nice to keep it to the three of us, again. You know?"

"Oh. But I was thinking of inviting Georges –"

"Yes, going forward, why not," – although truthfully, I could give a few reasons – "but maybe *this* time, we could just keep it to you, I and Marilyne? Like before?"

"Um."

"Please, Yves."

"All right."

We left it there. I knew I was only doing it for Marilyne, but I couldn't help feeling somehow contaminated. Imagine: Philippe Favrier grovelling to *Yves!* But it was done; I'd apologised. And I'd managed to keep Clooney out of the dinner, which was a significant victory. Just because he wasn't a rival didn't mean he wasn't irritating.

This new Yves-shaped arrow that I had to my bow, together with the success of the puppy, prompted me to call Marilyne. As usual, she was in a clinic, but I left a message with her secretary. Then I fidgeted around the apartment, fussing Infelix and dusting surfaces and repeatedly checking that my phone was on, until she rang back. It was probably no more than half an hour, but I cuddled a thousand cats and wiped down a thousand tables in that time.

"Marilyne?"

"Hello, *cheri*. How are you? Everything okay?"

"Yes, darling, of course. I was just ringing to check that everything was okay with *you*."

"Oh yes. And thank you so much for the gift! Did you see what I did with it?"

"Expert as ever, darling!"

"It was very unexpected, Philippe, but utterly charming. I suppose this means either that I have been very good, or *you* have been very bad." I knew what she meant, of course; her voice was light, but there was sprung steel beneath its silvery tones.

"Look, I'm sorry, Marilyne. It's just that I've been thinking about Antoine a lot, and how I nearly lost you then, back in Paris, and how ever since we moved to Geneva things have been difficult for me, you know. And then I thought I was losing you to Clooney, Marilyne, I really did, and you have no idea how that hurt because of, you know, how he is, the way he talks to me."

I heard her sigh. "But you no longer think this, correct? You have come to your senses?"

I hesitated; some impulse of caution held me back.

"Philippe?"

"It would really help me, Marilyne, if you could just tell me. In straight language. It would just help. You know what I mean."

"Philippe! I am not having, have not had, and will never have an affair with Georges. Okay?"

I breathed deeply. "Thank you, darling. Thank you so much. And I'm sorry for everything. I really am."

"It is Yves you need to apologise to as much as me. He—"

"I have done, Marilyne! I phoned him just now! It's all cleared up between us. And I've arranged another dinner with Yves! Put this in your diary, darling." I mentioned the date, and squirmed with pleasure as I listened to her little sounds of surprise and delight. "So you see, Marilyne, I've been busy."

"Well done, sweetheart! Look, put a bottle of Pinot Gris in the fridge, will you? For later. And I know tomorrow is Saturday, but maybe you could take the morning off? Because I'm having Monday off, in lieu of all the work I had to do for the Cardiac Glycosides Symposium, so we can have a long weekend, for once, all right? Good! But now, please *cheri*, get yourself to La Market Jaune and do some work. It's important for your state of mind."

Now that I was back on the medication regularly, my kidneys had gone into overdrive. Maybe there's a rebound effect or something, but the urgency seemed worse than ever, and I only just made it to La Market Jaune in time that morning. But made it I did, with only a little down-below dampness, and oh, it was good to be back among my *bandes dessinées*!

Strangely, nothing much had changed in the shop. I felt that there should have been some fundamental shift in being after my unprecedented absence, that things could not have remained unchanged. But the bell still went *tinkle-tink, tinkle-tink* when I opened and shut the door; and the BDs were still there in their racks, parading their bright, glossy covers. The only change was an overflowing mailbox; I looked at the A4 envelopes and shuddered with papery pleasure.

Tinkle-tink.

I looked up, preparing for Laurence, but it was not Laurence. It was Clooney.

Clooney? Clooney!

He didn't see me at first – I was sitting at my desk, behind the counter at the back of the shop – but I saw him. He stalked in with a carnassial smile, dark eyes glinting with sadistic anticipation. He quartered the shop boustrophedon-style, examining every shelf. As he walked past Orphan's Corner, he stopped to finger the latest issue of *Madame Médecin*. His grin widened, and he shook his head slightly, as if to say: *This is too good – just too good!* He approached the counter, and I stood.

"*Bonjour*, Georges."

"Philippe! *Salut*!"

"Are you lost?"

"Of course not, Philippe. I walked here expressly to visit your fine establishment." He rubbed his hands together slowly, as if to caress his own skin.

"I am afraid I don't do medical textbooks. Or sex manuals."

"Ha, ha. No matter – I have many of those at home already. One category is well-thumbed, the other less so." He looked at me askance, gauging my reaction. I wasn't going to bite, however, not now that things were getting better between Marilyne and I. No point in jeopardising my progress just to have a go at Clooney.

"Then how may I help you? After all, you've been very clear that *bandes dessinées* do not meet your criteria for great art."

"It's certainly true that I would not read them *myself*, Philippe. But I have a friend, a dear friend, who is partial to this, ah, *modality* of literature." There it was! The 'for a friend' excuse, from Clooney, of all people! I fought to keep a straight face as he continued. "So I have come to you as the, ah, fount of all knowledge regarding graphic art. What should I buy for one whose interests are, ah, eclectic, yet intensely focused on the modern? I fear your *oeuvres* from the twentieth century" – he waved a nonchalant arm around La Market Jaune – "will be of little interest. Might you recommend something a little more *en pointe,* perhaps even somewhat *avante garde*?"

"Mm-hm. Might this *friend* also have a particular interest in the medical world?"

Clooney's eyes gleamed; he nodded in a vigorous parody of enthusiasm. "Yes, truly. But his interests are, one might say, more inclined to the machinery of health, the clockwork of anatomy rather than the chemistry of cures. Plumbing rather than pharmaceuticals. *Pseudo*-medicine, perhaps. Do you see?"

I gave him a long look, gnawing at the plaster on my thumb. I thought about saying things, unforgiveable things. But no; it was clear that he was simply trying to rattle my cage. My interrogation of Yves, and my chat with Marilyne, had put Clooney out of the picture. He was a mischief-maker, yes; but nothing more. And now that I observed him in this new light, I could not believe how I'd ever thought Marilyne might have found anything attractive about this conceited dandy. Doubtless he'd heard about my suspicions, somehow – maybe from Yves – and thought he'd pop round to stir things up. Well, it wasn't going to work; but I *would* sell him a BD. And waste a good deal of his time into the bargain. So I took him around shelf after shelf, talking him through this artist and that, this series and the other. Eventually, he plumped for something by Michel Leduc, the Quebecois artist who'd devised a world populated by cyborg-type characters with visible internal machinery. Their anatomies were a bit steampunk – more cogs than circuit boards – but the concept seemed to satisfy Clooney's pretended needs. He gave me a skin-deep "*merci*" and strode off with his purchase hidden under one arm.

When he'd left, I did a little pleasure-dance behind the counter, or maybe it was a victory dance. It certainly felt like I'd reached a critical turning point. Consider: Marilyne and I were speaking again; Marilyne was not having an affair with Clooney; Clooney was thereby demoted from gorgeous love-rival to effeminate irritant; thus deprived of power, Clooney's ability to disturb my balance was much diminished; hence the ease – the cool, calm, collected ease – with which I had dealt with his unexpected visit. And I'd sold him a BD, to boot! Yes, I positively danced. The Book shows me kicking out a leg here, and throwing up an arm there, eyes shut and eyebrows raised in cartoon joy. I collect my mail. I open the envelopes. Another two issues of *Madame Médecin,* but ha! – who cares? The artist's power to vex me has been dissolved in joy. I merely glance at their titles and set them aside with the other entries, for later review. I laugh loud and long, and wave at a tram clunking by. *La Market Jaune, La Market Jaune, La Market Jaune . . .*

At the same time, however, the frames in this sequence of the Book are scattered with discordant notes. In particular, the BDs in my shop are painted intensely, and oddly distorted. I am shown examining one; down its spine, I see the words *EP Jacobs.* I look puzzled, as though I am asking: *What might they whisper, my beautiful BDs, had I ears to hear their little voices?*

But before I could think too much about this, I heard a true, albeit fractured, sound.

Tinkle-tink. I twisted round to face the shop door.

"*Bonjour!*" The greeting set the surface of my undrunk coffee rippling in rings – centripetal and then centrifugal.

"Laurence – this is a little late in the day for you, is it not?"

"My friend!" He strode to the counter. I half-expected some reference to our encounter on the bridge, but no. He had come to impart information and opinion, and that he would do, without wasting any of his valuable time.

"There is photographic evidence for a close association between Hergé and Edgar Jacobs," he roared. "Did you know this, my friend?"

"Of course. They worked together for a while. Everyone knows that."

"But do you know *where* the photographs were taken, my friend?"

"I'm sure you are about to tell me."

"The location of their *folie à deux* was none else than Doré et Fils, here in Geneva!" His triumphant bellow set off a sympathetic echo from the shop door bell – *tinkle-tink*.

"Really? How do you know?" Somehow, I couldn't help pretending to take a polite interest in Laurence's disjointed utterances, even though I knew from experience that a meaningful conversation with him was impossible. And indeed, he completely ignored my question, following instead some script in his head that seemed to have been worked out long before he entered my shop that morning.

"The art gallery, my friend! Observe, understand, learn, act!" He winked at me, turned his twisted body around and left.

And yes, that was it, surely; that must have been what the BDs would have told me had I still been listening to their voices. Planche 8, Numero 8, in the window of Doré et Fils. Laurence must have seen it too. I pulled out my phone; its wallpaper sprang out at me, bathing my face with a radiance of culture, demanding my attention, insistent, a call that could not be denied.

I thumbed the Doré et Fils number into my phone. I paced the kitchen while I waited for them to pick up.

"Hello, Doré et Fils, may I help you?" I recognised the voice: Miss Slavic Cheekbones again.

"Yes. This is Philippe Favrier." Long pause; for a second, I thought we'd been cut off.

"Hello, M'sieu Fournier. How can I help you?"

"*Favrier!* Not Fournier. Favrier."

"I do apologise, M'sieu Favrier."

"Mm." Another long pause.

"M'sieu Favrier? The nature of your enquiry?"

"It has not changed since my previous visit." Really, what was the matter with these people? "Obviously. The Jacobs artwork from La Market Jaune. In your window."

"Ah yes, M'sieur. The graphic art sample. I must tell you that the vendor, for whom we are acting, is inviting offers—"

"Madame, we have been through this. You were kind enough to explain the situation fully, perhaps three weeks ago, when I visited your shop. You will doubtless recall the very generous offer that I made. I regret that I have been incommunicado – business obligations, naturally – but I am now phoning to gauge the vendor's reaction to the offer, and to pay a deposit if required."

"M'sieu made an offer? Permit me to check against the registry, please . . . Your name, M'sieu?"

"Favrier!"

"Favrier, of course . . . One second, if you please, M'sieu, while I retrieve our notes from the system . . . Ah! . . . Ah, yes. I can confirm that we still have your offer in the register, M'sieu Favrier, and the vendor's response is imminent. We—"

"Imminent? What does that mean? Why can't you just tell me now whether or not the offer is sufficient? If the vendor believes it to be too low, I can adjust it, can I not?"

"M'sieu, as I believe we discussed, our hands are tied. In effect, the vendor has requested a blind auction, and we are bound by his instructions. But if M'sieu wishes to raise his offer, of course we can adjust the registry entry accordingly—"

"No! My offer is already exceptionally generous. And I can go higher, but I want that to be by discussion with the vendor, blind auction or no blind auction. Just tell the vendor my name, will you: Favrier. Philippe Favrier. I have no doubt it will mean something to *him*."

"As you please, M'sieu. May I be of assistance in any other way?"

"The time-scale, Madame. When is your *process* to be completed?"

"The final decision will be made tomorrow morning. Following that, M'sieu Favrier, the item may be collected by the purchaser immediately."

That was better: I could hear the encouragement in her voice; clearly, the item was as good as mine. I congratulated myself for not having been drawn into the trap of putting in higher and higher blind bids.

"Goodbye, Madame!"

I hung up, and then spent more time ogling my phone photo of Planche 8, Numero 8, 1953. Where should I put it: in the apartment or in the shop? There were so many places it could go, and it would look good in all of them. Everything was good; *life* was good.

Yes, that was it: life was *good*. I had won Marilyne back, defeated Clooney, and soon would possess the divine Jacobs artwork at a decent price. There was a bottle of Pinot Gris in the fridge, it was Friday evening and Marilyne would be coming home early. I lived in the best of all possible worlds.

I woke, the next day, to the best of all possible mornings. Marilyne's soft warmth stretched and nuzzled alongside me; my lazy, sleepy hug pulled her close and found the linear, crusted scabs across her belly. She winced and sighed as I traced them with my fingers.

"Coffee, Philippe." She spoke through a delicate yawn; a gossamer lock slipped into her mouth's corner. I pushed it aside to kiss the soft confluence of her lips. A dimple appeared. "Coffee."

In the kitchen, Infelix waltzed with my ankles as I set the kettle off and filled the cafetière. I raised my foot to rub his furry stomach with my toes; he arched and mewed. While the coffee brewed, I fed him and spot-cleaned the litter tray. "You can stay in today, Infelix," I whispered. "In fact, you can do whatever you like today."

I was about to leave the kitchen with a tray of coffee and croissants when I remembered I'd not taken my morning dose of the Favrier drug. I hesitated; I took a step back; I placed the tray on the table and looked in the direction of the bathroom. The problem was, I probably didn't remember to take it last night, either, what with one lovely thing and another. I took a step away from the kitchen table – and then I thought, just once, just this once, let me fully live this bright morning in all its singing colours, this beautiful morning when everyone is happy and everything is *right*. Just this once. I could always take the pill later. That's what I told myself, as I brought the tray to Marilyne. Time enough to mute life's true colours later.

She sat up, pulling the duvet to her neck and levelling it across her lap to make a platform for the tray. I got back in beside her while she sipped at the coffee. Her eyes smiled at me. I never understood how some people's eyes could be so readable; how can the sum of iris, pupil, sclera and lids express, in turn, joy and hatred, fury and pain, and love, love, love? Love has a colour, and it is violet-blue; blue has a song, and sings it sweetly.

"What's that, Philippe?"

"What's what, darling?"

"That tune. You were humming something."

"Was I? Just a happy tune, darling."

She reached across, found my hand and squeezed it, setting off a peal of tiny pleasure-bells. "I am *so* glad we've found the smiley Philippe again. I was getting worried that you were going all Paris on me. All those things you were saying about Clooney and me . . ." She took her hand back in favour of a croissant. "You see – and I think this has been the case since Antoine – I don't have the resilience I once had, Philippe. I can't be strong for both of us, all the time. I need you to keep going too. You know what I mean. Resist, until your father's shares come through. Then it will be easy."

Yes, I knew what she meant. Resist the suffocating pressure of the Normal; push back against its efforts to squeeze you into its cookie-cut shapes. Above all, don't let it drive a wedge between us, don't let it throw a spanner into our relationship's delicately balanced machinery. But it's hard to push back without a private income; so come on, Favrier Pharma.

"Don't worry, Marilyne. All is good now."

"And in La Market Jaune? How's your competition going?"

"It's okay. At least, kind of. I've let things slip a little recently, but it's not a problem. I can just pick things up from where I left off and start again."

"Good. You really need that kind of external focus for your mind, or you *will* start getting ideas."

"Ideas?"

"You know. Seeing things which aren't there. Like with Clooney and me."

We were silent for a little minute, Marilyne and I; at least we didn't speak. But bedclothes rustled; cups chinked; Yves' printed knife pressed through soft pastry. And somewhere, something whispered to me. *She's trying too hard. Something's wrong.* I glanced at Marilyne. She raised an eyebrow, gave me an arch look and continued chewing croissant.

"Marilyne . . ."

"Mmm?"

"Just thinking about it . . . thinking *back* . . ." I hesitated; she chewed more slowly, keeping her eyes on me. The violet-blue had changed subtly, as if sun-bathed petals had been shadowed by a high cloud. "You mentioning the Competition reminded me, you see . . ."

"Reminded you of what, *cheri*?"

"Well, there's still this question of who *is* the author of *Madame Médecin*, isn't there? If it's not Clooney, then who *is* it?"

Marilyne frowned, looked away, looked back at me, head on one side, mouth down-turned in a kind of *What the hell is this?* expression.

"You've lost me, Philippe. Who is *Madame Médecin*?"

Seriously? I thought. But I explained anyway: I reminded her of how *Madame Médecin* was an elaborate joke at our – *my* – expense, a cruel, mocking parody of our life. I pulled a random issue from the pile of entries under the bed – *still* there! – to show her. "And the point is, Marilyne, it could only be done by somebody who knows us reasonably well. So: if not Clooney, who?"

She nodded; the blue of deep water in a limpid sea. "Okay – I remember now. The weird competition entry, that BD where the criminal mastermind looks like you. Listen, Philippe – many of the correspondences you describe could have happened by chance, or through third-hand knowledge. Nothing suggests to me that the artist has any close connection to us as a couple. Nothing at all. I grant you they must know *you* – Mr Arch-Villain resembles you too closely to be a happenstance, that's true. But Madame Médecin is just a stereotype. Even if you believe her occupation reflects mine – which is highly debatable! – it's the kind of similarity which could have resulted from you mentioning to somebody that your wife was a doctor. Truly, Philippe, the artist is almost certainly somebody you met at Comic Con at some point. They are only being mischievous, and at some point they will identify themselves. In fact, maybe you should let them win the competition – that might bring them out of the woodwork."

She threw *Madame Médecin and the Implants of Youth* to the floor. "Otherwise, *cheri*, let's hear no more about it. Okay? And now – it is Saturday, so the gym beckons! Will you come?"

"No."

"As you wish, dear-heart. What then are your plans for the morning, if you are not working?"

"I shall go to Doré et Fils, to collect something. You know – the Jacobs original."

She stiffened, half in and half out of jogging bottoms. "To *collect* it? Whatever do you mean?"

"They said the vendor would make his decision today. I think he'll find my offer *very* acceptable. They pretty much told me so."

"You made an offer?"

"Oh, sorry, did I not tell you? I could not pass up on such an opportunity, darling. I'm sure you understand."

She hesitated; her eyes took on a dark expression I could not read. "Just remind me, what did you offer, *cheri*?"

I told her; she relaxed. Obviously, she too realised my bid was bound to be accepted. "Ah – I see. Well, good luck, darling. But try not to be upset if you don't get it okay? There will be a lot of interest in that kind of item. *Ciao*!"

"*Ciao*, darling."

And the sound of the door closing behind her almost, but not quite, smothered the small, whispered question that now nuzzled at my ear unceasingly: *If not Clooney – then who?*

Chapter 20

I didn't take the tram to Doré et Fils that day. Something about it repelled me; with its rounded angles and pre-ordained route, it was like a coffin sliding along crematorium tracks to a beckoning incinerator. And the faces of the bodies inside: such a gallery of vapid, unreasoning hostility! The vehicle was just a giant, armoured slug that ingested the sluggish Normal only to vomit them up at their Normal destinations; so it seemed. I shuddered, and walked on over Geneva pavements. Pedestrians milled, crowding me with their stink, staring doltishly. To avoid their eyes, I kept mine to the ground, orienting my steps by ground-level landmarks. *Here, where the cobbles take on the grey of a cannon barrel, I proceed; here, where the steps fan out like a regulated, rounded cascade of stone, I descend; there, where the tram tracks cross my path again, I turn left*; and so on. In this way, I progressed without incident, without meeting a Normal eye, until – barely three streets away from Doré et Fils – someone spat on the ground in front of me. I stopped, head down; the frothy saliva turned the stone a darker grey. All around it and about were scores of similar marks, as if the paving-stone, in a semicircle around the spitter's feet, had been freckled by exposure to a monochrome sun.

"My friend!" A bassoon rumble. Somehow, it lacked its normal vigour, yet – somehow – it drenched the air with tones of dark foreboding.

"Laurence."

He leant forward as far as his spinal deformity would allow, and spat again. Then he turned and threw an arm to one side in a reckless gesture of command. His other hand cradled some kind of thin, flat package.

"Continue!" he bellowed, like a doleful foghorn. "Continue!"

"Are you well, Laurence?"

"No. But that, my friend, is better than the alternative. As you know."

"I am perfectly healthy, in all regards!" Sometimes Laurence was *very* irritating.

He tapped his nose and winked in a vulgar representation of secrets shared and unshared. "Here, all is confidential. But soon, you will see something of interest – I guarantee it, my friend!"

"I look forward to it."

"The shop-window, do you hear? You have not heard the last of that! Continue!"

I continued. The Book shows me spitting surreptitiously to one side, attracting a look of disgust from a perfectly-dressed Genevoise in four-inch heels. Some days, it was if Laurence infected me with his habits, and there was nothing I could do about it. But I was approaching Doré et Fils; it was time to wear the mask. I patted my pocket; my wallet, weighted with credit cards, reassured. I took a deep breath and walked towards the art gallery, towards Planche 8. There it was, in its usual place in the gallery window; all as before, except for one thing: the label beneath it had been obscured by a sticker, with capitals of arterial red, that simply proclaimed: *VENDU.*

Vendu: sold! Something happened to the light; the sun went behind a cloud, or maybe came out from behind one. I can't remember; the Book doesn't specify. But I was suddenly aware of my image in the window, hands to the side of my head in a parody of horror. Indeed, the Book gives my reflection something of the tormented face from Munch's *Scream.* Was my mouth really open like that? But I pull myself together with words of admonishment: *Always looking on the black side, Philippe!* Indeed, shadows flow from behind buildings and press hotly at my feet; their darkness groans like a distant torment. *Paint a future less black,* my thought bubble insists. *It is marked 'Vendu' because it has been sold to M. Philippe Favrier,* I tell myself. *M. Favrier needs only enter the shop and claim what is rightfully his,* I assert.

I entered; *Reeeeeeee.* Miss Cheekbones looked up: *Meeeeeee.* All around, glorious paintings welcomed me with the hue and cry of pigment, with the chimes and tones of colourful paradise.

"I have come to claim what is rightfully mine!" Maybe I was too excited; my voice seemed louder than it should have been. My heart chirred and kicked. Miss Cheekbones raised both eyebrows, her professional smile aborted.

"*Bonjour* —"

"Favrier! Philippe Favrier!"

"Of course, M'sieu, naturally I remember —"

"Naturally? Ha!" I could have said more regarding this little deceit – how many times had she called me Fournier? – but under the circumstances I thought I'd grant mercy. "The Jacobs piece. I am here to pay."

"To pay? M'sieu Favrier, we appreciate your interest, as does the vendor, but unfortunately, M'sieu, I must inform you that the piece is sold—"

"What! I mean, I *know*. Sold to *me*." But something was wrong; I could see it in the way the galleried paintings leant forward from the walls, as though to bear witness, or to judge; in the way the room's perspectives and angles had shifted slightly, illustrating an off-kilter world in which I was always just off-balance. I put a hand on the countertop for support. Miss Slavic Cheekbones glanced at my fist, and then at me, and then quickly away, and then down at her computer.

"If M'sieu will bear with me, I will bring up the records . . ." Her fingers tickled the keyboard, and she read from a screen. "Yes. I must tell you, M'sieu, that a number of parties were interested in this item. Many offers were made, and several – I regret – were higher than the figure M'sieu indicated he would be willing to pay. *Enfin,* a very generous offer was made and accepted very recently . . . the party clearly wished to make certain of a successful bid. The vendor is very happy. We are not seeking further offers, M'sieu, by instruction. Perhaps I could interest you in—"

"But I phoned you! You said I could pick it up today!" I was aware that my voice was loud, too loud, but I couldn't help it. Injustice leads to rage; the relationship is immutable. Even the paintings knew it; their colours seethed and burned and hissed.

"I do not remember saying exactly that, M'sieu, but if there has been a misunderstanding then of course I apologise—"

"This is outrageous!"

I could see that she knew she was in the wrong; the way her eyes went a bit wide and then a bit shifty, the way she swallowed and started looking nervously around.

"*Je suis desolée . . .*"

Well, being sorry wasn't good enough, and I told her so. There's a whole page of the Book devoted to that episode; I see myself stamping around the shop, shouting and swearing, spittle flying from my mouth. Miss Slavic Cheekbones was almost in tears by the time I'd had my say, and quite right too. As I stormed out of the gallery, I turned around in the doorway and pointed at her. "You haven't heard the last of this!" I roared. A cliché, I know, but it was all I could think of as a parting shot.

I stamped away from that den of liars with some high, otherworldly note keening in my ears, as though a demon played a monotone flute as a backdrop for my pain. And had I not heard that note before? Indeed, now I considered it, I saw that key parts of my life kept repeating themselves, up and down, round and round, the same peaks and troughs, the same twists and turns. As if I were trapped on some kind of satanic carousel, as if I were part of a show repeated *ad infinitum* on for the public's amusement. Today, on *Mock the Afflicted*, let's have a laugh at Philippe Favrier! See him get all excited by a piece of unique art, uniquely meaningful to silly little Favrier and his silly little shop, only to lose said piece at the last minute! See him wriggle and squirm like a . . . like a . . .

Like a cartoon baddie caught by the cops. Like PseudoFifre losing out, yet again, to the voluptuous Madame Médecin.

Yes. Damn him. Damn her. Damn this eternal carousel.

*

"Hello, Philippe."

"Yves!" He was standing by the tram stop down the road from Doré et Fils. I hated the way he stared at me.

"Are you all right, Philippe?"

"Why wouldn't I be?"

"I don't know."

"So what made you ask, then?"

"You had that look. You know." Yves made a pitiful attempt at pulling his features into something that resembled emotion: gaping mouth, wide eyes, raised eyebrows. "Like in the BDs. You know."

"Really? *Really?* And you want to know why that was, Yves? Just ask the bastards in Doré et Fils! Go on!" I gestured down the street, towards the art gallery. Yves' slow, dull glance followed my hand. "They sold what was rightfully mine. Original art from *La Marque Jaune*. They sold it."

He nodded in slow motion, while something akin to understanding struggled beneath his blurred features. "Oh yes. I know the one. Marilyne mentioned it. You really wanted that, didn't you?" The rudiments of a smile pulled at his mouth. "Don't worry. I'm sure it's all for the best."

All for the best? What planet was this idiot from? Would it be 'all for the best' if I took his rucksack, full of the twisted anatomies of his odious creations, and threw it beneath the wheels of the tram? We shall see. I reached towards him – but too late. He was getting on the tram, and other Normals were pushing after him. He was out of reach. I walked on the pavement alongside as he walked down the tram's aisle, and when he took a seat at the window, I shouted through it: "No, it bloody well is not all for the best!" I pulled a face at him through the glass, tugging and twisting my ears and stretching my mouth into a leering grimace. I may have pulled too hard – one of my ears felt sore – but what else could I do? I am an emotional person.

And, as Yves's tram clink-clunked into the distance, those emotions were still too strong by far for me to return home. But my feet hurt, and I was miserable, and the heat of the day enervated. I wanted to sit down somewhere cool and dark, somewhere where I would not be disturbed. What to do? La Market Jaune, of course; as always, I had the keys with me. So, *tinkle-tink,* and hey presto, just like that, all Geneva's dull inhabitants were shut away, all its tedious Normality dammed. As if the phrase 'Proprietor: Philippe Favrier' could keep at bay the boring hordes engulfed by Geneva commerce each morning and excreted each afternoon by the same banks and shops.

I sat at my desk and took off my shoes and socks. I flexed and bent my feet; the cool floor soothed their hot ache. Barefooted, I made a coffee in the micro-kitchen, and sat down again. I clenched my fists and snarled at the shop's low ceiling. I turned on the computer, went to the Facebook page of Doré et Fils and posted a withering account of their behaviour; I logged onto Trustpilot and left the most damning review I could construct. I wrote a letter to the *Tribune de Genève*; my excoriating prose denounced the management and staff of the art gallery – crooks all! – and vilified the corrupt, venal individuals who chose to sell art of historical value through such an outlet. I searched Google for an hour in a futile attempt to uncover the home address of Doré and his damned Fils. Then it occurred to me that if the bastards at Doré et Fils had sold my Edgar Jacobs artwork to another buyer, why then, I would buy a better one from another dealer. So I spent another hour or more on the Internet, scouring the websites of every gallery from New York to London, from Copenhagen to Tokyo. But they had nothing, of course, nothing at all; at least, they had Kim Deitch artwork from *The Boulevard of Broken Dreams;* a *Krazy Kat* cartoon signed by Herriman; an early Spiegelman (pre-*Maus*); various prints from Archie Comics; a David Lloyd from *V for Vendetta;* an Eduardo Risso (*100 Bullets*); hordes of manga – but of Edgar Jacobs? Neither hair nor hide. Defeated, I made another coffee. And then I remembered that I'd not turned on my phone that day.

Three missed calls and three text messages from Marilyne:

Back from gym. How'd it go?

Just had lunch – couldn't wait any longer! Are you coming back?

Philippe where ARE you??!

I thumbed out a quick response: *Back soon. Awful news.* And I know I shouldn't have, perhaps, but then I turned the phone off again. She'd be angry but I was in no mood to speak to anyone, and I think that was understandable.

I paced the shop, up and down the rows of BDs in their bright colours, running my fingers over their smooth corners, listening to their individual, hushed voices. I stalked past Thorgal and *L'Echo des Savanes* to Orphan's Corner. There, I turned to walk along the back of the window display (Jijé and Michel Leduc). And then I passed the mailbox on the door. Almost absent-mindedly, I lifted its lid. Some Saturday junk mail, and an A4-sized manila envelope. I turned it over and around. On the front, nothing but my shop's name, La Market Jaune, in childishly clumsy hand-writing. No return address on the reverse. The Book shows me pulling a face; my thought bubble says, *Now what,* as I open the envelope.

And I should have known *Now what*, I really should have. But I went ahead, like the stupid man that I am, and began slowly pulling out the contents, and even when I knew what they were, I continued pulling them out. Bring it on, was my attitude; nothing, but nothing, can make my day any worse, so I am ready for you, Madame Médecin, I am ready for whatever you might throw at me.

Only, I wasn't. Not for this one.

It began as one would expect, with a stupid title: *Issue #10: Madame Médecin and the Thwarting of PseudoFifre.* But there was a slight change of emphasis in the storyline; rather than unleashing medical problems on the Swiss populace, PseudoFifre tried a sneaky direct attack on Madame Médecin. She was sunbathing by Lac Léman, in a bikini (of course) when PseudoFifre tried to set off explosive that had been packed into the tubular supports of Madame Médecin's deckchair. But Madame Médecin activated a novel heart pacemaker that her lab technicians had been developing, and which she just happened to have with her. This blocked the electronic signal that would have triggered the explosion. She walked innocently away, all sculpted legs and rounded derrière, and PseudoFifre sneaked up to the chair, like the evil gnome from any fairy tale, to find out what went wrong. He took out the detonator to look at it more closely. Then Madame Médecin turned off the pacemaker, and the detonator promptly exploded in PseudoFifre's hand. "You didn't think of that, did you?" crows Madame Médecin gleefully, all perfect breasts and perfect teeth. The final frame shows PseudoFifre, with a bandaged hand, glowering in his headquarters and plotting revenge.

Okay. I had to read that entry twice, three times, maybe more, and each time the fury grew, spreading through my stomach like an ulcer, draining me of strength, pounding in my temples, until I was nothing but hatred held together by human skin, a jelly of vitriol knocked out of a man-shaped mould. Or rather, a PseudoFifre-shaped mould. It was clear that the author no longer cared whether I knew or not; indeed, he or she *wanted* me to know – or, perhaps, *knew* I knew. And it wasn't the puerile drawings that hurt so much as the *intent* to hurt; the cheap, cowardly, anonymous spite. That, and the betrayal. The bandaged hand? Obviously, that signified the plaster around the base of my thumb from the paper cut Marilyne had given me. And okay, I'd kept the plaster there for a while, but even so, the artist had to be someone who'd seen me recently. Not just some random nobody from last year's Comic Con, as Marilyne had absurdly suggested. And the dialogue given to Madame Médecin – "You didn't think of that, did you?" – could have come from none other than Marilyne, from the very *contretemps* when she'd given me the paper cut that led to the bandaged thumb. What had she said? . . . *but who then pays the rent . . . you didn't think of that, did you?* No; wait! She'd also said something very similar when berating me after I'd gone drinking with Yves! *I could have called the police, Philippe! But you didn't think of that, did you?* And again – the Book records her words in unambiguous, Comic Pro clarity – "Why did you simply not borrow Yves' phone? Something else that you didn't think of, perhaps!"

So there it was. I was not just being persecuted by someone known to both Marilyne and me. It was far worse than that. Marilyne herself was in league with my persecutor. The creator of *Madame Médecin* was in direct contact with Marilyne; they were collaborating in some way or ways, who knew how closely. There was no other plausible explanation. There was no longer any doubt.

Chapter 21

Even the Book cannot adequately represent the crippling nature of this blow. The artist does his best; he illustrates me in hideous close-up, face-on, lividly underlit; my eyes stare up from my downwardly inclined face as if rolling back into their sockets; my skin is greenish, my teeth bared; plewds run down my forehead as if from a melting scalp. But the actual impact on me was far greater than such an image might signal. It was as though the universe had twisted on some axis, and now showed me that all my perspectives, all the lines and angles of that beautiful geometry by which Marilyne and I had built our sanctuary from the Normal – that architecture was skewed, asymmetric, ugly. The protection it gave, that I had depended upon, was worse than an illusion – it was a deliberate deceit. Great fists seized my viscera; intestines, heart and lungs were crushed; I could hardly breathe, and something kicked and clutched behind my ribs. Somewhere far away, I heard a continuous rising sound, like a siren; I tore at my ears, but it stayed, it stayed, and as it ascended so did the clear note of my anguish. There is no pain like love's betrayal, none, and it makes a sound like no other sound. It paints the world with a colour for which there is no word in any language.

Things fell into place, now. Marilyne's recent fits of pique had nothing to do with Infelix on the roof, nor with my drunken evening with Yves. No, these were just excuses to cover the real reasons behind her behaviour, and I'd been too stupid to see it – too *stupid*. This had been part of a plan, her plan, *their* plan, all the time. But how long was 'all the time'? How long had I been a fool, how long laughed at and, presumably, cuckolded? And by *whom*? I heard a mocking whisper from Orphan's Corner: *You didn't think of that, did you?* It was taken up by the others, and echoed softly around La Market Jaune. I put my hands to my ears, and rubbed and pulled at them; as usual, the sound of skin on skin half-blocked the whispering, but couldn't completely silence it. *You know the how; now uncover the who.*

I remembered Clooney: his mocking smile, his hand on Marilyne's arm, his hand on Marilyne's back. But I'd already investigated Clooney via my interrogation of Yves. So: if not Clooney, who? I ground my teeth until the enamel protested and my jaw ached. I would find out and have my pound of flesh, even if it was my last act in this life. But I knew I had to be careful about jumping to conclusions. Keep calm, Philippe. Apply logic.

And with that decision – to be *logical* – the high siren note of betrayal and despair disappeared beyond hearing, and everything around me and in front of me, in space and time, took on a bright, spot-lit clarity. I had never been so focused, so determined. I went to Orphan's Corner and collected all the unsold *Madame Médecin* entries. I bundled them into my shoulder bag, locked up the shop, and left. I now had a task, and nothing, nothing would distract me from its execution.

I walked again – the tram's slow claustrophobia and limping progress would have been intolerable to my tight-sprung energy. When I got back to the Old City, I shouldered open the door to our apartment block, and went up the stairs two-by-two, all four stories. I unlocked the door to Number 4b, *Madame Médecin* holding onto my arm, and was greeted by – what?

Silence. Marilyne was not there.

You'd think that would have meant peace, but it didn't. The silence was charged with anger and tension. It whispered at me. I stood just inside the apartment door, looking down the short hallway that led to living room and kitchen and our two bedrooms, listening to the sub-audible. *Philippe.*

In the kitchen, I laid out *Madame Médecin* on the table. I placed Yves' printed knife at her throat, as if to weigh the paper against non-existent currents of air. For no reason other than force of habit, I turned on my mobile, and, just like that – as though she could somehow *spy* on me – it rang.

"Hello?"

"Philippe?

"Yes."

"Where have you *been*? And you turned your phone off again!"

"I had to finish some work. In the shop. Accounts."

"But what was the awful news, Philippe? You scared me!"

"Awful news?"

"That's what you said. In your text."

"Oh yes." That other pain, which had been pushed into insignificance by *Madame Médecin* and Marilyne's betrayal, struck me again. Losing Planche 8 was nothing compared to losing – to being *betrayed* by – Marilyne, but it still hurt, in an additive kind of way. Doré et Fils had given me a body-blow while Marilyne had stabbed me in the heart, that was true, but the body-blow also was significant. "Yes, awful.

Doré et Fils. The bastards sold Planche 8 to somebody else. After all my discussions with them. After my clear instructions. The bastards."

"Oh, *that*." She actually sounded relieved! I couldn't believe it; if anything could demonstrate how little she understood me, how little she cared about my feelings, *that* was it: the cursory, blasé manner in which she responded to the theft of Planche 8. "Don't worry about *that,* darling. Really, don't. These things – they are less important than you think. I promise. Oh, Philippe – when you said 'awful news,' I thought – well, I didn't know what to think."

Yes, you did, I said to myself. You thought maybe people were beginning to wonder about the wonderful Marilyne. About disturbed autopsies. About missing organs. About Antoine. That's the awful news you fear. But out loud, I said nothing.

"So I came out looking for you, darling. I went to all the usual places. I even went to La Market Jaune – but you must have just left . . ." She paused, as though waiting for affirmation, but still I said nothing.

"Philippe – are you quite sure you are well? You have been diligent, I hope – you know, with the pills?"

"As always, *cherie*."

"Good. Good. Well, I shall come home, then. Okay?"

"Okay."

"Love you, darling."

"Love you." Not.

What kind of a crap-filled, unjust, cruel life was this? After a childhood such as mine, after all my difficulties wrestling with the Normal, after faithfully supporting Marilyne no matter what, after spending years scratching out a living from La Market Jaune, surely I deserved better than betrayal and theft?

In the Book, the rest of that day is vague; the artist provides scattered images in an imprecise order. Infelix pesters me, and I chase him around the flat until he takes refuge under the bed, where he caterwauls until I leave the room. I take *Madame Médecin* to the bathroom, open the bathroom cabinet, reverse the pedestal mirror and study my – no, *his!* – profile; I compare it with what screams from each page of *The Thwarting of PseudoFifre*. Rage and horror almost break me. I open the bathroom window and howl at the rooftops like a dog. I collapse in front of the toilet and retch emptily into its bowl, again and again. I hear Marilyne's key in the lock and hide all the *Madame Médecin* issues under the bed; Infelix darts out and runs to the lounge. Marilyne appears; speech bubbles are littered with fragments of dialogue:

"Philippe? I am still worried about you . . ."

"I can't believe you left your phone turned off again, after all we've said—"

"Are you ill, dear-heart? Are you sure you are not ill again?"

"What is wrong, Philippe? I can see something's wrong. Please talk to me."

"Well, if you're *sure*—"

"Really, there is time enough for everything in this world, including adding to your graphic art collection. So don't worry, darling, okay?"

Oh, she said all the things that a loving, faithful Marilyne would have said, no doubt about that. But I knew what she was doing now. I could see it in the way her smile left no impression in her eyes; the way they remained flat, cold, empty. The eyes of a traitor who knows to speak nicely. *She is dangerous,* something whispered; and I saw that it was true. In the Book, I smile back. I make reassuring words, for all the world as if I think she loves me still.

"But I am perfectly well, darling."

"The phone ran out of battery – only realised when I got home. It's okay now, look—"

"I am sick of the Normal, Marilyne. That's all."

"I *am* talking to you, darling. And I've told you that nothing's wrong. Other than the small matter of Planche 8."

"Thank you, *cherie*. Very reassuring."

These conversations must have happened at various places around the flat, for the Book presents each scrap of dialogue in a different room, as if I am pacing a gaol and she is following me watchfully, shaking her gaoler's bundle of keys. And with each word of hers, my hatred grew within me like a madstone, heavy and hard. For so many years I'd accommodated her: I'd moved to Paris; I'd let her collect the things she collected; I'd taken the pills she suggested, with catastrophic consequences for my life and art; I'd done whatever she wanted, all the time; I'd even helped her with Antoine's heart. And all that time she'd been betraying me, mocking me, with some unknown Other; some enemy. Well, I'd be the compliant fool no more. So while she yawned at the kitchen table and thumbed through her text messages, I went to the bathroom, pressed each and every one of the Favrier pills from the blister pack, and flushed them down the toilet. Then I lay beneath the duvet, foetally huddled, eyes dishonestly shut, while Marilyne got ready for bed. I lay still, still, and pretended not to feel her touch, and listened to her breathing slow and settle. My thoughts swarmed, but I moved not a muscle.

The decision to cease my medication brought me a kind of bitter peace; it was if I had crossed some kind of Rubicon, and thereby made life simpler by eliminating choices previously open to me. And that peace, such as it was, eventually brought sleep. And that night I dreamed again.

I was sitting cross-legged on an endless, level grey plain. Ashy dust covered the ground, as if some immense field had been incinerated and levelled, and all remnants crushed to powder. Not even a dead cinder remained. In front of me was Antoine's jar, buried to half its depth. I could only just see the pinky, domed apex of its contents. As I watched, the heart moved. At first, a little shrug, like a sleeper moving a shoulder; then again. And then a slow writhe, which became faster and more urgent until I could no longer see what the jar contained, but only the concept of movement. And then the jar's lid split, and the contents boiled forth into a column, a rapid vertical growth that bifurcated into a Y-shape. This column, now the deep, brown-red of a scab, became still, pregnant with significance. I gazed at it, knowing that some message was being presented to me, but unable to discern its meaning. After a little while, the tree – as I now saw it to be – began to grow again, but more slowly. Its branches and twigs twined around and back in a complex, many-layered, symmetrical pattern – an arborisation of design, not chance. *Yggdrasil!* I called out; but there was no answer, and I felt like a stupid child. The tree's growth continued, but more slowly. Buds moved; petals opened; golden flowers blossomed forth. And what flowers! Like open, inviting hands dripping with yellow honey. And on each palm, as if marked with the stigmata of love betrayed, there were words written in Marilyne's neat cursive. I squinted at them, but could not read them; the flowers were too far away, and the writing too small, and the paralysis of dreams did not permit me to walk closer. But as I craned forward, I saw that the tree also moved towards me – at least the branches stretched out, and the flowers offered their pretty yellow palms. Now I could read their messages. Some said: *I know what you are.* Or: *See, the woman who stole Antoine's heart away.* Others were more succinct: *Remember Paris* or *PseudoFifre – ha ha!* And finally, one that was repeated, more and more often, until at last I saw that every flower carried the same message: *You didn't think of that, did you?* And at this point, I became aware of something, no someone, sat at the base of the tree, engaged in some busy pursuit. Fat Yves, with his 3D-printer. As I watched, he fed material into the machine, while the machine printed the growing tree. But what material was he using? Not plastic, no; it was Antoine's heart! *Stop!* I shrieked, and, with superhuman effort, overcame my limbs' paralysis and crawled towards him over the dust. My journey took an aeon of aeons; galaxies were born and died beyond the grey horizon before I reached the tree's base, and when I did so, Yves was no longer there. The tree had died and fallen; it lay on the ground, an eternal symbol of destruction. I ran my hands across its smooth trunk, its soft contours, and found that it was Marilyne.

I don't recall waking from that dream. But I must have; the Book shows me at the kitchen table in the pre-dawn hours. I have been drawing, profusely, and painting; one of the pictures shows a recumbent woman on an ashen plain. She is dead, arms spread like branches. All around her, their yellow acid-bright against the grey dust, the buds of little roses lie scattered.

Chapter 22

The next morning, I awoke to the susurration of still objects. Furniture, walls, books, pictures: each breathed its own dead note. I reached out an arm; the sheets next to me were cold, cold.

In the kitchen, two Post-its hissed and spat at me from the fridge: like water on a hot pan. *You were up in the night, dear-heart, so I let you sleep!* The second said: *Have gone shopping – decided I want a new dress!* Shopping – today? Of course; Marilyne said she was taking this Monday as holiday. To make it a long weekend for the two of us. But shopping is more interesting than Philippe, it seems.

I kicked at Infelix; Infelix dodged, put back his ears and protested as only a cat can. In the bathroom, red-brown tissues littered the sink and floor; Yves' printed knife lay on the sink's edge. Once, I would have cleaned up after her: no more. "No more of *anything*," says my speech bubble. In the Book, I am, quite literally, a picture of despair. See how I finger the peeling plaster at the base of my thumb; see how I pull it back to reveal first, like a tide-mark, the black scurf that marked the plaster's position, and then just beyond that, the damp flesh now turned sickly white. See how I fight back tears; not for the wound, but for what it meant.

Indeed, the paper cut was now hardly visible. But unhealed pain requires unhealed flesh, so I picked up Yves' printed knife and placed its tip to my skin. *If Marilyne can, so can I.* I pushed it in, just a little, and drew it carefully along its pre-ordained route. Such a tiny, thin pain! It sounded like a violin's high tremolo. I repeated the exercise; it was easier the second time, and the tremolo more muted and lower in tone. Maybe I did it a few times, I don't know; the Book doesn't say. It wasn't a big deal – just enough for the paper cut's rebirth. Because it was *important*, that cut; it bled unhealed meaning. I found a new plaster in the bathroom cabinet – careful! – and dressed my small wound, taking care to follow the footprint of previous dressings. There was something pious about this whole process, and I left the bathroom invigorated, as if flesh's mortification gave sustenance in and of itself. Maybe this was how Marilyne felt after she paid her dues for the mirror's vanity.

Back in the bedroom, I pulled *Madame Médecin* from her hiding place and sat, propped up by pillows, while she spread her exaggerated femininity in front of me. It was time to discover who Marilyne truly loved, who she traitorously hid. Logic required me to consider three key factors: ability, motive, and opportunity. My persecutor had to enjoy some combination of these; the Bastard hid at the intersect of those three sets. That was indisputable.

First, ability. I had already established, during my investigation of Clooney, that the Bastard had to be an artist of some form, and have more than a passing familiarity with BDs. That kind of draughtsmanship simply could not flourish entirely in a vacuum, and, importantly, could not be completely hidden. Somehow, somewhere, it would be evident, like water escaping from a pipe.

Secondly, motive. What could possibly be driving the Bastard to persecute me in this way? Part of it, undoubtedly, was love or lust, and truthfully, he wouldn't be the first to chance his luck with Marilyne. Men had often trailed after her, usually until some hint of what she kept hidden raised their hackles and sent them scurrying away for Normal love. But if that was all it was, why didn't he satisfy himself with a clandestine affair? Why humiliate me in a ridiculous lampoon, and then *send* it to me, as if inviting discovery? What did he want? Try as I might, I could only think of two possibilities – revenge and money – and each took me down only a succession of dead-ends.

Finally, opportunity. There were two points to note here. First, the Bastard must have studied me closely in order to produce a likeness that was, I now realised, painfully accurate. Such observational acuity comes only from real life, not from films or photographs. Second, he must have seen Marilyne and I recently, that is, *after* she gave me the paper cut (because the plaster on my thumb had been noted), and *after* her heavy-handed reiterations of *You didn't think of that* (because that dialogue had been quoted in *Madame Médecin,* obviously as a result of Marilyne reporting it to the Bastard). Therefore, the Bastard either lived in Geneva or visited very frequently.

And then something foul and stinking raised its dark shape, the damned Inkling again, and it whispered in my ear, and reminded me of the ghost of a memory. I leafed through the issues, and found the one titled *The Thwarting of PseudoFifre*, and I turned page after PseudoFifre-sodden, ignominious page, and yes! Look there, where the impotently furious PseudoFifre returns to his laboratory – guess what? His underground lab, with the shelves and the electronic displays, and the counter behind which PseudoFifre sits when he is plotting, this all exactly corresponds to the layout of La Market Jaune! How could I have not noticed this before? Clearly, the Bastard was familiar even with my shop – my *sanctuary,* damn it!

So: the Bastard must be one whose life had brought him close to La Market Jaune on one or more occasions.

Good. The application of logic, had, I felt, delivered results. Indubitably, the Bastard lived or worked in Geneva, probably in a part of the city relatively close to La Market Jaune; had some manifest artistic ability; and was motivated by some obscure desire for revenge or some illogical expectation of wealth. I cogitated on this; I gnawed at a knuckle; I pulled at my ears. But nothing; no breakthrough. I had stencilled an outline that I could not fill in.

Perhaps if I read through all the *Madame Médecin* issues again, slowly and carefully? I picked the comics up, reflecting that the Bastard's hands had touched those very pages. I brought them to my face and smelt them: nothing but the odour of cartridge ink and paper. I spread them out on the bed. There were ten separate issues. They had arrived at irregular intervals from the very start of the Competition. And when did I start the Competition? My thoughts fought through mind-fug. Two or three entries had already arrived when the *Tribune de Genève* did a small piece on the contest; Marilyne and I had been gloating over the article when Yves gate-crashed our Café Titeuf rendezvous. That was in early spring, according to the Book. So, the first *Madame Médecin* probably made its putrid presence felt in February or March, shortly before we'd bumped into Yves.

I dug out *Issue #1* and opened it. It began with Madame Médecin pertly walking towards a hospital. Now that I looked, I saw the distinctive ring-shaped shelter in the hospital forecourt that marked it out – uniquely and unmistakably – as the main building of the Hôpitaux Universitaires de Genève. Where Marilyne worked, of course. The next panel cut to PseudoFifre sitting alone at a café (and, my God, it was the Café Titeuf! – is nothing sacred?), convulsed with evil laughter at the thought of the antibiotic-resistant bacteria he has just developed in his secret underground laboratory. When most of humanity has been wiped out, he will loot the world. But Madame Médecin happens to be sitting at the next table, and overhears his deadly plans. Cue frenetic activity by Madame Médecin's team of ace lab technicians. Cut to a close up of Madame Médecin holding vials of a new super-antibiotic just in front of her outstanding cleavage. Bravo! Madame Médecin's genius has saved the world from a megapandemic; cue applause from admiring laboratory technicians.

Issue #2: pretty much the same story, but different pictures; just replace 'antibiotic-resistant bacteria' with 'bio-engineered prion disease', and 'super-antibiotic' with 'anti-prion suppositories'. Ditto issues #3-9, where Madame Médecin deals with, respectively, a deliberately mutated form of the leprosy bacillus that tracks to the heart; COVID-X98 virus, cunningly engineered to trigger a ferocious pandemic; a form of infectious psoriasis that has been designed to peel the entire patient like a banana; radio waves which cause instant narcolepsy; orthopaedic implants modified with microprocessor chips which turn the implant recipients into PseudoFifre's slaves; a computer virus that spreads via the internet and causes LCD screens to emit blinding rays; and a self-propagating nanobot which hitchhikes on pollen grains to enter people's airways whence it causes the afflicted to vomit up their own lungs. In each case, a monodimensional, humourless plot with a monodimensional, humourless solution.

In fact, that was another key criterion for the Bastard. He'd have had to be pretty challenged on the imagination front. Likely, quite dull, as a person. The kind of person, probably, that you just wouldn't notice. Like Yves.

Yves. Now that I thought about it, the Bastard could actually be somewhat similar to Yves. Maybe it would be helpful if I looked for suspects with some resemblance to a boring lab technician.

Yves . . .

Wait. The *Madame Médecin* entries had only begun to appear after Yves moved to Geneva. *Just* afterwards. What had he said to us in Café Titeuf? He'd said he'd moved to Geneva three months earlier – which was *exactly* when the first *Madame Médecin* issue landed on my desk!

He lived in Les Pâquis, just around the corner from La Market Jaune. He would pass my shop every single weekday on his way to work. Just by sitting in a tram, he'd have a direct view into the shop to where I sat at my desk behind the counter.

Yves! No!!

Steady, Philippe. Apply logic: Was he an artist? Could he draw? Well, what had Marilyne once said about his abilities? That was it: *A prosthesis designed and formed by Yves is as much a sculpture as any Henry Moore, and his works will one day be seen in the best galleries. I am convinced of it, Philippe.* The best galleries!

Memories gestated, burst forth and mewled painfully. In the Chat Noir, that night – Yves had commented on the plaster on my thumb. He'd *seen* the injury that later found its way onto the hand of my ridiculous cartoon alter-ego.

And there was something else, nagging away at me. I racked my brain again, and fragments of conversation resurfaced like old splinters pushing their way back up through flesh. His smug assertion: *Everybody loves Marilyne . . .* His little smile when he claimed that Clooney had no romantic feelings for Marilyne: *He's just not interested in women.* Yes; *Clooney's* not interested in women! But what about *you*, Yves? And this: *Georges is terrible at drawing.* Again: What about *you*, Yves? And what else did he say to me that night, when I was mocking his unsuccessful love-life? *You'd be surprised.* I felt my face cut off its blood supply and then drag it all back and pump it into my cheeks; humiliation and rage, the eternal blood-brothers.

Yves! Dear God, no, Marilyne, I thought. If you must be unfaithful, be so with a surgeon, a banker, one of the Swiss mafia, some *homme serieux,* anyone, even Georges Clooney, but please God, not Yves! That would be the final indignity, the deepest ignominy; to be judged less interesting, less attractive, less of a man than *Yves!*

But wait; again – employ logic, Philippe. You *must* remain logical. True, Yves had both opportunity and ability, it seemed; but what about *motive?* Revenge? Surely not; I'd never done anything to Yves. I'd hardly known he was there. Money, then? Again, unlikely; it's not as though I'd pay him to stop drawing *Madame Médecin.* Or to stop having an affair with my wife. So there was no money motive either. Unless . . . Ah. Of course.

At last. I understood everything. The shares. My shares.

It was obvious what they were trying to do, so obvious. I saw now that they had been working towards this for months; it explained all. They wished to provoke me somehow, to make me turn on one or both of them, to lose control; and then Marilyne would divorce me, and even if she only got half of my Favrier Pharma shares, she would be a very wealthy woman. Certainly, she would never need to work again. Nor Yves. And, in retrospect, this also explained Yves' odd, flat response to the news of my shareholding in Favrier Pharma, when I told him in the Chat Noir the other night; it *hadn't* really been news to him. He already knew, but was ineptly trying to pretend he didn't, to avoid raising my suspicions.

That was it. That was it. My fingers were trembling, and my breathing too fast; but I forced myself to remain calm. It was still possible, I told myself, that I had misunderstood something, that I was reading more into *Madame Médecin* than was there – literally. But deep down, I knew that my life had been irrevocably laid bare, exposed as a cruel comedy played out for God knows how many people. All the world's a stage, and all of us merely players; but I, I was even less than that – merely a cartoon cipher, a weasel-faced, balding goblin in a bad BD, openly mocked by my wife and her fat lover. I felt unmanned, emasculated by fury and despair and humiliation.

Yet I had to know more; I needed the entirety of my folly to be laid before me. So I re-read the issues, and now that I read them again, I saw that they just screamed *Yves wrote this* at me. How could I have missed it? The pedantic, unimaginative storyline; the absence of wit, of vivacity, of any kind of spark of inventiveness or originality; the restriction of settings to the biomedical world, which was the only world that Yves knew. It was all just so Yves. It was if he were putting plastic words into his 3D-printer, running the programme, and getting plastic stories back out, one after the other.

And the pictures; I didn't know that Yves could draw, but the fetishistic obsession with female curves displayed in *Madame Médecin* was exactly what I would have expected from his closed, closeted personality. And that triggered a new train of thought, and I saw his pale, damp hands all over Marilyne – *my* Marilyne – his podgy fingers, with the nails childishly bitten to the quick, touching her perfect skin, and it was all I could do to not rush out and go to Yves' workplace there and then, to rip off his balls and hold the bloody white eggs in front of his popping, bullfrog eyes.

But no, I thought. I had to be careful about this. I had the advantage now. Those two thought that I was weak and stupid – me, a Favrier! They thought they could cuckold me, and mock me in pictures, and rub my face in their betrayal by sending my goblin-featured caricature to my own BD Competition, in my own shop. They thought my unfaithful wife could laugh in my face and taunt me with the BD, as near as damn *tell* me what's going on. I would bear all of this, they thought, and there would be no consequences for them! They were wrong.

They are wrong, affirmed the clear whispers from around me; *and now you will show them.*

I put the collected adventures of *Madame Médecin* back under the bed, pushing aside the dusty pile of Competition entries – yes, still unread! – and got dressed. I looked again at the peeling plaster on my hand; its talismanic importance was unarguable. I retrieved Yves' knife from the bathroom and opened the cut again; deeper and longer. Oh, the colour of tremolos! Pain can paint the very air with its bloody violin. Then I sat, motionless, deep in thought, focused on one thing and one thing alone, turning the printed knife over and over in my hands.

In the Book, Marilyne comes home at lunch, breathless and happy. She notices nothing. "Wait there, *cheri*," she says, and runs into the bedroom, dodging Infelix's pleas for attention. "What do you think?" she says, moments later. I look at her; PseudoFifre looks at her. She is wearing a long cotton dress, a flowery print; it clings to her from shoulders to hips and then floats about, moulding first to one thigh and then to the other as she moves and twirls. Her hair is piled up in a bun; her long neck follows curves and tangents seen only in God's book of geometry. "What do you think?" She is looking at me; her smile suddenly unsure, her movements less natural.

"Beautiful," I say. "You are beautiful." And it is true.

"You like? Good. I'll wear it when we go to dinner with Yves . . ." My fists clench; I look up from under lowered brows. ". . . Anyway, look here . . ." She takes me through her other acquisitions, the ones she has not paid for. Childish things: a plastic torch with a Superman logo, a packet of fruit pastilles, a set of Top Trumps footballer cards. The things that a six-year-old boy might have liked. The things that Antoine might have liked, had he lived for the last five years, eleven months and three weeks. She spreads them out on the lounge table, crooning over them in a low voice. Her cheek is wet, and I sit still while PseudoFifre admires her acting prowess. Then she shakes her head, as if to shake off memories, and stands.

"Philippe – whatever would I do without you?" She walks over to me, bends, and kisses the top of my head. PseudoFifre plays with Yves' knife, turning it this way and that, this way and that. "Anyway, it's lunchtime, and I've bought a fresh baguette. Come on." PseudoFifre follows her into the kitchen.

"Let's finish off that soup, Philippe, okay?" As usual, she did not wait for a response; my acquiescence was, it seemed, a given. She pulled a saucepan from the fridge and put it on the hob. She put a breadboard on the kitchen table and slid the baguette half out of its bag. Then she looked around questioningly.

"Umm – ah! Philippe? The knife, please?" I hesitated and then passed her Yves' printed blade. She sliced the baguette crosswise, littering the breadboard with fragments of crust.

"I never worked that out," I said.

"What, dear-heart?"

"The knife. Why Yves gave you the knife. Seems a bit odd."

She looked at me askance. "Well? Did you expect *Yves* to give *me* something *Normal*?" Her laughter was like a pretty cascade. "Remember how proud he was. 'It's hard to print a cutting edge' – how many times did he tell us that?"

"Why did he not give it somebody else?"

"To whom? Who would receive a gift like that and not react Normally?"

"What else did he give you?"

"In Paris? Endless entertainment, dear-heart." She poked at my stomach with the knife's handle, and then stuck it into the breadboard, hilt a-tremble. "And now that he's in Switzerland, he will continue to do so. Seriously, when you're in a place like Geneva – because I agree with you, Philippe, it can be a little stuffy – it is *so* relaxing to talk to someone from the old days. Before, you know." She stepped towards me, threw her arms around me and hugged me tight. Her fine hair caught at my cheek and released it; the scent of her flesh enveloped me; her hand stroked the back of my neck and near stopped the heart of me; the press of her breasts sent shivers of desire all through me. I was paralysed. Then she stepped back, leaving her hands on my shoulders, and looked at me from her violet world. The smile had gone. "And – *seriously,* seriously – I am *so* glad you will be coming to dinner with Yves. It wouldn't be the same without you, darling, it really wouldn't. And I know you persuaded Yves not to invite Georges, this time" – her finger wagged at me; *Naughty,* it said – "and he's fine about that, he gets it, he really does. Only we do hope you'll come round to seeing Georges' finer points one day. Georges likes to tease, that's all – it's just his way."

"And Georges always gets his way. As does Yves, it seems."

Marilyne was stirring the soup, head bent over wisps of steam. I couldn't see her face. "Well, when two people want to go the *same* way, there's no argument, is there?" She poured out the soup, and looked up with the bright, happy smile that first made me love her. "Here you are, dear-heart! *Bon appetit!*"

The Book shows the rest of that day spent in inconclusive verbal feinting and sparring. I throw out subtle suggestions regarding Yves, and Marilyne blithely shrugs them off as if she no longer cares whether I know or not. But one thing gradually becomes clear to me: this dinner with Yves will be, must be, the last dinner, the dinner when I confront them and unmask Judas. But how? PseudoFifre sinks into contemplation; Marilyne laughs.

"You're doing that thing with your ears again! What are you thinking about now, Philippe?"

"Nothing, *cherie,*" I say, and wonder how she cannot see the murder in PseudoFifre's smile.

"Are you sure you're alright, Philippe?"

"Never better, dearest."

In the dream, PseudoFifre and I sit on a high peak. *Look,* he says, extending his skinny arm; his gesture encompasses the panorama of lands spread before us. So I look. And now I see that the toytown fields and farms in fact are the roofs of the Old City. The tiled slope on which I squat is treacherous; its vertiginous gradient sways in all directions, and I am overcome with nausea. PseudoFifre grabs me by the hair and twists my head, so that I must look back, over my shoulder, up the roof's slope behind me. I see the bathroom window; Marilyne is peering out of it. She sees me and smiles: *Bon appetit!* Then she picks up Antoine's jar from the windowsill and rolls it down the roof towards me. *No!* I shout. *No, Marilyne!* But she has gone, and the jar is rolling past me, gathering speed exponentially as it clatters down the slope. I scramble after it, losing balance, falling into gravity's vortex. My hands grasp at grimy tiles; my fingers scrape the bricks of chimney stacks; my nails catch on the edges of lead flashing; my skin tears on sharp irregularities. The jar rolls off the roof's edge, and I follow it: down, down, down. Faster and faster. What dreadful momentum! I look to one side and see PseudoFifre, falling with me. He is holding a mirror. His reflection pleases him: *Never better*, he says. *Never better.* But now he is looking at me, and I have the mirror and I am staring at it, at him, at me. *No!* I scream. Down, down, down. And then: impact.

Chapter 23

The next day dawned strangely. In the Book, the artist's palette has subtly shifted; less green-blue, more orange-yellow. The colours have the brightness of fever; a close-up shows my sclera tinted with their livid hues, my eyes wide with surprise – or with recognition?

The latter, surely. I felt, that day, that my once hollow shell was now inhabited by something strong and familiar, by some prodigal thing that had left me years ago and had now returned. I felt like a pithed frog made whole again, wonderingly stretching undead limbs. My perceptions were heightened; when I drew the curtains, I felt the night sublimate like indigo smoke, caressing my skin with velvet touch as it fled the summer sun's roar. When Infelix's hungry approach disturbed the air, the whorls and eddies of his wake triggered rainbow iridescence, like oil on water. And somewhere, something whispered: *Ah, Philippe . . .*

Marilyne had left without waking me. This was normal, of course; and yet, for some reason, on this day, that knowledge appalled me. I fingered the plaster on my thumb; it was loose again, its edges peeling and black. I removed it, re-opened the cut with Yves' knife, and put a fresh plaster in place.

In the kitchen, burning yellow squares shrilled at me from the refrigerator door. I took them off, screwed them up and thrust them into my pocket. I made a coffee. Infelix attempted to trip me as I walked with it to the breakfast table; I responded appropriately. In the Book, one panel's foreground is taken up by the cat's outraged face: "*MIYOWL!*" he screeches, in bold capitals. Behind and to the right I am visible, equally outraged, planting my foot on his rear; my leg trails blurgits. Coffee slops over the cup's rim as I kick out. My speech bubble reads, "*Take that, you little *&?!*!*" Italicised. Comic Pro.

Infelix fled; I stalked him around the flat, pulling faces. When I finally caught him, I took him by the scruff of the neck and pushed him through the bathroom window. Spreadeagled on the tiled slope, he flattened his ears at me before turning tail. I believe he knew, somehow, that I just didn't care anymore.

On the way to La Market Jaune that Tuesday morning, I breathed against the tram window and drew a love-heart in the condensation. Then I rubbed away the moisture inside the outline to make a heart-shaped window in the misted glass. Through this, I watched Geneva roll past: cafés and grocers, chocolatiers and jewellers. A city whose culture depends on money and its disbursement; a city where status is determined by snobbery. The greys and whites of its buildings reached my ears as a bass-rich rumble, like a threatening sea; the calls of its pedestrians assaulted my senses like the caught spray of a Jackson Pollock. And the yellow writing on the windows of La Market Jaune glowed like molten iron and sung to me with voices of liquid silk; they were so beautiful, like one of Arvo Pärt's choral pieces, that I forgot to get off the tram. Or maybe it was a conscious decision, I don't know – the Book isn't clear. But once I realised I'd missed my stop, it's certain that I stayed on the tram deliberately, all the way to the Jardin Botanique, at the north end of Geneva, where the tram tracks turn back on themselves and head back into Geneva centre. There I alighted; perhaps I hoped for the peace and tranquillity that the Jardin once was able to give me. Or perhaps I simply was not ready to retrace my steps; perhaps I needed to go on. But to what? Something awaited me, I was sure, even if it was only Being or Becoming. 'Only', I say! What else is there, but to Be or Become? I carried on, then, walking by the lake's shore. I observed swans that observed me, their dripping bills hung with green lake-weed. I ducked down into the underpass, beneath the main road, and up again into the Jardin Botanique.

Giant cedars loomed. Looking up at their high sway, I became dizzy, and had to stop momentarily. I held a hand to my down-turned head while my vision buzzed. When I raised my eyes again, an old glasshouse stood in front of me: a great pile of gleaming panels and white frames, its shape and dimensions conceived, surely, in some Victorian's opiated fantasy. It drew me in, that delicate monster, with warm green whispers; it drew me in. And why not? The wind from the lake was cold.

Within the glasshouse, it became clear that what from the outside had appeared clean and precise and carefully organised – a hospital for plants – was a deceit, a scab over putrefaction. Rivulets of moisture ran, like sweat, down panels blushing with the black-green of moulds and algae; steam rose in miasmal wisps and clung to skin and lungs; plants of some disease-ridden jungle vaulted and twined and budded and bloomed. Everywhere the vegetal stink of slow growth and rapid decay; everywhere the susurration of green in all its infinite variety, punctuated by chimes of fruit and flowers: here a pus-hued blossom, waving styles and stigmas in obscene excitement; over there, berries like scarlet blood-clots, inviting a dangerous consumption. A hideous, contrived wonderland where everything was emetic and all said, *Eat me . . .*

I walked on, but it was like walking amongst enemies, enemies . . . A woman with a pushchair, first obstructing me with pointed malice and then, as if to mock, withdrawing to one side of the walkway and snapping, "Excusez-*moi*," while her child looked on like one of Breughel's small ape-creatures. Older children staring with unconcealed hostility and then, once I'd passed, turning to murmur secrets and point at my back. An old man with a stick pausing in his decrepit ambulation, and gurning like a retard. Still, I walked on, farther and farther into the warm innards of the glasshouse, until I saw a cruelly familiar figure by a raised bed, gesticulating at a shrub with assumed authority; as if to *Be* him were to *Become* an expert on any subject under the sun. Clooney! Why here? Was he not at the hospital? With Marilyne? But who was that with him, that he now spoke to; that woman with blonde hair, her face obscured by Clooney's shoulders? I strode forward, teeth a-grinding, fists clenched. Perhaps it is *both* Yves and Clooney! How many, Marilyne? How many?

He was still speaking when I reached them and grabbed his arm. He half-turned, head back, frowning at this assault on his person.

"Georges," I said. "How strange to see you here—" But I was no longer looking at him; I was looking at his female companion. Who was not Marilyne.

In fact, it was hard to understand how I thought she might have been Marilyne; she was taller, bigger-boned, her hair a darker shade of blonde and cut in a different way.

"Philippe—" he said. I let go of his arm and he took half a pace back. His companion nodded *Bonjour* to me; her eyes widened as if to intimidate me, but I would not be gainsaid.

"Where is Marilyne?" I asked.

"Marilyne? But Philippe – how would I know?" He sneered at me – the insolence! "Have you lost her among the bushes? That was careless." A smirk threatened to smear itself across his pretty face, but I took a step forward, and he became more serious.

"She did not come to the Jardin with *me*," I said. "And anyway, one man's loss is another's gain. Isn't that the expression?"

He hesitated, as though unsure how to answer; his dark, sharp eyes trying to read my face, to gauge the best lie. In the end, he went for a faux-friendly approach. "Truly, Philippe, if she is not at the hospital, then I don't know where she is. But of course, you would have phoned her secretary, no?" He paused, looking from one of my eyes to the other. I said nothing. "In any case, Marilyne has many demands on her time, and I am the least important of those; she does not share her schedule with such as I! You see, I simply play the, ah, *sous-fifre* to Marilyne's virtuoso performances."

And there it was. The clever-clever comment that he just could not resist, the smirk. *Sous-fifre*, how pseudo-funny, ha ha.

"And this botanically-themed outing is for what? To collect yellow roses, so that you have something to hurl at the virtuoso's feet?"

He frowned, and pulled a face as if he did not know what I was talking about, the liar, and looked to his companion. "Yellow roses? Ah! No – yellow *oleander,* Philippe. That is why I am pestering Chantal." Clooney gestured elegantly to his companion. "Chantal – may I introduce you to Philippe Favrier? Philippe is Marilyne's husband . . ."

"*Enchantée*," said Chantal, extending a hand. Here it comes, I thought. I could just see Clooney gearing up to say it.

". . . Philippe runs a, ah, an enterprise dedicated to the *bandes dessinées* . . . La Market Jaune . . . perhaps you have seen it?"

There it was. It was couched in dishonest politeness, of course, but there it was. This is Philippe Favrier, seller of comics; is it not amusing? This adult, this grown man – he is a comic seller. I looked at Clooney; I imagined him with his chest opened up and his naked heart gulping in the sudden cold.

Clooney continued. "And Chantal is Director of Research here at the Jardin Botanique. Thanks to her, Marilyne and I can source as much fresh yellow oleander as we need, whenever we need it."

"We'd have to prune it anyway," said Chantal. She smiled at me, as though to say, *Joke's on you*, while reaching over to the large shrub in the raised bed behind Clooney. She shook one of the lower branches, and the plant shuddered as if waking from a dream. Now that I looked more closely, I could see it was more of a small tree than a big shrub; perhaps three metres tall, it loomed over Clooney as though to envelop him, to crucify him on its smooth wood. Its long, thin leaves of venomous green clawed at the air, and its tubular flowers of acid yellow tucked their petals into each other in spirals that somehow reminded me of Escher's endless staircases. Its abundant growth blocked the light from the glasshouse windows behind it; the plant had caught us, all three, in its green shadow. And that scent!

What was it? Sugared apricots? Its sweetness annulled thought.

"You see, Philippe," Clooney spoke to me, but I saw that he glanced at Chantal with some soundless meaning, "yellow oleander – *Thevetia peruviana*" – he pointed to the plastic name tag around the tree's base – "contains chemicals with very interesting properties. Marilyne and I believe they could be turned into important drugs for heart conditions. They are structurally complex, and we don't have the budget to synthesize them *de novo*, but very fortunately, Chantal has this most excellent specimen, and with just a few leaves from time to time – thank you, Chantal – our technician can extract enough glycoside for our experiments." Clooney bent down and picked up a cool bag from the floor; he unzipped the insulated lid and showed me the livid green and yellow harvest. "But I must get this back to the lab now and freeze the leaves *toute suite*. Thank you again, Chantal, and I do regret we can't provide any thanks more concrete than an acknowledgement on the publication . . . you know as well as I how poorly funded we are in medical research."

"You should try botany," said Chantal. Clooney laughed, and so did she, and then they did the full treble cheek-kiss while completely ignoring me. They departed in opposite directions; from her I received a cool "*Au revoir*," and from him a sardonic glance and a typical Clooney-esque *double entendre*: "If I see Marilyne at the Hôpital, I will tell her you are looking for her. Otherwise, do pass on my very best regards to your beautiful virtuoso, and please tell her we will have the ah, only *slightly* adulterated pleasure of purified oleander extract by Wednesday."

But what's less funny, Georges, is that somebody will die for this slight adultery.

*

I left the stagnant air of the glasshouse soon after Clooney; soon enough to see him depart the Jardin Botanique on his own, walking quickly. I dawdled, wanting to get back to Geneva proper, but reluctant to negotiate trams and crowds. In the end, I opted for the long walk back alongside the lake. But it was hard on the feet, and as I approached Navigation, the lakeside stop where paddleboats full of tourists set off for Nyon or Montreux or returned therefrom, I had to rest. I sat on the waist-high, waist-thick stone wall that borders that part of the lake; my feet dangled over the jumbled boulders that served as a breakwater, two metres below. Across the water and to my right, the Jet d'Eau's silver plume lazily signalled the changeable alpine winds. Behind that, the city's skyline raised its squat angles to Mont Salève: great square buildings with rows of anonymous windows, their brows crowned with reminders of the city's business – Bank of This, Bank of That, Bank of The Other. From the moorings near the Jet, the wind brought me the remote clatter and slap of yachting impedimenta: masts and rigging and cables, all being tugged this way and that, all harassed by the same cool air that made my skin rise in goosebumps and my nose run. I dug in my pocket for a tissue, but only found a small, hard ball of crumpled paper. Yellow paper. Marilyne's Post-its that I'd taken from the fridge that morning and screwed up without reading. I flattened them out on my thigh.

Make SURE you feed Infelix this evening, said one. *Do NOT put him on the roof.* The other said: *Dinner with Yves soon!* and specified a day and date. Yes, Marilyne, another X@@??! dinner with Yves. I crushed the little yellow messages again, rolling them into rough spheres, and dropped them onto the rocks below my feet, where they bounced and rolled into the shallows.

I couldn't tell for sure if there was a real connection, but as the canary-yellow paper touched the water, the lake's surface – almost imperceptibly, yet unmistakably – heaved towards me and back: a long, slow swell in which unnumbered millions of tons of water moved by millimetres, as though to vomit up the bilious taste of Marilyne's loveless messages. And Lac Léman's discomfort transmitted itself to me; I felt uneasy here, as though some monstrous fish observed me from the lake's bed, plotting a fate for me beyond human comprehension. Uneasy? Worse – a sudden terror clutched me and possessed me, and I ran, ran along the lakeside path, past all the hotels on the Quai du Mont-Blanc, past the Pont du Mont-Blanc and onto the Pont des Bergues. Here, I knew, I could cross onto the southern shore and get back to the Old City, unless my enemies stopped me. "Aside!" I bellowed, as I weaved through knots of pedestrians. "Stand aside! Make way!" But this surfeit of energy was almost too much for me, and by the time I reached the apartment I was weeping uncontrollably, my breath coming in gasps. The door slammed behind me; its echo died. And there, there, there behind the dead echo, where they had always waited in all their bright colours, were the whispers of my dreams. *Oh, Philippe . . .*

You can't bottle things up so long and not expect a kickback. The dreams were sad, and angry, and frightened; some were fractured, some in pain. It was like listening to a crowd of banshee mothers howling for the souls of their lost children. *Oh, Philippe . . .* It was like it was in Paris, after Antoine, but much, much worse. It was like returning to your family after a long journey, and finding them changed, finding that where love once had been was now only malice and spite. Such dreams! They tore at me. The one that was Marilyne, surely, would have helped me; but that one wasn't there. Yet I could hear it, louder than the others.

Riiiiing . . .

"Philippe?"

"This is Philippe."

"What on earth is going on?" Her voice was like a serrated blade, a buzz of pain. It cut me. "I've had Georges on the phone – he says he saw you in the Jardin Botanique."

"Clooney? He passes on his best regards, and looks forward to the pleasure of adultery."

"Never mind that. He says that you were looking for *me*. In the *Jardin*. Is that correct?"

"I lost you."

Her long, deep sigh escaped the phone. It echoed around the room. "Listen, Philippe. I am tired. I too am tired. Okay? But we, *you,* must be strong. You must. And I am going to book you for some bloods, Philippe, because I think your treatment is losing efficacy, and we may need to increase the dose. Just until we can finish, you know, all this, and go to be on our own. Okay?"

"Finish all this."

"Be strong, Philippe. Be strong. And for God's sake, check that you have taken your medication. Okay? Love you. See you later, darling."

"Yes."

In the bathroom, I held Antoine. When I put my ear to the jar, I thought I could hear the weak cries of a sick baby. A mewling that bewailed the cruelty of genetics. One random deletion in a critical cardiac gene, and *paf!* Your life will comprise seven days of gasping pain; no more, no less. Stitch up as many hearts you like, Marilyne, we lost the only one that mattered.

The bathroom walls lower and loom. The air catches in my throat, and something flutters in my chest. I cannot breathe. Cradling Antoine in the crook of one arm, I struggle with the window's catch. The fresh air brings Infelix, wet and hungry. He almost pushes the mirror from the sill, but I do not care. I gulp at Switzerland's cold winds like a lungfish emerging from a burning lake into a frozen desert.

Chapter 24

We are close to the end now. I am beginning to understand the *who* and the *how*. Open the Book, then, and let us read of how that day ended, and of who the next day brought.

I slept deeply that night, as though some decision I'd made in some subconscious part of me had relaxed me – or directed my body to conserve energy for challenges to come. The Book records no dreams, but dream I must have, for I was drawing again: my most recent picture, the recumbent woman seen from behind, has been modified. A mirror has now been drawn in front of her, so that the observer can see her face, and her face is Marilyne's. Truly, my creative faculty had returned. Yet it seemed changed, somehow: joyless and resentful, like a mortally ill person dragged from anaesthesia back into the dull pain of awareness.

Marilyne, of course, was not there when I awoke; by the time I'd breakfasted she'd probably split the sternum of her second patient of the day. She'd left no Post-its; only a heart-shaped, foil-wrapped chocolate, stolen from God knows where, placed centrally on the table. The wrapper was the same bright yellow as her Post-its; on its underside, a small label asserted *Rainforest Friendly* beneath a stylised tree motif.

We tug at our ears again, and PseudoFifre grumbles to himself. Yes, we tugged at our ears, and I don't know whether there was any causal relationship, but it seemed appropriate that it was then that I had the idea. It was almost as though it had been there, bubbling away in a lower circle of our mind, ever since I'd bumped into Clooney in the Jardin Botanique. Perhaps it had been gestating even before then; maybe it was conceived when I'd glanced at Marilyne's paper on the isolation and use of novel *Thevetia peruviana* cardiotoxins.

Indeed: *Thevetia peruviana*, also known as yellow oleander. A native of South America, and present in excellent form, with its custard-coloured, trumpet-shaped blossoms, and long, thin, pale green leaves, in the South American collection of the Jardin Botanique in Geneva. Yellow oleander: commonly called the suicide tree.

Yes. The suicide tree, the toxins of which were the subject of the publication that Marilyne and Clooney were writing; the publication with which Marilyne had given me the paper cut for which she had never apologised. The situation was taking on a pleasing symmetry. It was, I felt, like working on a jigsaw puzzle. You just know when the pieces really fit.

From then on, I refined my plans without pause, energised by a black passion that recognised no barrier, that simply took what it needed for its inescapable purpose. I went to La Market Jaune each day, but kept the shop shut – this to forestall Laurence's early-morning visitations and thereby enable me to work without distraction. Even so, the BDs called to me continually: *Philippe,* they said. *Philippe.* Sometimes I would answer, but mostly I sat behind the counter, watching their vivid pigments shift and breathe in a slow, toxic pulsation, and listening to their pages' susurration. *Are we not beautiful?* they said. *We know what you are,* they said. At lunch I would always leave them; sometimes to march furiously down to the lake, sometimes to pace up to Carouge and back, not returning until mid-afternoon. In the Book, I see that the Geneva of this period has the feel of graphic art noir: muted colours, exaggerated shadows, threatening perspectives. I see too that I am muttering to myself during my perambulations: my ideas bubble naturally into speech, and pedestrians step aside respectfully so as to impede neither my physical nor my mental progress.

Finally, one muggy, pollen-filled day, I found that PseudoFifre was ready, his plans complete. I didn't enter the shop at all; instead, I went to the hardware section of a large supermarket in Geneva centre. I knew exactly what I needed, and I didn't need much: a bottle of 70 percent alcohol, a packet of disposable latex gloves and a pair of Swiss-made secateurs.

That was it. That was all we needed to give the Book the ending it deserved.

Bizarre coincidence: as I came out, holding a bag containing my purchases, I saw Clooney and Yves walking down the Rue du Rhône, talking animatedly. Yes, that figured; Clooney would have been in on it as well. He'd have split his sides at the thought of the sad, little comic-seller being – at one and the same time – both immortally mocked in cartoons and also cuckolded by the cartoons' dull artist. He'd have been laughing about it with half the hospital. Deathlessly funny!

Those stupid, stupid people. How could they have forgotten the dangers of the Ninth Art? I'd told them, over and over again – dull Yves and patronising Clooney and Marilyne's *grande école* chums back in Paris, I'd told them all – *cartoons can kill!* Consider their history, I'd said; consider their impact, from Daumier's *Gargantua* to Denmark's Jyllands-Posten images, two hundred and fifty years later. Throughout this period, I'd said, the illustrated caricature has been a delicate, and often indelicate, weapon of extraordinary power. I'd used those very words. To be ridiculed in the printed word is one thing, I'd said, but to be the subject of a fully illustrated humiliation provides an exquisite ignominy all of its own. To be caricatured in sequential art is not like a spoken insult, which fades soon after its own echo; it is, for the victim, momentously permanent. It is forever; it is *deathless.* Fools, to play with fire so!

So Clooney's participation in the deceit demanded a response, but he'd had only a bit part; I'd deal with him at a later point. Once my shares vested. I'd buy up the Hôpitaux, no, the *entire* Swiss medical system; in fact, I'd bribe every cardiology department in the Western world, just to make sure he'd never work in medicine again. Plenty of time for Clooney; it was the betrayal by Yves and Marilyne that was the bitterest pill to swallow. That had to be my immediate concern. *Do things in order, or chaos ensues.* Right again, Dad.

Those days brought me a kind of understanding, a kind of superficial peace. I now knew what I was. I had to accept my place in the world, and my place was not to rub shoulders with Swiss shoppers – how their eyes stare! – nor to pace dark cobbles beneath the threatening perpendicularities of the Old City. No, my place was in La Market Jaune: with my art, with my books, and, God help me, even with Laurence, my brother in the fraternity of the Ninth Art and in much else besides. *I know what you are, my friend.*

Yes, Laurence knew what I was, and I knew what I was; yet, as if to accommodate some masochistic impulse, I would again and again stare at my own profile in the mirrored mirrors. Each reiterated confirmation multiplied my pain. It was as Clooney had said. It was as Marilyne had said. It was as I myself had already seen. I was PseudoFifre. The cipher, the underling, the laughing-stock.

At this point, the Book shows PseudoFifre tearing at an ear with one hand, while the other clutches at the empty, silent air. I pace the apartment in a surfeit of agony. And now that I look closely at the Book, I see that there is no longer any difference between the depictions of myself in my own life story and the drawings of PseudoFifre in *Madame Médecin*. There is no more pretence.

It is over, whisper my BDs. *It is over, sous-fifre.*

Thenceforth, I proceeded with a new certainty. My thoughts were laser-sharp, my decision as unambiguous as birth and death: *it is time to begin*. So I collected all the items that I needed. From the spice rack, the empty biopsy sample tube that I'd labelled *Heart M*. From the cellar, an old food processor (an unwanted wedding present that we'd intended to give away, but never had). Then, the 70 percent alcohol in its plastic bottle with a child-resistant top. The brand-new, ultra-sharp secateurs. The disposable latex gloves. A cool bag and cool blocks. Coffee filter papers. Here we go, I thought. PseudoFifre's final plan is coming together.

And in the Book, our speech bubble says: "Yes. It is over, and therefore it is time to begin."

Chapter 25

Memory is a powerful thing. But of all memories, mine is perhaps the most formidable. See how the Book has captured me in a sequence of stills, adorned with speech bubbles and drawn in dramatically exaggerated perspective! See how it pins, like butterflies to a board, the evanescent hues of experience! Here, for example: Marilyne lies next to Yves, and looks at me with disgust and anger in those impossibly violet eyes. "You stupid man . . ." she says, "you stupid, stupid man . . ."

But I don't want to think about that. And I really don't want to think about Yves any more. Not now. Not ever.

Let us return then to the relevant part of the Book; let us do things properly, in the correct order. Let us read of how PseudoFifre executed his plan.

Over the next two weeks I made several visits to the Jardin Botanique, secateurs snagging at my pocket, and surreptitiously harvested foliage from the yellow oleander tree. I took only small amounts; first from one part of the plant, and then from another. *How powerful is yellow! How bright our leaves, how delicate our poisons! Oh Philippe – can you not see?* On my final visit, I went so far as to snap off a small branch, laden with blossom, and bent and twisted it into my rucksack. I stopped after that, suspecting that I was pushing my luck. After all, Chantal was also cutting back the oleander's growth, and at some point she would notice the additional denudation.

I always took the plant material back to the micro-kitchen in La Market Jaune, never to the apartment. There, my preparation method was invariant. I would macerate fresh oleander foliage in the food processor, add 70 percent alcohol and leave the chopped-up plant matter steeping overnight. The next day, I would separate the alcoholic solution from the plant mash by passing it through coffee filter paper and into a mug. I would then gently warm the clear filtrate to evaporate some of the alcohol, thereby producing a more concentrated toxin. This I stored in the sample tube and refrigerated. After two weeks I had about thirty millilitres of chilled, mineral-yellow liquid: *Heart M*. Cold and sulphurous, it was full of bilious intent; when agitated it didn't form itself into discrete, sociable drops like water, but spread itself over the interior surface of the tube, as though seeking to escape, to attack. It iced my spine just looking at it. Always dangerous to call someone stupid, I told myself; very dangerous.

Perhaps Marilyne and Yves had forgotten that alcoholic extraction of plant alkaloids was the basis of Favrier Pharma's first drugs. Perhaps they never knew.

Throughout, I pretended that things were normal at La Market Jaune; at least, I reverted to normal opening times. I dropped the ball a bit in that I never got around to judging the Competition entries, and had to put a notice in the window regretting the postponement of the Competition until further notice. But frankly, I no longer cared. I even accepted Laurence's visits and his booming disapproval of the continuing poor standards of my merchandise. Because Laurence and I, we were linked, whether I liked it or not. We knew what we were. Life sorts you and places you, and, squeal and protest all you like, you'll sit in the place life has set for you. So I accepted Laurence, as the leper accepts the bell.

"*Bonjour!*"

"*Bonjour*, Laurence."

Silence; even the BDs held their peace.

"Why do you follow me, my friend?"

"I'm not following you, Laurence."

"Perpetrator of falsehoods!" Laurence's outrage was all-consuming; the shop's foundations shuddered before his rage. He turned aside to lecture an audience of BDs, which nudged each other, all agog.

"My friends! I first became aware of him, this *marchand de guano,* at the Hôpitaux! Since then, he has dogged me unceasingly! Yet I made no complaint. Can a man kill a flea by chiding? It is kismet, I tell you, my friends, kismet! I seek only to help, to educate, to enlighten! There is crysipclas, yes, but there is also ankylosing spondylitis, macular degeneration, and idiosyncratic discharges of countless forms! Have I not advised you of this? The eternal truths arrayed in your pages speak to my veracity!"

The BDs sat in their racks with the kind of rapt attention you see in children during their first ever theatre visit. Their bright pulsing had slowed and was focused on Laurence; his face was bathed in the glow of their colours – now jaundiced, now incarnadined, now tinged with the fever of verdigris.

"I took him in hand, this *marchand de tapis d'enfer*! I exposed him to concepts of the highest order! And yet . . . *Putain!*"

He shifted clumsily from foot to foot, and then hurriedly exited the shop. *Tinkle-tink.* Through the shop window, I saw him fumbling at his trousers.

"The glaciers melt!" he howled. "The Rhône is in spate!" A weak stream of urine sputtered discontinuously against the glass at the base of my shop window. Spurt, splash, drop and dribble. I dimly heard the rebuke of pedestrians.

"It's the pills, you idiot," I said. "Stop taking the pills. They make no difference, anyway." But Laurence couldn't hear me.

On the way home one evening, instead of walking straight to my usual tram stop, I detoured past Doré et Fils, and looked through the window. The Edgar Jacobs had gone; there was just a blank space, an absence, a bitter, painful void where it once had been. If I had needed any further confirmation that the whole world was against me and always had been, that provided it. Damn everybody and everything! I turned away, as alone as I'd been as a child; as alone as I'd always been. And guess what? There was Miss Slavic Cheekbones again, walking away, heading in the direction I'd just come from. She looked back like a thief expecting pursuit, saw me shaking my raised fist, and broke into the kind of tip-toe run dictated by high heels. *Go and catch her and slap her silly Slavic face,* something said to me. But something quieter said, *Careful, Philippe. Wear the mask. The yellow time approaches.* And, as if to confirm these little whispers, from the corner of my eye I caught a flash of gold moving past me. A tram, and there, in the window seat, someone held a bunch of yellow roses. Not the big showy variety that fall to pieces in a couple of days, but small, neat ones, their petals chastely gripping each other. The sort that Marilyne loved. And nursing these drops of gold, staring straight ahead with a deliberate smirk – *I have seen you, and the sight amuses me* – was Clooney. I'd have spat against the window if I'd been close enough.

*

As PseudoFifre's schemes took shape, I took care to behave normally; that is, to behave as though nothing had changed. But Marilyne was too bright not to suspect that something was up. She sensed it in some way. I could tell from the subtle probes she employed, like a doctor prodding a patient's belly. *Does this hurt? How about this?* The closer we got to dinner with Yves, the more she prodded.

"So . . . nearly five years of La Market Jaune! Five years next week, in fact – am I right?"

"Mm-hm."

"Fantastic! You should be very proud. And what are your plans for the next five years?"

"More of the same."

"Hey, I've an idea! How about franchising? Offer a franchise to each city in France. Even Quebec. Why not?"

"*Oui.* Why not."

She sighed, and stepped closer to me, where I was dissecting a piece of Gruyère into micro-slices. She put a hand on my shoulder, and it was all I could do not to hit it away and jump up screaming, *Betrayer! Deceiver!*

"*Cheri,* what is it? You will say, won't you, if – you know – you are upset?"

"Mm-hm."

"You must tell me, if you are out of sorts, Philippe. You must. We two especially, in this world – we need each other. Do you not see that? You must see that; you especially must see that."

"Especially me? *Especially* me? Because I'm especially stupid, you mean?"

"No. That's not what I mean, as you well know."

"Then?"

"I mean that, especially after *Paris* – after Antoine – you must realise that between you and I on the one hand, and the drop on the other, there is only a perpetually refreshed act of will. Do you not agree? People like us, we walk a knife-edge, a scalpel-edge, each day. And we cannot keep our balance without someone to hold on to. So you *must* communicate with me. You understand? Please, Philippe . . ."

After a brief silence, she tried again, with a false cheerfulness that another time would have touched me, no, *vanquished* me, with its fragility.

"So, no little animals for me this week, *cheri*? Have you seen what I did with the puppy heart? Look."

I looked. It was indeed a work of art – her best yet. Rather than cutting off the major blood vessels close to their junctions with the heart, she'd left some of their length in place. Somehow, she'd plaited together three of the larger veins, and then formed the plait into a heart shape – a Valentine heart, I mean, not an anatomical heart. And then she'd arranged the remaining vessels so that they radiated out and away in a pleasing pattern, like a frozen explosion of angiogenesis. I looked closer. Thin wires inserted down each vessel to hold it in place – that's how she'd done it. Presumably, the wires passed through the wall of the heart and into the card on which it was mounted. She'd obviously washed the dissection very diligently – the isopropanol was free of the usual sediment.

"It's your best yet," I said, with a little smile. Two can play at this game, dear Marilyne.

"And it was all thanks to you. A great find, darling – thank you so much." She kissed me with an artifice of tenderness that made me want to sing and die and love and kill, all at once. Then she turned, and went towards the bathroom for her end-of-day washing and cutting.

"Don't forget," she said, through a yawn. "Dinner with Yves tomorrow. Have you a clean shirt?"

So soon? Fate marches with a fast step, I thought. But I was prepared.

My dreams that night were chaotic, but intense. Thin wires had sprouted forth from my heart and through my flesh. These connected me to Geneva's thick tram cables, strung above the roads. Tied thus, I trundled desperately along the tracks, obsessed with making it to the next stop on time. Something fateful awaited me there, I knew. As I approached the stop, I slowed down, fighting the momentum; my heart went flippety-flop. Without surprise, I saw that I was in a part of Geneva I knew well: La Market Jaune was reflected yellowly on my flanks, in vivid capitals. What joy! But instead of sounding the normal tram bell, I could only make a weak *tinkle-tink* sound as I halted. A single passenger awaited: Laurence. He approached me, groin first. *Have you seen my divine javelin, my magnificent endowment?* he bellowed. *Observe! I make a gift of it, this spear, this sceptre of King Ottokar, for all the nurses at Les Hôpitaux . . .* Disgusted, I looked away from him to La Market Jaune. Through the window, I saw Marilyne; she was naked. A line of men snaked back from the shop door. She looked at me, laughing. *Get to the back of the queue, Philippe,* she said. She pointed with her chin to where fat Yves waited, a puppy's heart in each hand. I turned back to Marilyne, weeping, but she had disappeared. I had to find her, so – *tinkle-tink* – I headed off down the tracks to the Old City. I tried to climb the hill to our apartment block, but the tram tracks didn't go in that direction; I fought and struggled, but the wires held me back. I pulled and pulled, and at last something gave way in my chest, and I was free. I ran up the hill; at the top, I paused to look back. I saw my heart suspended from the tram wires; *tinkle-tink*, it went, softly, *tinkle-tink*, as it headed off, following the tracks. I knew where it was going, where it could only go: to that tram stop called Terminus. The end of the line. Then, in the way of dreams, I found suddenly that I was in the apartment, so I walked to the kitchen, where Marilyne was having breakfast. She sat at the table, a clean bowl before her. *Well, dear-heart?* she said. *Do you have something for me?* But it was too late; I was empty inside. I had no heart to give her, not even my own.

Chapter 26

"What are you doing up at this time in the morning?" asked Marilyne. She seemed surprised to see me in the kitchen so early.

"I have a lot to do today."

"Ah." She let the silence grow, and I knew what she was thinking: *You have a lot of BDs to sell – how comic.* After a little while, she said, as though by afterthought: "You haven't forgotten about dinner with Yves tonight, have you?"

"How could I forget?"

"Good. And don't get any ideas about going out for a drink with him first, Philippe, please."

"Don't worry," I said, "I won't be going out for a drink with Yves again. Ever." I looked at her directly when saying this, holding her gaze. It was foolish of me, I knew. And indeed, for a minute I thought I had gone too far, for she gave me a troubled glance from under her long, beautiful lashes. Those eyes: so blue, so violet, so treacherous and lovely.

"I can't say I'm sorry," she said. "You came back in such a mess, that last time."

I gave a non-committal grunt, and shrugged. She looked exasperated, but carried on.

"Speaking of Yves, darling, please try not to be rude tonight, if you can. He thinks well of you, I know he does. And he was nothing but supportive in Paris . . ."

I bet he was, I thought. *Very supportive.*

"I will try, darling," I said.

"By the way," she said, "Today, I won't be coming home after work, so I'll see you *chez* Yves, okay? I have to pick something up in town, from the shops, before they close. I'll just go straight to Yves' flat from there." As casual as that. As though Yves' flat were her second home. Maybe it was.

"Really? I expect you'll have your shower there too, will you?"

"Ha! That would frighten Yves! No, he'll just have to put up with me sitting at the table dripping with blood and shedding pieces of patient. Needs must."

"The need being? What are you buying that can't wait?"

"Tut-tut. Ask me no questions, and I'll tell you no lies." And she left for work, while the blood pounded in my temples until I thought the vessels would rupture. Her heels laughed at me down the communal stairs: *clack-clack, Philippe, clack-clack.* Tell me no lies, indeed.

But in fact, this worked to my advantage, somewhat. I had to test the potency of my little creation today, in any case. No point in going through all this just to give my faithless wife and her lover a stomach upset. By not returning to the flat this evening, Marilyne was presenting me the ideal opportunity.

I left La Market Jaune at lunchtime that day and went to the apartment. With me, I brought a packet of frozen peas purchased from Migros; nestled against this cooling block was my tube of *Heart M.* Once inside the apartment, I opened the bathroom window; Infelix peered at me from the roof, but did not approach. He had become cautious of Philippe's boot in recent days. So I went to the kitchen, rattled the box of cat biscuits, and pushed the cat-food bowl along the floor with my foot. Infelix appeared with Pavlovian inevitability. From the cupboard, I took a tin of tuna in spring water. I opened it, and wafted it under the cat's nose. He lashed his tail, and started winding himself around my feet, his irises frosted with greed. I spooned a third of the tuna into a feeding bowl. Then I took a plastic drinking straw, and using a pen, marked the straw exactly one centimetre from its end. I lowered the straw into the *Thevetia* extract until the one centimetre mark was just about covered by the delicate yellow of certain death. Then, with my thumb over the top end, I raised the plastic tube, now containing a carefully measured one straw-centimetre of poison. This I transferred to the bowl of tuna, gently blowing through the end of the straw to eject the last drop. Finally, I used Yves' knife to carefully mix and mash *Heart M* into the fish.

Predictably, Infelix got stuck in as though on the point of starvation. It was not until he'd eaten most of the tuna that he started to twig that something might be wrong. He looked up, as though alarmed, and retreated from the bowl. Greed prevailed, however, and he approached the fish from another angle. This time, he didn't stop until the bowl was licked clean. Then he walked away, and washed his face. At least he started to, but then his life changed rather rapidly. He yowled and looked uncomfortable; he tried to scamper off – as if to flee his fate – but his back legs had developed a kind of spastic shudder. Then, for some reason, he dragged himself towards me with his front legs alone, crying as only a cat can cry. When he reached my feet, his front legs also gave way; he lay there, dribbling, breathing heavily but slowly, and looking around as if for escape. Finally, very gently, his neck muscles let go, and his head sunk slowly to the floor, and stayed there. His lungs dragged at the air in rattling, gasping breaths, which got slower and slower. I put my hand on his chest; his heart was pounding like a mad thing, *ba-bub, ba-bub, ba-bub*. And it was odd, because I felt the lungs stop, heard his breathing cease, but the heart kept going. It was as though it was refusing to give up, still insanely pumping unoxygenated blood to a suffocating brain. I kept my hand there, and after perhaps a minute, I felt his little engine cease its hopeless race in mid-step: *ba-bub, ba-bub, ba –*.

The afternoon was quite straightforward after that. I cleaned up the kitchen – Infelix had emptied his bladder in death – and wrapped the body in several plastic supermarket bags, taped into a tight bundle. To make sure the little corpse would sink, I'd put the sternal retractor in the innermost bag, and punched several holes in the bundle to allow air and other gases to escape. I put this package inside a final carrier bag and left the flat, swinging my burden jauntily in one hand, while the other caressed my shoulder-bag and its cargo of *Madame Médecins* (every issue; it seemed somehow right that she should witness Infelix's end). I was almost carefree; between taking a life and not taking it, I had discovered, there is only the smallest of separations. A step that can be bridged by no more than one's intangible will.

A couple of Normals were standing at the tram stop. They looked at me vacantly; I grinned cheerily, made a play of picking up a couple of pieces of litter – a cigarette packet and a sandwich carton – and waved them at my audience before putting them in the Migros bag with dead Infelix. Play the good citizen, Philippe; raise no suspicions, not at this juncture. I felt their eyes on me as I walked on, but they said nothing; my camouflage was perfect.

Once out of their sight, instead of taking my normal tram from the Old City towards Cornavin station, I crossed the road and jumped on one heading in the opposite direction, towards Carouge. At the Pont de Carouge, where Laurence had witnessed me vomiting into the Arve, I alighted and walked down the residential street that follows the river's bank. I dodged through the opening in the railings and descended the steps to the swift Arve. A few hundred yards upstream, the river thundered over black rocks in a set of mini-rapids; in front of me, however, the water was untroubled, though its flow was fast. I waited until I was sure that there were no dog walkers nearby, took the weighted bundle of dead cat from the carrier bag, and threw it far out. It was gone immediately; and I, another Rubicon behind me, shouldered my burden of *Madame Médecin*, and departed.

Killing a cat – killing *anything* – isn't that out of the ordinary, when you come to think about it. I mean, it sounds strange until you actually do it, and then it's just something else that you do. Like selling BDs, or painting your dreams, or watching your wife cut the dead heart from your one-week-old son. What's the difference? There is none; none at all.

The Book shows PseudoFifre ambling along the Arve's bank and back up the concrete steps that warm afternoon. He has no particular expression on his face. He is a creature living in the moment, in the calm water between the rapids, in that state of grace that exists between one death and another. His journey back to La Market Jaune is erratic; he gets off the tram two stops early, walks across the road (*Madame Médecin* rubs at his thigh; the bag's strap cuts at his shoulder), and takes another tram all the way back to the Pont de Carouge, before reversing direction yet again. It is as though he wishes to prolong the gracious state, to revel in it; or to revisit his actions and reconsider. To rewind time, perhaps, to turn back the Book's pages; I don't know.

In the shop, I sat behind my counter, watching the trams follow their contrary routes; absurdly, I found myself mentally tracking them, in each direction, counting off each stop by memory: *that way leads up to the Jardin, this way only to Terminus.* I paced the aisles between my ranks of glossy, vivid BDs; I listened to the eternal, revenant whispering: *Today, Philippe.* I dragged and tore at my ears. *We know what you are.* I placed all the *Madame Médecins* in a pile on my desk and once again read them through, marking each humiliation, each betrayal, each irrevocable wound. It was as though a great hand had clutched my heart and now sought to drag it forth and pin it to a piece of white card. I replaced the *Madame Médecin* collection in my bag, to take home with me again. They seemed heavier than they should be – the weight of bitterness perhaps; the unexpected density of despair. No matter; I would keep them next to me forever, I decided, to forever remind me of why today came to be.

When I eventually left La Market Jaune, I was a worn and hollow man; exhausted, in the true meaning of the word. Emptied. And yet a small thing flip-flapped crazily in my empty chest. I could swear it made a little sound – *tinkle-tink.* I could hear it, just behind the rattle and clack of the tram.

At home, I showered. Oddly, I caught myself opening the bathroom window and making little *psss-psss* sounds to the rooftops. But Infelix would never come scampering back across the tiles, now. That chapter of the Book was closed.

Forever. *It's not your fault, Philippe. You must do what you must do.* "I know," I said. *It is Yves and Marilyne who bear the guilt.* I took a blue cool block from the freezer and wrapped some kitchen paper around it to soak up any condensation. Then I retrieved the biopsy tube of *Thevetia* extract – *Heart M,* glowing like the very essence of aureolin – and nestled it against the cool block in my shoulder-bag. My cold yellow poison was further protected by a packet of latex gloves and by the collected editions of *Madame Médecin*. Finally, I shoved in two chilled bottles of wine – a Chasselas and a Pinot Gris.

I shut the door of the apartment behind me, firmly. The slam had a different quality, somehow, a new finality. The door's closure left a charged emptiness. It enveloped me and followed me, humming in my ears. And now that I re-read this part of the Book, it is though I live it afresh. Look.

Chapter 27

Look: PseudoFifre catches the tram to Les Pâquis, where treacherous Yves lives dully in his brown flat, surrounded by little plastic monsters. Look at them: the woman with six breasts, the crab-thing, the little imps that leer and cavort. The weight of *Madame Médecin* bumps against PseudoFifre's hip as he walks from the tram stop. He passes walls scrawled with foul words and walks over pavements smeared with the excrement of small dogs. The bag's strap hurts his shoulder; for comfort, he pushes one hand beneath the leather band. He walks up the steps to the door of the vertiginous apartment block that cradles his arch-enemies. His mind is empty; he pulls at his ears, but hears still the yellow echo of slammed doors that can never again be opened. He presses the buzzer on the door.

"*Oui?*"

"This is Philippe."

"*Bien.* Come in."

I pushed open the door during its brief moment of acquiescence, and mounted the stairs. Only three floors. Yves had already opened the door of the flat. He seemed vaguely discomfited; his plump face attempted to form itself into the semblance of puzzlement.

"Where's Marilyne?"

"She had to go into town straight after work, to pick up something from the shops. She's coming here directly."

"Oh. Okay."

"In fact, I thought she might be here already. Are you sure she's not in the wardrobe, or under the bed, or something?" I just couldn't help myself.

"Yes, I'm sure. Would you like a drink?"

"Thanks, but I'll wait until Marilyne gets here. Let me put the wine in the fridge, though." I patted my bag.

He followed me into the kitchen, and shuffled from foot to foot while I made room in the fridge for the wine. I reached into my bag and took out the two bottles, carefully shielding the other items from his view; it wouldn't do for him to see all the *Madame Médecins* bundled together in there. Even Yves might smell a rat if the rat was large enough.

"So how are you, Philippe?" I could almost hear the cogs turning in Yves' brain: *This is the kind of thing that people say, so I'd better say it.*

"Very well." And you know, in a way it was true. Colours were vivid, and sounds clear. I felt that I was hearing things to which I'd been deaf for too long, seeing pigments in their full, unveiled splendour. I didn't need to pee all the time, and I'd been dreaming again. So yes, I was very well, thank you.

I shut the fridge door, and looked around the dull, sepia-brown kitchen. All was as Yves-like as ever. The only splash of colour, I noticed, came from the yellow roses on the table. Dwarf roses, in the late bud stage.

"Nice flowers. Are they for our benefit?"

"Somebody gave them to me." He looked embarrassed. As well he might, I thought.

"Ah. A secret admirer."

"Yes." Just like that! He just didn't care any more, whether I knew or not!

"Listen, Philippe . . ."

"Yes?"

"There's something I ought to tell you . . . Marilyne suggested I should . . ."

"Oh yes?" Here it comes, I thought. I was standing by the work counter; it would be easy for me to reach across and pull the largest knife from the block.

"You remember when I withdrew from the medical course? Back in Paris?"

"Continue. I'm all ears."

"Well, you aren't, not really. But your ears *are* looking sore. Have you been pulling at them again? Marilyne says you do that. She finds it quite cute, sometimes."

"Get to the point!"

"Okay. Well, I gave up medicine because I was having a lot of difficulties . . . on the social level. People. I still find it difficult. But I finally worked things out, back in Paris. Marilyne helped me. I didn't tell anyone. Now she thinks I should I tell you. She thinks it's the right time. The right time to tell you. She said you'd understand, if I did."

"But Yves, I understand perfectly . . ." I took a knife from the block and moved a little closer. He was within reach, now, carefully regarding me with his pudgy, expressionless face. A buzzer sounded, making us both jump.

"That must be Marilyne." Yves walked to the doorway intercom, pressed a button and spoke into it.

"Yes?"

"*Bonsoir*! It's Marilyne!" Even the intercom's crackle couldn't hide her boundless vivacity.

"Oh good. Come in." Standing just behind him, gripping the knife, I could see two vertebrae making bumps in the oily skin of his neck. Just beneath and between these, of course, was the little bundle of nerves that carried pretty much everything that made Yves' life worth living. He turned round.

"You won't need the carving knife," he said. "We're having stew."

We went into the hallway, and listened to Marilyne's heels coming *clack-clack* up the stairs. Yves opened the door as they got closer, and there she was, looking happy and excited, fresh as a new-bloomed flower in spite of having, that day, cut to the core one or more human beings. She had a parcel under one arm, about the size of a laptop, and the way she held it against her side pulled at her dress and emphasised her curves. You know, I almost stopped the whole thing there and then, she looked so joyful, and I remembered why I had married her. But then I saw her kiss Yves on both cheeks; I saw her put her hand on Yves' shoulder and give it a little squeeze.

PseudoFifre turns on his heel and goes to the kitchen.

"I'll open the wine," I said, over my shoulder. "Chasselas for me, and Pinot Gris for you two, okay?" Because Yves would always drink what Marilyne was having, and Marilyne liked Pinot Gris.

PseudoFifre takes the wine from the fridge, and places it on the table, where it grows beads of condensation. He takes three glasses from the cupboard. He opens the Pinot Gris, pours half a glass, and drinks it down in one. Now the bottle can accommodate the planned addition. PseudoFifre reaches down into the bag beside the fridge, and removes the biopsy tube from its kitchen-towel cocoon next to the cool block. *How beautiful is yellow!*

And into the straw-yellow Alsace Domaines Schlumberger Pinot Gris, 12 percent, I poured the identically coloured alcoholic extract, 70 percent, of *Thevetia peruviana*. Yellow oleander, also known as the suicide tree. I had carefully measured the volume to give at least the same dose per kilogram body weight, when spread between one unfaithful wife and one fat lab technician, and assuming ingestion of one small glass of wine each, as the dose that I had shown to be lethal within minutes in a seven kilogram cat. I remember thinking to myself as I measured it out, just before leaving the apartment that evening: You see, my friends; you see, I am not stupid.

PseudoFifre gently agitates the wine bottle, holding it up to the light, until he can no longer see the refractive discontinuities that betray incomplete mixing. He pours out two generous glasses of Pinot Gris-*Thevetia*, and takes them through to the sitting room. Madame Médecin stops talking with her side-kick as PseudoFifre enters the room. But it doesn't matter anymore.

"Thank you, *cheri!*"

"*Merci*, Philippe."

"My very great pleasure."

I returned to the kitchen, and opened the bottle of Chasselas. I drank down a large glass immediately, and poured another. Normally, alcohol affects me quickly, especially on an empty stomach, but that evening I might as well have been drinking double-distilled water. I went back to the lounge, bringing both bottles of wine with me. I noticed that Yves had drunk half of his already, and gave him a refill.

Marilyne was raising her glass. But, weirdly, everything seemed to have slowed down. Betwixt cup and Marilyne's rosebud lip, an entire universe was born from a black singularity and expanded into black nothingness. The smile that dimpled her clear cheeks spoke of the infinite. And I could not stand it.

"I'll just check on the stew," I said.

"It's fine," said Yves. "I'm timing it. It'll be ready in eighteen and a half minutes."

But I was already in the kitchen. You'd have thought my heart would have been in overdrive; in fact, when I put my hand to my chest, I felt nothing. A hollow man.

PseudoFifre paces Yves' kitchen in an excess of dark tension. He takes exaggerated steps, raising his knees almost to his chest. The night makes mirrors of the kitchen windows; he admires his own grip-toothed rictus, and turns from side to side, seeking that familiar profile. He sees his hands rising to his ears, but stops them, and instead extends his arms as though to embrace and draw in all the inchoate darkness that lies behind his grinning image.

Not your fault, Philippe.

"Philippe? You're taking a long time to check a stew which didn't need checking."

"Just coming, *cherie*."

Yves and Marilyne looked at me as I returned to the lounge; Yves blankly, Marilyne with some puzzlement. But she made nothing of it. Instead, she got up and stood beside Yves, one hand protectively on his shoulder.

"So, *cheri*, Yves says he has made a little confession?" Looking back, I am amazed that I didn't crush my wine glass into splinters. But I wore the mask and sat down as though all were normal.

"Indeed, he was in the middle of doing so when you arrived. But the interruption was of no consequence. You see – *I already knew*!"

PseudoFifre coolly takes another sip of wine, and stares icily at them. He has a cruel, triumphant smile on his face. Madame Médecin pauses, unsure of how to proceed. She tries to hide her confusion with a small laugh.

"Really? Well, there you are, Yves – all that time and effort back in Paris was wasted. You should simply have gone to Philippe for your diagnosis."

"Diagnosis? What are you talking about, *cherie*?"

But Marilyne was no longer attending to me. She was looking at Yves. I hadn't expected him to go first; I thought it would be the other way round, because of his greater weight. But he had been drinking more quickly, and had moved onto a second glass, so I suppose it cancelled out. He got even more pop-eyed than normal, went very white and clutched his gut. Well, Alfred E. Neuman, I thought – What Me Worry? Marilyne was straight over there, checking him over and doing the things doctors do when they suspect something's badly wrong. But she didn't just suspect, she knew.

"Call for an ambulance, Philippe," she snapped. "Immediately."

"My phone's in my coat," I said. "I'll just get it." You see, Marilyne? Philippe brought his phone with him. Hasn't he been *good*.

I went into the hall, and took the phone from my coat, which was hanging from a hook next to Marilyne's. But I didn't make that phone call. I just sat there and listened to the sounds from the living room – Yves gasping, and Marilyne speaking in a low, urgent voice. Yves eventually made a dreadful groaning, gasping sound; this was followed by a wail from Marilyne:

"Philippe . . .!"

I walked into the living room. Yves was stretched out on the floor. It seemed that Marilyne had tried to put him in the recovery position, but it didn't look to me like he was going to recover from anything. His eyes were half-open, and there was white froth around his lips. He was very still.

Marilyne was next to him, semi-reclined. The poison had already stopped her legs working, and was now interfering with her arms. She looked sick and scared, and there was a pleading look in her eyes.

"Philippe . . . the ambulance . . . you must tell them it is an emergency . . ." She was having difficulty speaking.

I glanced from her to Yves, and back again.

"Lover-boy's not looking so good now, eh?"

That was when she knew. I could see it in her eyes. The shock and pain registered at first, and her lips made a silent *Oh,* or maybe it was a *No.* But then her understanding was replaced with a different emotion. Anger, certainly, but also something else: disgust. Disgust. She was lying down, now, next to Yves, and she said something, very quietly, but I heard it clearly.

"Oh, you stupid man . . . you stupid, stupid man . . ."

That broke the floodgates, as far as I was concerned. Even now, she dared to call me stupid! I wanted her to beg for forgiveness, not so that I could have the relief of forgiving, but so that she could acknowledge the pain she had caused me, the agonies of humiliation that I had suffered. Just that admission of guilt would have healed me. But no; she had to call me *stupid.* I went to the kitchen and got my bag. I came back, and upended it, so that all the copies of *Madame Médecin*, all ten issues, fell out onto the floor. Marilyne by now could only move her head. I grabbed each *Madame Médecin* issue, one by one, and held each one in front of her face, one after the other. I was shouting at her at the same time, but I can't remember the words; the Book doesn't say. I threw the last *Madame Médecin* down, spitefully, so that it landed on Yves. The parcel that Marilyne had brought back from the shops that day had somehow ended up on the floor beside her, and I stamped on it savagely, hearing the contents crunch and grind. Marilyne's breathing was now deep and laboured, and her eyes were looking into some inward middle distance, some deep blue world. Exhaustion overwhelmed me; my legs were overcome by an immense weakness. I knelt down, and laid my head on the softness of her breast, one last time. I felt its last rise and shuddering fall, and then I listened to her heart. It didn't want to give up; I listened to it to the end, through her stilled lungs: *ba-bum, ba-bum, ba –*.

When I get up, there is a dark patch on Madame Médecin's blouse. PseudoFifre has been weeping. Who would have thought it?

I stayed with the two of them until the morning; with them, and with all of Yves' little monsters. These higgledy-piggledy creations watched me mutely as if to bear witness to my own vigil. The doll with six breasts lounged and leered, onc hand on its own plastic thigh; her sister gazed at me in agonised triumph, legs spread to reveal a vulva stretched to breaking point by the emergence of a monstrous, hare-lipped baby, grimacing at the world; the imp with an arm for a penis waved at me obscenely. These and the others kept me company until dawn. Then, the grey light exposed a Geneva I had never seen before. The same buildings, in the same places, with the same people in the same streets; but an utterly different world. There was less correspondence between the Geneva of that morning and that of the morning before than there was between New York and ancient, vanished Ur. Everything had changed, forever, and irreversibly. I had had my revenge, and I was infinitely diminished by it.

Chapter 28

I do not know how I found the energy to clean up, nor where it came from. Nevertheless, I made myself put on latex gloves and begin. I carefully emptied the bottle of Pinot Gris into the toilet, avoiding splashes, and flushed it repeatedly; the empty bottle went into my bag. I shovelled all of the *Madame Médecins* into my bag too; I did this blindly, hardly able to bear the sight of the wretched things. I wiped down the outside of the bottle of Chasselas, washed out Yves' and Marilyne's wine glasses, then pressed their hands and fingers around the outside of the glasses and the bottle. Then I half-filled each glass with Chasselas, and left the bottle on the table. I didn't bother trying to remove fingerprints elsewhere; I figured that it wouldn't be surprising if my prints were found somewhere in Yves' apartment, given that we were known to be friends, but it would be curious if some surfaces were found to have *no* prints. Remember *Rooky Cop,* I thought. You are not stupid, Philippe; oh no.

As I was cleaning up, I caught sight of a dog-eared book with a heart on the cover. I picked it up expecting to find more evidence of Marilyne's perfidy, but it was innocuous: *On-The-Spectrum Relationships: A Guide for Adults with*

Autistic Spectrum Disorder. No doubt this would have been used to fuel Yves' imagination for the next episode of *Madame Médecin*. Not any more, lover-boy. And that got me thinking: maybe he'd been working on the next issue? If there was something else in the pipeline, I had to see it; I had to know all. So I searched the flat as diligently as I knew how. But the only BD I found was a genuine one – a Michel Leduc cyborg thing – and the only work in progress I found was in plastic. In the spare bedroom that he'd given over to 3D-printing, on the printer's fabrication bed, was a half-made creation. Not one of his teratomatous mannikins, this; it was a head-and-shoulders *oeuvre*, a printed bust. When I saw it, it was facing away from me. But I was pretty sure I knew what it would be: PseudoFifre, obviously. What had Yves said to me, on the phone, when we were arranging to meet at the Chat Noir? *But I might be able to show it to you, at some point. If it gets close to what I want it to be. In fact, I'd like to see if you can guess what it is.* "Okay, Yves," I said out loud, as I walked around to the front of the printer. "My guess is PseudoFifre."

But my guess was wrong. It wasn't PseudoFifre; it was Clooney. Close to a perfect likeness. Unmistakable. And next to it was a print-out of a picture of Clooney and Yves (Clooney grins at the camera, while Yves looks shyly to one side; behind them rise the yews and pines of the Jardin Botanique). I mused on this, and wondered, but found no answer that made any sense. So I left the printer and its sneering bust, and continued my search of Yves' flat. I found nothing of any interest. Many of his little mutants, several prosthetic limbs, some structures which appeared to be prostheses for no limb yet permitted by evolution. Reluctantly, I had to admit Marilyne had been right; Yves might well have been *one of us*. Even so, eventually I tired of rummaging through the plastic embodiments of Yves' odd mind. It was time to leave.

Still wearing gloves, I turned up the heat in the apartment to maximum, and closed the shutters tight. Then I took my bag and left. Two lovers mysteriously died, that's all; the rapid decomposition that is inevitable in a heated flat in summer would, surely, make it impossible to determine the cause of death. Hopefully, there wouldn't be any forensically identifiable traces of poison in the bodies within a day or two; and even if there were, so what? Marilyne was working on those very poisons in the laboratory. It was perfect.

And yet this panel of the Book shows me empty in the moment of my triumph; I exit Yves' flat, and descend the stairs with a vacant, desolate gaze that I can only describe as soulless. Yes, I had lost my soul, and I didn't know where to find it. I remember that long descent distinctly: the worn concrete steps, the chipped paint, every mark on the wall. The Book shows them in agonising detail, and illustrates each tread I trod, and I tell you, each step felt like it took me closer to hell. Indeed, the artwork in the Book has dramatically altered; its black desolation has something of the nightmare in it, reminiscent of Venditti's *Surrogates* series, as drawn by Brett Weldele. What had Venditti said about his inspiration? *"If you could create a persona and send it out into the real world – where it would do your work for you, and so on – then you would never have to go back to being yourself . . ."* Had I sent PseudoFifre, or had he sent me? We no longer knew.

I walked around to the back of Yves' apartment block, and left the Pinot Gris bottle with the other bottles in the glass recycling bin. They would be collected in the next hour. Then I went to the shop. I walked, because I didn't feel like sitting in a tram with people around me; I just wouldn't have coped. At any minute, I feared, I might have stood up and shrieked, *Murderer! I am a murderer!*

And now that I walked from Les Pâquis to La Market Jaune, it struck me that although my shop really was quite close to Yves' apartment – so he would have had ample opportunity to come in and study it, in order to faithfully reproduce its layout in PseudoFifre's subterranean lair – in fact, I had never actually seen him *inside* the shop.

Once in his hide-out, PseudoFifre continues covering his tracks. The bottle of *Thevetia* extract goes into a bag of rubbish, along with the food processor, and is put aside for disposal in the Arve later that night. He cleans out the whole kitchenette, including the mini-fridge, scrubbing away with bleach until there is no trace of any activity there other than coffee-making. He mops the floor. Then he deliberately breaks the mop and bucket, and puts them aside for plastics recycling. By the end of the day, every link that could be made between PseudoFifre and *Madame Médecin*'s death will be destroyed or dispersed beyond retrieval. PseudoFifre's revenge is complete.

I should have felt lighter at that point. It was over, and justice had been done. But I felt no relief. I could only hear Marilyne's voice: *Oh, you stupid man . . . . you stupid, stupid man . . .* It seemed to whisper to me from the wheels of the tram as it clunked and trundled past outside the shop; and the reversed writing in the tram window – *La Market Jaune, La Market Jaune* – I now saw, was the yellow of oleander blossom, the bilious signal of the suicide tree, pointing back to an unattainable past that I already missed so terribly. *You stupid man.*

Behave normally, I told myself; Normally. Of course. I opened the shop and sat behind my computer. There was a gap on one of the shelves in Orphan's Corner; it whispered at me. *Put them back, you stupid man.* So I took the *Madame Médecin*s out of my bag. There was something else in there with them. A package: the one Marilyne had brought with her to Yves' flat, the one I had stamped on and crushed in front of her. How did that get in there? I opened it, gently tearing apart the careful wrapping. A framed picture, now ruined beyond repair where my importunate feet had crushed the glass into the delicate paper, slicing and scraping Edgar Jacobs' careful line drawings. The irreplaceable Planche 8 from that most iconic Blake and Mortimer opus– *La Marque Jaune*. I read the note.

Darling – how could I let you buy this for yourself when I could buy it for you? And there was a LOT of competition, by the way! Five years today – you have done so well, and I am so proud of you! Let's celebrate tonight, and nurse our hangovers tomorrow chez Café Titeuf! Much love, M.

The phone rang; not my mobile, but the shop landline. *Da-ring, Da-ring. Stupid, stupid.*

"Hello?"

"Is that La Market Jaune? Purveyors of the, ah, Ninth Art?"

"Yes."

"Is that, ah, Philippe?"

"Speaking."

"Ah, Philippe, this is Georges."

Clooney? What did *he* want?

"What do *you* want?"

"Ha ha, charming. Of course, I am sorry to disturb you, but I was wondering if you knew where Yves might be?

He isn't answering the door this morning, and his phone seems to be turned off."

"Why would I know where Yves might be?"

"Well, you two had dinner with him last night." Clooney sounded peeved. "I wanted to take him to the opera, and then to dinner afterwards, but he preferred to spend his evening with Philippe and Marilyne. So instead, we agreed to go swimming first thing this morning. But he's not there."

Clooney started to say something else, but I put the phone down. Something rose in my throat; something bitter and spiny, something that tasted of an irrevocable horror that I refused to contemplate. *You know he's gay, don't you? On-the-Spectrum Relationships.* Yves and Clooney. Yves and Clooney. The shop door opened. *Tinkle-tink, tinkle-tink; stupid man, stupid man.*

In marched Laurence, with the fire of battle in his cold blue eyes, his shirt held together at the front by brown twine tied in a tidy bow. He was agitated about something, staring like a maniac. He waved papers at me, some kind of document, and strode towards the counter, flushed and aggressive.

"This has gone on long enough!" he bellowed. "It is too much, I tell you, too much! I insist you place my work in its proper place, alongside the works of the great Hergé! In the window, as is proper! Do you hear me?"

And he slapped the papers down on the counter, right in front of us. The proofs for a BD. He was breathing heavily, leaning over the counter, his exhalations like fresh excrement and rotting garlic. I looked at what he had brought. There was something familiar about the artwork.

We read the title, PseudoFifre and I: *Issue #11: Madame Médecin and the Fall of PseudoFifre.*

PseudoFifre starts to laugh, incontinently; and as he laughs, tears spring from his eyes and run down his cheeks.

"Oh, you stupid man!" he says, while Laurence glares at him. He pulls at his ears until the blood runs, while the tears flow and fall; but do they spring from joy or sorrow? And what kind of fall awaits PseudoFifre; how far, and to what end? Good questions, these, or stupid? It hardly matters, because the Book cannot answer them. It has ended; its last chapter is complete. From here, all pages are empty, forever; empty of colour, of life, of Marilyne. From here, there is nothing: neither plewds of grief, nor emanata of regret, nor even the lucaflects of an eternal, shining emptiness. PseudoFifre would add them if he could, but, oh Marilyne, I cannot draw, and you have receded, and I am alone, and it is like Paris again and oh God I do not know what I have done – oh, Marilyne!

Acknowledgements

Many thanks to Anil Menon, Miranda Miller, Ben Henley and Krysta Winsheimer for clear-sighted and instructive comments and suggestions; to Eros Espinoza for unforgettable artwork and for being so easy to work with; and to Angel Belsey of Deixis Press for taking a chance on an unknown writer and for breaking the publishing mould, again and again.